Hair of the Dog

Books by Susan Slater

The Dan Mahoney Mysteries
Flash Flood
Rollover
Hair of the Dog

Other Novels
Five O'Clock Shadow

Hair of the Dog

A Dan Mahoney Mystery

Susan Slater

Poisoned Pen Press

First Edition 2015

10 9 8 7 6 5 4 3 2 1

Library of Congress Catalog Card Number: 2014958041

ISBN: 9781464204180   Hardcover
      9781464204203   Trade Paperback

Poisoned Pen Press
6962 E. First Ave., Ste. 103
Scottsdale, AZ 85251
www.poisonedpenpress.com
info@poisonedpenpress.com

Printed in the United States of America

I want to commend all who rescue, train, and find homes for these special dogs. It was not the message of this work of fiction to debate the pros and cons of dog racing. But I would like to pay tribute to those who tirelessly work for the dogs' welfare. Following the ending of *Hair of the Dog* find a way that you can get involved if you wish to be supportive. A Ticket Home guarantees a dog's transport to a new life.

Acknowledgments

First of all, a heartfelt thank you to Godwin Kelly, sports editor of the *Daytona News Journal*. Godwin, I think you must know everyone in town! I so appreciate the intro to track personnel especially, President Dan Francati. When Dan realized what kind of information I needed, he had kennel owner/trainer Melody Alves give me a call. Melody could not have been more thorough. I got a wonderful feel for the dogs, the trainers, and the Daytona Beach Kennel Club and Poker Room itself. I met Mary Louden, president of Prison Greyhounds and would like to recognize the great work that this group does in finding homes for some wonderful animals. So, Godwin, Dan, Melody, Mary—this book is for you. I hope I did the subject matter justice.

Chapter One

Morning. The gold-orange glow shimmered in the narrow window high above him barely illuminating the computers and file cabinets. He turned over and rubbed his right hip bone. Musta slept on that spring poking up through the cotton batting. Cheap mattress, cheap cot, but when he was working with the dogs late, he could sleep in the office—didn't have to travel ten miles to get home. On his bicycle. If his mother had taught him one thing, it was not to look the gift horse in the mouth and to thank the Lord for small favors. All in all, he didn't have no regrets.

He could hear the dogs. Mostly barking but there were a couple howlers out there. And it was breakfast time. They never waited much past sunrise to let him know they were expecting a bowl of raw meat and kibble. These dogs were as precious as race horses, even if they only chased a mechanical rabbit a couple times a week. He swung his legs over the cot's side and sat up, taking a deep breath. Acrid smoke settled around his head and the deep breath sent him to his knees in a spasm of coughing. Fire. Oh, God, help him. He had to get the dogs out. The barking was at a fever pitch now. Had the fire reached the kennels? He grabbed his pillow and pressed it to his nose and mouth. Better. He could take them to the turnout. That area of scruffy grass where potential bettors could size up the day's might-be stars. No time for muzzles. Bites would be the least of his worries about now.

He moved the pillow away from his mouth, "Sadie? Come here, girl." She never left his side that sleek, brown-eyed silver greyhound. Knew without words that he'd saved her life some four years back. Slept with him curled into a ball at the foot of the cot. Shared his lunch and dinner. She was a real pushover for shrimp fried rice and pot stickers. Frantically he tried to see in the haze. The office door was open. That was odd. Could he have forgotten to latch it? Oh well, he'd find her outside in the hall or maybe in the kennel. She wouldn't be far.

But he couldn't go out in his skivvies. He put the pillow down and pulled on overalls, no time for a shirt or shoes and, bending low, pillow again over his mouth and nose, with eyes squinted almost shut, he sprinted for the door. And went sprawling. Through the doorway, crashing with a thud on one knee, slamming head-first onto the tile, shoulder scraping against the doorjamb, propelled forward, splayed out on all fours. And all because he caught his foot on…on…on a body. He pushed up, sitting back hard on his haunches, then bolted upright, heart pounding, slipping in the blood pooling beside the inert man dressed in Levis and plaid shirt, lying facedown, but with a knife handle sticking straight up out of his back. He couldn't stop his hands from shaking. He backed up against the wall knowing the keening sounds were his, a low-pitched wail that rose in intensity. *Help me. God and my mama, help me.*

The smoke was thick now. He had to do something. He bent over, dropped to all fours, grasped the knife handle and closed his eyes. The jerk threw him backwards as the knife slipped out easily and clattered across the tile. It was out, but he knew it wouldn't matter none to the man on the floor. He was dead. Absolutely, totally not getting up anytime soon. He knelt beside the body and leaning across it firmly put his left hand on the shoulder opposite, and right hand around the man's upper arm and pulled. The man flopped over against his thigh, then slipped down leaving a smear of red and settled into the pooled blood.

"Jackson?"

He stared down at the biggest kennel owner at the Daytona track. But no time to wonder about what had happened, that fire wasn't slowing down. Smoke billowed thick above his head. He grabbed up the pillow, and squinting into the acrid gray cloud, raced along the corridor to the room of large metal crates lining every wall, each holding a dog. Much less smoke back here. He tossed the pillow aside and set to work. He started with the crates closest to the hall. He twisted handles and jerked doors open as fast as he could, stopping only to cross the hall and throw wide the double doors to the outside.

Dogs pushed against him, jostling to enter the run that emptied into the observation and exercise area. Fifty dogs. All being held over for Thursday's races, with a hundred more arriving that morning. They had sent a whole bunch for training earlier that evening. And now the transport carrying the new racers was due at nine. Thank the Lord they hadn't gotten here yet. He needed to make sure the dogs still kenneled at the track were all accounted for. But no counting now. He'd save that for later; he needed to keep going. He didn't stop until the last crate had been opened and the last greyhound had bolted for what they thought might be freedom. But had he gotten everyone out the exit? Dogs were everywhere, and the smoke wasn't clearing. Thin tendrils hung in the air.

Only one thing to do. He grabbed two packages of stew meat from a fridge in the hall and waved handfuls above his head to get the attention of the errant few still circling frantically. He led them through the exit to safety, slamming the door behind him.

Still, no Sadie. He yelled her name but doubted she could hear over the raucous, panicked dogs. Had she run with the pack and was already safely out in the chain-link enclosure? He could have easily missed her in all the confusion. Maybe she was fighting over turf or circling the fence looking for him right now. The smoke was thinner outdoors, but behind him, the office was engulfed in flames. No time to check now. She'd wait for him. She wouldn't run away.

The body. Oh no. He'd forgotten. He wasn't thinking straight. He should have pulled it out of the doorway. He couldn't just leave it to burn. Dead or not, that wasn't showing respect to the family. He knew Jackson had a mother. You could find her every Wednesday when the programs were free, putting down a big chunk of her Social Security check at a betting window. He had to give Jackson back to his mama.

He started to run. The closer to the office, the thicker the smoke. He dropped to all fours and crawled forward. He stopped. Had he passed the office? No. He was in front of the door. There was the blood spot darker now around the edges. But no body. Jackson was gone. Maybe he'd been wrong about him being dead; maybe Jackson had crawled away. And he took his knife with him. There wasn't any knife where it used to be. That was a puzzle. What if the body had been a dream?

He could hear sirens, trucks turning in from South Williamson Road. Tendrils of fire now licked out of the office coming way too close to his clothing. No more wondering, he needed to leave. He crawled backwards and then stood and ran toward the dogs. He needed to do a count and find Sadie and then feed the dogs their breakfast. He'd grab some muzzles—he hoped there hadn't already been fights. Funny how some dogs were just jealous and needed to have their way. He'd bet old Pete had already put the chomp on somebody. Sadie'd be smart. She'd stay out of the way. He tried to whistle for her but there was too much noise. She'd never be able to hear him.

Chapter Two

Dan liked to watch her look at the ring. Hold out her left hand, ring finger crooked ever so slightly, then turned slowly to let the light catch the faceted sapphire flanked by 4-C perfect diamonds. Tiffany stones, a platinum setting with a world of memories. The case in Wagon Mound, New Mexico, had put a crimp in her sabbatical and left him with a cast on his wrist, but the ending was pretty nice. Yeah, she liked it. And he liked being engaged. It gave him a feeling of permanence—somehow grounded and warm and fuzzy all mixed up together. They'd shelved Ireland, not forever, just for now. There was still some time left before she had to return to the university. The sabbatical was for a full year. And just maybe she wouldn't return. Elaine had held true to her promise—she'd enrolled online in a six-month course for a certificate in private investigation. Time would tell, but co-mingling a shingle might not be a bad thing.

He tried to be persuasive with United Life and Casualty about getting a couple weeks' vacation before picking up a new case. Played the engagement card. Didn't he need a little time with his fiancée? Pointed out how between Tatum, New Mexico, and then Wagon Mound, the summer and fall had been a little hectic. Two cases wrapped up pretty neatly with some big savings for the company. Instead, UL&C came back with a tantalizing opportunity in Daytona Beach, Florida, and suggested he combine business with pleasure—hinted they'd look the other

way if his work time got a little heavy on the beach side. Not a
bad offer. Now he needed to convince Elaine.

"What would you say to a little vacation/work combination?"
They were starting their day at a Starbucks in Santa Fe. And like
a broken record, Dan kicked himself again for not buying coffee-
shop stock way back when. He wished hindsight didn't have a
way of defining his life. But he was turning that around. The
woman in front of him wearing his engagement ring would attest
to that. And, boy, did he have good taste. He noticed for the
umpteenth time how nicely her jeans accentuated every curve.

"Sounds great. When do we leave?" Elaine leaned forward,
elbows on the table. With her hair pulled to the side, secured
by a magenta scarf sporting little turquoise howling coyotes, she
looked thirty—not forty-six. He wondered if there would ever
be a time when someone would mistake him for her father. He
had to stop thinking that way. Fifty-two wasn't that much older.
Could six years make that big of a difference? Any gray in his hair
stopped at the temples. No, he could shave off a couple years, too.

"Tomorrow." He almost cringed. He was used to taking off
at a moment's notice, but he wasn't sure about Elaine. Did she
really know what she was signing on for?

"You're kidding!"

"Nope. Fire at a greyhound track cost the life of five dogs
yesterday. Five heavily insured ones. UL&C wants me on the
scene as quickly as possible."

"And this track happens to be?"

"In Daytona Beach."

"Florida? NASCAR heaven, by any other name?"

"The same. But I might throw in Atlantic Ocean, miles of
fantastic beach, company-guaranteed R&R—" Dan paused.
That last might be a bit of a fib, but they did say they'd look the
other way if billables were stretched to cover beach time. He
figured a couple long weekends wouldn't be questioned.

"*Guaranteed* R&R? Well, then, count me in."

Why did he think she didn't sound convinced? A touch of
sarcasm even? If truth be known, maybe he wasn't convinced

either. He needed to stop letting work interfere with his love life—now that he had one.

> > >

He was able to get a flight into DAB, the Daytona Beach airport and, after setting up two-weeks' boarding at Simon's favorite Pet Paradise doggy resort in Albuquerque, they were on their way. The Rottweiler was usually pretty good about short bouts of separation—the pool at the boarding facility was a favorite. Heated, no less. Dan watched from the parking lot as the big dog dove in and knocked two Labs out of the way, paddling to get a ball. It wasn't exactly comforting, but Dan realized he might not be missed at all.

Enterprise met them when they landed. The LR2 was low-end Land Rover but would more than meet their needs for the next week or so. Great for cruising the beach. The GPS was a welcome addition and Dan quickly punched in the dog track's address—960 S. Williamson Blvd. Someone said the world's largest year-round flea market was nearby. A square couple acres of other peoples' castoffs and a few booths of rinky-dink, made-in-China collectibles—using that term loosely. He could probably do without anything they had to offer. Wasn't he trying to cut back on the junk—that stuff that never got thrown out? He'd never use a word like "hoarder" to describe himself, but the Nordic Track under the bed was vintage. Really vintage. And wasn't he planning on combining households fairly quickly? Shut down that apartment in Chicago. Add Elaine's stuff to his stuff…Settle into that comfy house or apartment together. That might push him to a forced "throw-out" of keepsakes. No, there couldn't be a flea market visit anytime soon unless he was setting up a booth.

Anyway, there was no time to take a look today. He needed to check in at the track even before finding a place to stay. UL&C was adamant about closing the time-gap. Seventy-two hours post event wasn't bad; still every hour out diluted the quality of information gathered in an investigation. It was always amazing how quickly memories started to fade. Or took on aspects of fabrication.

Dealing with animals put a big emotional tag on the package: a breeder's hopes and dreams, plus an owner's money, in addition to a live animal with its own feelings. UL&C was one of the few large insurance companies that still insured animals—race horses, Alpaca farms, cattle, show dogs, working dogs…it wasn't his favorite kind of case, but, then, what was? Necklaces belonging to little eighty-five-year-old women? Jewels that survived the *Titanic* only to meet their doom in a small town robbery? He sighed. Wagon Mound wouldn't be soon forgotten. So he guessed there wasn't a favorite or an easy case. Five dead dogs already put this one out of the running.

〉〉〉

The track's parking lot would probably hold five hundred cars. In its heyday that kind of space would have been needed, but now dog racing was supplemented by other types of gambling—horse racing, harness racing, and multiple types of card games. Some of these were closed-circuit only, like horse racing, and some were live on the premises. From the looks of the people walking through the doors, this was just another form of retiree recreation. Dan didn't think he'd seen one person under sixty in five minutes.

"Not sure how long I'll be gone. I'll leave the car keys unless you want to tag along?"

"I think I'll take a walk. Too much sitting for one day." Elaine gave him a quick kiss on the cheek.

"That was a little chaste."

"Don't look now, but we seem to be of interest to about fifty elderly women on the tour bus behind you."

"Should we give them something to stare at?" Elaine barely dodged what was going to be a pat on her backside.

"You're terrible. Go to work." Elaine laughed and waved once before heading back down the entrance road.

〉〉〉

The late afternoon was beautiful. Wasn't October one of Florida's best months? Humidity low, lots of sunshine, only a whisper of a breeze—she could get used to this. Even if the amount of green almost made her eyes hurt. A person couldn't come from the high desert of New Mexico and not be almost overcome by the sheer vastness of vibrant color. Spread before her was a carpet of grass, short stocky palms and majestic towering ones, flowering plants edging the sidewalks, thick oak trees hung with Spanish moss, and looming over everything, giant pines. Yes, pines this close to the ocean. It surprised her, but she remembered reading that the area was known for its turpentine production in years past. She idly wondered if the pines were indigenous or from stock that was brought in. They were certainly flourishing.

She took a deep breath and stretched. It felt so good to walk after hours on a plane and in an airport. She turned down a recently mowed grassy path that ran along a hedge row and was startled to flush two white ibises from a nearby drainage ditch. It looked like dinner had been a tiny frog, judging from the frantic hopping of several amphibians. Though more than able to fly, the ibises simply looked at her, then sauntered onto the asphalt and continued their slow walk across the parking lot. They seemed so tame.

A rustling in the hedge row caused her to turn back. Was she being foolish to go off walking by herself? There were snakes and alligators in this state. A man on the plane made it sound like every puddle potentially housed an alligator. He shared tales of cities in the surrounding area keeping alligator handlers permanently on city payrolls. Farfetched? He seemed convincing.

But this wasn't an alligator. A very elegant gray muzzle poked out of the hedge and two liquid brown eyes seemed to implore Elaine to come closer.

"My what a pretty girl you are." She liked to be exact—call a boy, a boy, and a girl, a girl. Not that any dog was ever insulted and the telltale parts of this one's anatomy were still covered by brush. Something, however, just screamed female. Something ultra feminine in the arch of the neck and delicate, soft ears angled outward from each side of the head.

Elaine knelt in the grass and held out a hand. The greyhound was interested but wasn't about to let a stranger coax her from the safety of the bushes.

"You are so smart. You know I don't have a treat. If you come out, I bet I could find one." She was mentally kicking herself for leaving the bag of airline pretzels in the SUV.

"Okay, what if I come to you?" Elaine got up slowly keeping an eye on her new friend. "Now, isn't this better?" She let the dog sniff her hand and then gently patted her head. An expensive braided leather collar sported an etched metal plate with the name, Sadie.

"Sadie. See, I know your name." Elaine watched the greyhound's eyes. Calling her by name had made a difference. Trust? She thought so. The start of it anyway. The dog picked up something off the ground and walked out of the thicket, dropping the "present" at Elaine's feet.

"Ah, a gift for me." Elaine leaned over but stopped short of picking up the latex glove. She could only hope that it wasn't some contagion-bearing cast off from a clinic or lab because it was probably a pretty good guess that the bronze-red stains were blood. And lesson one of private eye training? Trust your instincts and if something presents itself as possible evidence, bag it. This was certainly worthy of being saved, even if she wasn't certain why. Elaine slipped the scarf from around her shoulders and fashioned a leash, securing one end to Sadie's collar.

"I don't want you taking off after any rabbits." But the dog didn't seem the least bit interested in going anywhere. She leaned into Elaine's knee and just stood there seeming to enjoy the closeness of a human. It was then that Elaine noticed the singed hair—a good-sized patch along her side that exposed the rounded, but uneven protrusion of ribs covered by bare skin. Two smaller burn-holes on her right shoulder with a pink rawness showing through seemed to be the sum-total of injuries. A little Neosporin was called for. The dog had been in the fire and must have gotten loose in the confusion. Was she a racer? Elaine thought not. This one was too much of a pet.

Elaine turned toward the SUV. If she'd thought the dog would be reluctant to follow, she was wrong. Sadie walked smartly beside her, nose just touching Elaine's thigh. Elaine grabbed her purse and a couple plastic bags from the backseat of the car—travel garbage bags—and walked back to the bloody glove. Gingerly picking up one corner of the glove using the second plastic bag, she sealed it in the first, then put one bag inside the other, rolled them up, and put both in her purse.

"Now what to do with you." Elaine patted the dog on the head. "I bet there's someone looking for his or her best friend."

Suddenly Sadie gave a tug on her leash and a pronounced "woof." If her wagging tail was any indication, the young woman hurrying toward them must be the owner or a very close friend.

"You're Sadie's owner?"

"No, well, sort of, yes, I guess by default. I know her owner." The young woman had dropped to her knees and was hugging and patting Sadie, only stopping to plant a resounding kiss on the dog's muzzle. "You gave us quite a scare. You naughty girl." The hugs and tone of voice weren't scolding, just full of concern.

She seemed close to the dog for someone not her owner. Confused, Elaine let her catch her breath before more questions. The young woman was twenty-something in jeans and tee-shirt and sandals. Seemed to be the standard uniform for this part of the world, Elaine decided.

"I'm Elaine Linden. My fiancé is the insurance investigator for the track's losses from the fire."

"Melody Paget. I'm a trainer at the track." She stood and offered her hand but kept her left hand on Sadie.

"How do you know this dog?"

"Sadie's owner worked for me. General maintenance—fed, cleaned, helped with turn-out, and getting dogs to the starting box. He was good. The dogs loved him. He'd been working with the dogs all his life."

"I detect the use of past-tense here."

"He—" Melody suddenly burst into tears. "He's in jail. They say he murdered an owner, then set the fire to cover it up."

"Murder?"

"It's been in all the papers—a front page story in *The News-Journal* for two days going. You're not local?"

"No, we just flew in. I don't believe my fiancé knew there had been a murder. Apparently several dogs also perished?"

"Top of their line. Not just any dogs. Two currently being raced and three that were young but coming on strong. I was working with one of them. Lots of promise." Melody pulled a Kleenex from a pocket and blew her nose. "It's a travesty. Dog racing has enough problems without this sort of thing. It's a terrible setback for the owners."

"Have you been taking care of Sadie?"

"She's been gone. Ran away the night of the fire. I put up flyers everywhere."

"Well, I know you're happy to see her. And I know her owner will be relieved." Elaine bent over to untie the scarf-leash.

"Uh, look, it's not a good idea that I take her if you're thinking of handing her off to me. Politics, and all that. My boss put her owner in jail. I'm not sure my getting involved would go over very well—you know, looking like I was doing him a favor. Sort of aiding and abetting the enemy. You haven't met Dixie."

"And Dixie is?"

"A kennel owner and co-owner of this." A half-turn toward the building in back and a sweep of her arm took in the Daytona Beach Kennel Club and Poker Room. "She's about as high up as you can get and likes to throw her weight around. But please don't get me wrong—she's done a lot for the track. She brought in a full-time vet, a grounds expert who keeps the track in superb condition. She turned the restaurant around…she's pretty much kept us in business."

"Sounds like she's the insured party."

"She is."

"So, tell me about Sadie's owner. You sounded skeptical when you mentioned he was in jail."

"I am skeptical—but you didn't hear that here. He's a dear sweet man who lives for his dog and the dogs he cares for. He's, um, maybe a little slow—he does fine as long as his life doesn't get complicated. But the morning of the fire? He didn't just run off, he saved almost every dog and then stayed around to calm them and feed them. He even broke up fights and muzzled the more aggressive ones. Now, does that sound like someone who has just committed murder?"

"No, it doesn't. Does this man have a name?"

"Fucher Crumm."

"Future Crumb?"

"Pronounced Foo-cher—spelled F-u-c-h-e-r. It's German, I think. And the last name is with two m's, in case you're thinking a 'b'. Everyone misspells both names. In fact, it's misspelled on his birth certificate. He showed me once. Seems his mother in the throes of labor yelled out, 'make way for the fucher,' and the nurse in attendance jotted down *the future* thinking it was a comment on this new addition to the family tree."

"That is a cross to bear. I wouldn't enjoy correcting my name all the time. Is he well liked?"

"Yeah. At least he should be. Just about everyone around here owes him money."

"I wouldn't think he'd make enough in maintenance to be generous to others."

"Oh, he doesn't. He got a big-buck settlement after the accident."

"Something happened here at the track?"

"Well, I hate to gossip but it's all been in the papers. Fucher used to drink. A lot. One afternoon a couple years ago he was walking home from a bar and got hit by a City truck—in a crosswalk. Lawyers proved the driver was texting so Fucher cleared over six hundred thousand dollars after paying off the lawyers. When his lawyer handed him a check, he asked if he could just have it all in twenties."

Elaine tried to imagine how big a stack of money that would be. Six hundred thousand in twenties. No wonder he was popular.

"He probably doesn't have much of it left. He bought a new

bike and moved to a nice apartment and bought a race dog. That's something to show for the money, I guess. But that's about all."

"Fucher owns a track dog?"

"Yeah, he put him out with me for training. He's twenty months but a comer. Nero's Song. Sadie's pup. Sadie was an expensive brood bitch in her heyday. Then she started having seizures. She was a Scottish import—never raced but passed on some top notch bloodlines. Fucher paid big bucks for Nero—a full fifty thousand."

"I had no idea dogs could be so expensive."

"Fifty thousand is pretty much top of the line. You can pay anywhere from five to fifty thousand and have a track-worthy dog."

"Will you race him here?"

"No, this is just an intermediate track. With his bloodlines and promise, we'll start him in the Miami area—at an 'A' track."

"When will that be?"

"I'm not sure, but we're not that far away."

Elaine leaned down to give Sadie a pat. "I feel like I'm in the midst of doggy-royalty."

"You sort of are."

"So what are you thinking of doing with Sadie?"

"Trainers here don't have the room with their other dogs—I mean even if they wanted to risk the wrath of witch-lady." Melody paused, "I could ask Fred Manson. He's in charge of maintenance but he's like Fucher's mentor—keeps an eye on him—a real father-figure, I suppose is the best description. But I know he lives in an apartment that doesn't take dogs. I'm not kidding—I'm stuck on this one. It would mean the world to Fucher if you'd take her." She held out a leash.

"Me? I don't think—"

"Please? It would give me time to find a permanent home, that is, if Fucher isn't out soon. Think about it. There aren't a lot of options. We can't take her to a shelter and risk possible euthanasia."

Euthanasia sounded a little melodramatic but probably was a possibility. "You know, Dan and I may not be here very long.

Sounds like the case is pretty straightforward—answers already in place."

"Any amount of time would be a gift." The hand that held the leash was still extended toward Elaine. "Please?"

One more glance at the liquid brown eyes, and Elaine knew she'd been had. She took the leash and snapped it in place and removed her scarf. "Okay, but we'll stay in touch. Close touch."

"Do you think you could do one last favor?"

"What's that?" Elaine was a little leery. It was bad enough she was going to have to explain all this to Dan and had somehow, in all innocence, acquired a live animal to take care of when she'd only wanted to go for a walk.

"Could you contact Fucher and tell him you have Sadie?"

"I don't know the man. Wouldn't that information be better coming from you?"

But Elaine didn't give Melody a chance to use politics again. "No, I can see that it wouldn't. Okay, tell me how I can reach him."

>>>

"We're going where?" Dan glanced at the dog on the backseat and then at Elaine.

"Volusia County Correctional Center."

"A jail?" Why had this not appeared at the top of his "fun things to do in Daytona" list for the afternoon? But he listened quietly to the tale of Fucher Crumm and agreed with her that the poor man was probably frantic over his pet. He turned and looked at Sadie who was doing a pretty good "doggy in the window" act—head hanging slightly, eyes imploring, finally with a sigh putting her head on her paws. Resignation. A doggy take on "oh woe is me." But he could see how Elaine was suckered in. For that matter, wasn't he?

"Inside, right now, someone must have mentioned his name. Fucher's worked here for years."

"Yeah. I heard his name a lot. Everyone's talking about the fire and the kennel owner who was found dead. And, I gotta say, with a fair amount of disbelief. Not that anyone was coming right out and saying they didn't think he could start a fire, let alone kill. Everyone I spoke with was pretty tight-lipped. But they are emphasizing all the good things this man does. It's just that somebody wields real behind-the-scenes power."

"Melody mentioned a woman who's part owner. Seemed very afraid of crossing her—even thought taking care of Sadie would brand her a traitor."

"I think I know who she's talking about. I have a meeting tomorrow with Dixie Halifax. Pretty much the head honcho, from what I can see. All I know is she's the one who's insured."

"I don't envy you your job."

"Yeah, and it doesn't make things any easier that this kennel owner, Jackson Sanchez, the guy who was killed, didn't think Fucher should be handling dogs—thought his handicap kept him from making good decisions about their care. It seemed he'd made a stink about it. Reported some medicine mix-up to the track veterinarian."

"Interesting. I got the idea Fucher was well accepted. Or at least relied upon."

Elaine quickly relayed the story of the six hundred thousand dollars all in twenties.

A low whistle, "That would make anyone popular."

"Was Fucher's job in danger?"

"I kinda got that idea. I don't think any action had been taken—maybe more of a threat—but I guess this Fucher was pretty distraught. I'd like to be able to throw my opinion in the mix, size up Fucher myself. And I need a first-hand account of the fire for UL&C. I'll try and set up an interview for a later date. So, I guess a visit to the jail isn't a bad idea."

Chapter Three

"Sadie, Sadie, Sadie…" The rhythm was soothing. "Sadie, Sadie, Sadie." Fucher blew his nose but didn't stop rocking. He sat on the edge of the bottom bunk bed and kept his eyes tight closed. Where was she? Why hadn't someone called him? Why couldn't he go home? She could be sick or injured. She'd wonder why he wasn't there. "Help me, help me, help me…"

He couldn't imagine how she'd gotten out. Outside the entire compound. That didn't seem possible. He always took her to the track. She'd trot along beside his bicycle or ride in the cart he pulled behind. On the days when Fred picked him up, she rode up front in the truck's cab. She was never away from him. Never. Until now.

"Hey, you in there." The guard banged a baton on the bars of his cell. "You got company." The guard unlocked the cell door and stepped inside.

"Did they find Sadie?" Fucher jumped up hitting his head on the upper bunk. "Is it Mel or Fred? Did they come to get me?"

"Take it easy, cowboy. I don't know anything about this Sadie. An' I don't know who's visiting, but I'm gonna take you to the visitors' area. Gotta wear these." The guard indicated the ankle shackles in his hand and not so kindly pushed Fucher back down on the bed's edge.

"Stick those tootsies straight out."

Fucher held both feet in the air and waited while the guard clipped the bracelets in place.

They were too tight and hurt—rubbed his skin leaving bright red lines around his ankles. Fucher pulled himself upright and took a step. It wasn't easy to walk with his feet bound together. He tried to hurry but stumbled. Once the guard just let him fall. But it was okay. He could hop and go pretty fast. It had to be news about Sadie. Maybe Melody had brought Sadie to see him. Or Fred. Sadie'd be okay with them. But he didn't think they'd let a dog in. Still, Sadie would've gone back to the track and everybody knew her there. He bet Melody or Fred had found her. She'd be safe. Melody would take care of her. He'd give Mel some money for food. Yes, yes, Mel would know what to do. He tried to jump faster.

"This is it." The guard indicated a door on his right.

Fucher looked through the glass partition. The room was small with only a metal table and four chairs. And two strangers—a man and some lady he'd never seen before. So, it wasn't about Sadie and Fred. No one had found her. He couldn't hold back the sobs or the wailing. The guard had opened the door but Fucher braced himself against the casing and wouldn't budge. "Sadie, Sadie, Sadie…" He banged his head sideways against the metal door jamb in the cement block wall until the guard roughly jerked him back.

"Mr. Crumm, we have Sadie. Sadie is fine." Elaine stood, took a step forward. "I took video for you to see. Here." She held up her phone. "Come join us. We have lots to talk about." Elaine pulled a Kleenex from her pocket and held it out. "We're going to take care of Sadie for you but we need to know what she eats."

Elaine studied the thin, blond-haired man in the orange jumpsuit. Burr haircut, scraggly beard, watery blue eyes. Was he thirty yet? He seemed young, vulnerable, and scared to death. There was just something so terribly wrong with the picture. Did he even understand why he was there? Elaine moved a chair out from the table. "Come sit with us. My name is Elaine. I really want you to see the video."

Fucher hiccoughed loudly and stopped wailing, yet still hung back. "I don't know you. How'd you get Sadie?"

"I know you don't know us. I found Sadie at the track this afternoon. Melody told me where to find you. We want to help." Again, Elaine extended her hand, palm up.

Reluctantly, Fucher stepped into the room and shuffled to the chair.

"This is my fiancé, Dan Mahoney. Dan is going to be working at the track investigating the fire."

Fucher glanced at Dan before leaning toward Elaine and dropping his voice to a whisper. "Is he a cop?"

Dan leaned forward, "No, Fucher, I'm not with the police. I work for an insurance company. Here, look at Elaine's video." It had taken some arm-twisting and a really compassionate warden to bring a phone into the jail. But he could see why the official had listened to him. It would be expensive to put Fucher on a twenty-four-hour watch when knowing his dog was well taken care of negated any worry of his injuring himself. It was nice to see law enforcement that cared.

Fucher gingerly took the phone and was immediately engrossed. At first he frowned; then, laughed and touched the screen with his finger. "She's pretty. I love her."

"I know you do. That's why we want to take good care of her for you. We're here to get your help," Elaine added.

"She's in the car right now. When we leave, I'll go down first and walk her around the parking lot. Maybe the guard will let you watch us from a window up here."

Dan told himself he'd make that happen even if he had to go over the guard's head again. A little extra insurance that Fucher would know that Sadie was well. He might be stretching the compassion thing a little, but Dan didn't think so.

"I'd like that. I think she'll know I'm looking at her." Fucher, now relaxed, leaned back in the chair. "Did you get her something to eat?"

"On the way over we stopped for a McDonalds cheeseburger." Elaine watched as Fucher frowned.

"That's not good food for a dog."

"I didn't let her eat the bun." Elaine hoped that bit of news got them back in his good graces.

"That's better, but she needs raw meat and kibble. She'll even eat a raw carrot."

Elaine took a pen and pad out of her purse. "What kind of kibble and raw meat?" She wasn't sure about a carrot-eating dog but it wouldn't hurt to try her. She made a note of raw carrots.

"Regular beef stew meat. I get it at Sam's. And I feed Natural Balance kibble. She likes the duck or venison best. Sometimes for her coat I get her the fish one—it has Salmon. She weighs sixty-three pounds so she gets one cup of raw meat and five cups of kibble every day. No treats. Unless it's a carrot."

He probably took better care of Sadie than himself, Elaine thought. That dog was his whole life. She couldn't believe she'd tried to dodge bringing this much joy to someone.

"You know, I have lots of her food at home. You could go there and get everything. And her eye drops—she's allergic to grass. And she'd really like her bed. And—"

"Whoa. I'm not sure we can take everything but it would be good to get her food and medicine." Dan had visions of a hotel room overrun with dog toys and beds and food…and allergic to grass? What a little doggy princess. He briefly thought of Simon's good German ruggedness. Now that was a dog.

"They took my keys but you can ask Mrs. Carter. She's my landlady and she can let you in. An' Mel has a key and so does Fred. They're my friends."

Elaine wrote down his address. Thank God for GPS. She had no idea where his townhouse was located and Fucher's directions left a lot to be desired. He didn't remember a lot of the streets and tried to fill in with landmarks. A telephone pole with lots of advertisements stapled onto it didn't seem trustworthy, but neither did "that coffee place that wasn't Starbucks close to a corner across from a firehouse that wasn't really a firehouse but had a fire truck out in front."

Finally, she had everything that would help. Dan left after setting up an appointment for the following afternoon to talk about the fire. Promising more pictures of Sadie probably got him a second visit. That and the fact Fucher would get to see Sadie in the flesh two days in a row.

The guard shushed him, but seeing Fucher jumping up and down, calling out for Sadie, even though the window was well fortified and protected by a maze of metal bars, was heart-warming. Elaine picked up her purse and keys at the first guard station and turnstile, then followed the Exit signs to the lobby. She couldn't help but shiver as each heavy steel door slammed shut behind her. Incarceration. A world she was glad to leave.

>>>

Elaine quickly filled Mrs. Carson in on how Sadie had been found.

"Sadie! Oh my, you gave us quite a scare, girl. You've been out on the streets all by yourself this whole time."

The woman making over Sadie hadn't taken the warnings about sunscreen seriously. Wrinkles and a deep tan signaled a lot of beach time and premature aging. Her age was difficult to determine, but Elaine guessed somewhere south of fifty.

"It was just so kind of you to go by the jail. There's no way that dear boy should be in there. I knew his mother; she worked for me. I have the ten units here—all townhouses but there's a lot of maintenance. Fucher paints, picks up the parking lot, and keeps the shrubs trimmed. All this in addition to his regular job at the track. That boy never stops. He's such a good worker, but so was his mother. She just passed this last Christmas. Oh my, I guess it's been almost a year now. Fucher took it so hard. I don't know what he would have done if he hadn't had Sadie."

"Mrs. Carson, is he current on his rent?" Elaine wasn't sure why she asked but how awful it would be if he lost his home, too. He certainly wasn't bringing in a salary where he was.

"Please, I'm Joan. Oh, let me tell you, he was smart to tie up this place for five full years. You know, when he got his accident money—I'm sure you've heard about that?" Elaine nodded. "Well, he paid me sixty thousand dollars. We drew up a contract and all. There's three years left on the lease."

"That was looking ahead."

"Every time he loaned anyone money or paid ahead for something, I made him draw up a contract. My brother's an attorney and he helped him. Now, let's go get this pretty girl's food. I know where the treats are."

At the word "treats" Sadie wagged her tail so hard her entire body wiggled. And it was obvious she knew the way. Elaine had to hang onto the leash as Sadie took off to follow Joan.

"Here, you can do the honors." She handed two door keys to Dan. "This one is for the door handle and this one for the deadbolt. I'm due for cataract surgery and have a terrible time with my aim at close range."

Elaine had no idea what she thought Fucher's apartment would look like but it wasn't this. Granted the furnishings probably came from T.J. Maxx or Tuesday Morning, yet the place was bright and cheerful and actually tastefully done. A navy throw over a not-so-new couch sported several neon-colored, satin-covered pillows in green, pink, and blue. A wooden rocker had been refinished in bright yellow with grass-green accents. Another pillow in a luminous dark green finished the look. Geometric designs in the large floor rug of muted greens and yellows tied everything together. The place was inviting.

"Where did you say you were staying?" Joan was moving toward the kitchen.

"We didn't. Haven't gotten that far. Miss Sadie here sort of rearranged our priorities." Dan patted the dog on the head. It'd take awhile to get used to the wasp "waist" and dainty feet. Compared to Simon she had the face of an anteater.

"Well, I don't know why I didn't think of this but I have a unit that's just freed up. End of Octoberfest, you know, for bikers. I always keep two or three units available for weekly rentals. Fully furnished, of course. This is a major tourist area. I make more money in the summer and during NASCAR and Bike Week than I do renting a unit on a yearly basis."

"Sounds great. Let's take a look." Dan caught Elaine's eye and an affirmative nod.

"Why not? It might be perfect for us."

"It's only two doors down. You could even leave the bulk of Sadie's food here. No need to lug it around. You'd have to take her bed, though, and her dishes. I'll help. I know where everything is." Joan picked up a dog toy. "I don't imagine you brought much with you? Household goods, that is. I keep small appliances in the garage—coffeemakers, toasters, microwaves, irons—well, you name it and I probably have it. We could get you fixed up in no time. Let's take a look."

The rental unit had been recently painted in what Elaine was beginning to call seascape colors—seafoam green, seaglass blue, seastorm gray. It was clean and bright and the furniture, though a little dark, looked comfortable.

"You'll find dishes above the sink to your right. There's a washer/dryer in this hall closet." The layout was dining room/ living room combination, kitchen with wraparound counter, and half bath all on the bottom floor, and two bedrooms and a bath upstairs. Far more room than a hotel would provide. Elaine might have to work on overlooking the frolicking seahorse wallpaper in the upstairs bath. Still, in all, it was very doable.

"Not sure of the timeframe but let's say two weeks with an option on a couple more." Dan wished he could be more exact, but that was another part of this job—a long weekend could turn into a month. He'd be haunted by one totally unplanned hospital stay in Wagon Mound, New Mexico, for years to come. That had added a few weeks to what was going to be a four-day investigation.

"Oh good, I just know this will work out. You're only three miles from the beach, you know. There's really lots to do. I have several pamphlets if I can put my hands on them. Let's get Sadie's stuff in here and then we'll go back to the office."

Sadie's bed turned out to be a giant sofa without feet— billowing pillows made up the base and stuck up a foot in height around the edge. But it was a favorite. Sadie never left it the entire time they were loading up dog food and dishes.

"Okay, girl, time to get this to your new home." Dan clipped the leash back on and picked up one corner of the cumbersome dog bed. "Good grief, do you have bricks in here?" There wasn't any picking it up, it was too big and too heavy. Elaine helped but the two of them more dragged than carried the monstrosity to its new home. Then, placing a water bowl and a dish of kibble beside it, Elaine called Sadie.

The dog didn't need to be encouraged. Sadie buried her nose in the bowl enameled with paw prints and gulped more than tasted her food.

"I wasn't thinking but I bet she hasn't eaten a full meal in three days."

Dan watched as Elaine filled Sadie's food bowl for a second time. Probably wouldn't hurt her. He'd never seen a fat grey-hound…that was like saying there were obese vegetarians. He picked up his jacket and headed toward the car. A few suitcases and they were home. It was a relief to have found a place so quickly.

Chapter Four

The office wasn't opulent unless you knew what you were looking at—it was more Spartan than comfy. But original artwork, and not just paintings, highlighted the entire room. Dan would have bet that oversized glass bowl on a pedestal in the corner was Chihuly. Dan pulled out his iPad and rechecked the list of losses. He was pretty certain he remembered other artwork kept in the kennel office and lost in the fire. Yep, there it was. Five prints by Bridget Riley; the last appraisal put each at roughly sixty-seven hundred dollars—or somewhere close to a thirty-three thousand, five-hundred-dollar loss. Still, it was less than the insured worth of one greyhound.

The woman behind the desk on the phone looked up and motioned him toward a chair. He didn't mind the wait. All the better to size up his surroundings. The room was monochrome—gray, black, white—with enormous splashes of color from the art scattered around. The eight-foot-long desk was chrome and glass, the sofa a black leather "sling" purely Scandinavian with matching chairs. He couldn't name the artist but the large bronzes of two greyhounds sitting on the edge of the desk were spectacular—each over two feet tall.

But it was the woman who held his attention. Who was it who said a pet owner starts taking on the characteristics of his charge as he grows older? He remembered his mother kiddingly saying if she didn't get her upper lip waxed regularly, she'd end up looking like the family pet—a Schnauzer named Toby.

So this was Dixie Halifax. Ash blond, thick hair worn short and brushed back from a somewhat long and narrow face, eyes a pale gray under pencil-thin brows. Gray-striped suit, white silk blouse, red plastic framed reading glasses perched low on an aquiline nose, pearls at each ear and a long rope of them looping almost to her waist. A four-carat diamond on her right hand. The lady liked the finer things in life.

He'd memorized the Wikipedia entry: born in 1952, lawyer, known for having worked several high-profile cases, was a junior clerk during the O.J. trial. She'd spent years representing various "mob-stars." Married to an F. Marconi (1983), but widowed before the age of thirty. No other marriages. No children. Earned a reputation for getting a couple of family "godfathers" out of prison on technicalities. Recognized more recently for her work with dog tracks across the United States mediating Grey2X demands to clean up the industry. In addition, she was a top breeder and importer of greyhounds. The Halifax kennel was touted as dog racing's winningest one.

She held the phone away from her face, "Mr. Mahoney, isn't it? I'm so sorry for this—I'll only be another minute." A smile that could have been a grimace before Dixie covered the mouthpiece, stood, and walked to the floor-to-ceiling windows at the far end of the office. Out of ear-shot, not that Dan had been listening in. The accent was right out of the South—maybe Memphis or Little Rock. Nothing soft or lilting like an accent from Mississippi or Georgia. There was a distinct twang to this one. A sound that made you lock up your back molars before you even realized you were grinding your teeth. But there was certainly nothing to dispel the greyhound analogy, viewing Ms. Halifax from behind. Lithe, sinewy calf muscles, broad shoulders above tiny, waspish waist…yes, she could be the human counterpart to the dogs she raced.

The extended call did give him a few more minutes to admire the five ceramic greyhound vases on the credenza behind the desk. Vases? They were half the size of cookie jars. Then it hit him. These were urns, not vases. Each had a ribbon; one had two ribbons tied around its neck. Their racing colors. Dan was sure of it. He had to be looking at what United Life & Casualty was just about to pay two hundred and fifty thousand for. He leaned forward. Each ribbon had last Tuesday's date stenciled in gold. And there was a gold plate around each dog's neck engraved with its name.

"Finished, at last. Again, I am so sorry. I really abhor rudeness." Dixie crossed the room, settled the phone in its cradle on the desk, then perched on the edge of the polished teak base swinging one leg that ended in the highest heel of any shoe Dan had ever seen. "I can't stand these—cripplers for certain." She flipped one heel off and used bare toes to pry her other foot free. "There, much more like it. Now, how can I help?"

Interesting, but shaking hands didn't seem to be a part of the greeting ritual. Some women were comfortable with the custom, some not. Dan would have bet Ms. Halifax would be a hand-shaker. He glanced at his notes and then back up to meet a particularly cool stare. "My questions are perfunctory. I'm sure some sound invasive and even threatening, but United Life & Casualty needs as complete a picture of what happened as we're able to ascertain."

"I understand completely. Your work can't be easy where animals are concerned."

"No, you're right, it isn't. Ms. Halifax—"

"Dixie, please."

"Dixie…I thought we could talk here, and then I'd like to take a look at the office in the kennel—what's left of it, that is."

"Not a problem. I have an appointment at eleven but we'll find someone to show you around."

"Then let me start by offering my condolences—I understand the dogs lost were from your kennel? Bred and raced by you?"

"Yes. Two were currently on the track; both were three-year-olds. The other three were my future—some months away from racing but already showing tremendous promise. No, I'm not being melodramatic. I don't know when I've seen such finely honed natural instincts. You know, every once in awhile you get a dog that just doesn't like to race. If the will isn't in them, it's next to impossible to put it in."

"Why were all five dogs at the track if only two raced?"

"The two were slated for races in two days. I usually don't take them back and forth between my kennel and the track unless they have more than one day between races. The three babies were beginning track training. Various trainers get the youngsters started at quarter, then half, distances before testing their abilities at a full five-sixteenths or seven-sixteenths of a mile. People don't realize it, but a greyhound only travels a length of 1,650 feet up to 2,310 feet from starting box to finish depending on the track. But they have to be brought up to that distance, no matter how small it seems. Is this your first time at a dog track?"

"I admit to being a novice. Fascinating stuff, though. How long have you been involved?"

"This is a life's dream come true. I'd raised greyhounds for over twenty years, but it wasn't until about five years ago that I had the opportunity to buy a half interest in Daytona Beach Kennel Club and Poker Room. It just seemed the logical next step after being in the breed for so long."

"Did you feel you were taking a chance?"

Daisy uncrossed her legs and leaned forward, "Because of the state of racing today?" Dan nodded. "I didn't, but my friends did; so did my parents. Greyhound racing does face a somewhat precarious future. None of us knows how much longer we'll be around. I've taken a lot of guff for getting in on the downslide. But today, this is one of the few tracks running in the black."

"You make me think that wasn't always so." Had he hit a sore-spot? Dixie hesitated and raked sharp, white teeth over her bottom lip. Stalling. Trying to decide how much or even what to say?"

"We've struggled. I won't say that we haven't, but our position is unique. Most tracks offer casinos the chance to piggyback on their dog racing gaming permits. It's a lot easier to open and maintain a casino if it's built around dog-racing. It's this combination of live dog racing, closed-circuit games or simulcast horse races that keeps the public coming back. I just don't know for how long. If you throw in the bad press—drugs, dogs injured and even killed—more tracks have closed in the last few years than are still open. But I see a bright future—maybe not as glorious as the one past, but the world will always produce gamblers, Mr. Mahoney. Wouldn't you agree?"

Dan nodded. Yeah, there would always be those who would put down a little money in hopes of making more of it. But the cost of running a place like this—the restaurant, the kennels, a vet—all this could get to be prohibitive without a healthy group of repeat bettors, and just how many of those could there be in Daytona Beach, Florida? But maybe there were other related businesses. "Is training a big part of the track's revenue?"

"Not like it used to be. Not too long ago we would have had dozens of dogs in training and a full roster of trainers."

"And today?"

"Maybe three full-time trainers use the track. The number of youngsters getting their start here has dwindled to under twenty."

"I understand you've been active with the…" Dan checked his notes, "Grey2K people—the group who wants to close all tracks—you've helped them draw up a plan to change the face of the sport?"

"I've done what I can. Mostly I've listened. I've offered my services *pro bono* because I'd be the first to say in a number of instances they've had a point. The sport has needed to be cleaned up—greed and live animals are not a good mix."

"I would agree with you." Wasn't greed the motivator of almost every case he'd ever worked? He wouldn't expect it to be any different with live animals. "Oh, I almost forgot to ask if all five of your dogs were housed with the others? I think some fifty dogs total?"

"Yes and no. They were kept in the kennel area but their crates were not mixed in with the others."

"How were their crates separated? On an opposite wall? Next to, or at the end of a row of crates?"

"Actually on a wall adjacent to the door."

"Were there other handlers in the area? Other than Mr. Crumm, that is."

"Not Tuesday evening."

"What about maintenance people—this Fred Manson, for example?"

"Fred was out of here by five-thirty."

"I understand there are night races. Wasn't this early for him to leave?"

"Not at all. Fred has a crew that does track upkeep for the late races. No need for him to stick around. On the other hand, Fucher often worked late—and just as often worked another handler's night shift. We've never thought we had to have more than one person overseeing the kennel at night, especially when there was a reduced number of animals. Usually we house one hundred and twenty dogs—sometimes more—and that necessitates more than one handler."

"I can imagine the feeding alone, even of fifty dogs, would be far too much for one person."

"Yes, although it's not as daunting as it sounds. There's a routine, of course, for handler and dogs. Fifty dogs can be checked and fed within an hour. After eating and exercise, the dogs settle down quickly."

"So you obviously trusted Mr. Crumm?"

"What am I supposed to say to that? I *did* trust him. He's handicapped, but he's been with the track for years. It's only been recently that there's been any trouble."

"What kind of trouble?"

"Oh, I hate to be the one tattling but over the past year, Fucher seemed paranoid—pugnacious, even. Thought people were out for his job. On one occasion he pushed a young trainer into a fence and squirted him with a water hose just for correcting him. Fucher thought the young man was trying to get him in trouble. I know that doesn't sound like a big deal, but it attests to his deteriorating state of mind. I think when he lost his mother, he just unraveled."

"That would have been around Christmas time?"

"Yes. He started to forget things. There was a mix-up with medications and one dog almost died."

"A dog belonging to Mr. Jackson Sanchez?"

"Yes. Jackson reported it to me and the racing commission. In fact, he was very vocal—told anyone who would listen. He requested that handicapped individuals not be entrusted with dogs."

"Do you employ more than one special needs individual here at the track?"

"No, no we don't. We've been pressed to expand our hiring to include educable individuals who could be trained to care for the dogs and to offer the training here at the track through Daytona State College. Several of the kennel owners objected and the idea just sort of faded away. I think the college was disappointed—saw some federal funds evaporate. You can imagine how saying no was received—in this day of 'give everyone a chance.' Don't misunderstand, I'm all for offering gainful employment to those less fortunate, but, still, how far can we go if our dogs are put in danger?"

"Were you planning on firing Mr. Crumm?" He thought Dixie looked surprised, or maybe it was the extra moment of hesitation; but he thought she paused to gain composure...and to think how to phrase the answer.

"I talked with Fucher very sternly. I wanted him to understand the gravity of the situation."

"Translate 'very sternly' for me. Were threats of firing made?"

Again, she didn't answer at once. There was some smoothing of her skirt and studying the floor. Theatrics? Dan wasn't certain. "I didn't threaten him but Jackson did."

"Did you overhear this?"

"Well, no, but Jackson admitted it. And at least one of the trainers witnessed it. It was not done with my approval."

"Do you think this threat was enough to push Fucher into an act of murder?"

"In the past I would have said no, but after this last year, I have to say there's nothing that I can point to that exonerates him."

"Would he have a job here if he were to get out on bail?"

"I certainly don't see that happening."

"Having a job here or getting out on bail?" Did lawyers study how to be vague or confusing? He guessed he knew the answer to that.

Again, that pregnant pause and some fidgeting with her skirt. "Neither, I guess."

Now it was Dan's turn to wait for more explanation but none seemed to be forthcoming. Time to change the subject. "I'd like you to take a moment and go over this list of what was lost in the fire. Make any corrections or additions. I'll pick it up from your assistant later. If you have pictures—more recent than we might have on file of both the artwork and the dogs—I'd appreciate those. In the meantime I'd like to tour the kennel."

Dixie picked up the phone. A couple calls and a young woman knocked at the door. Dixie introduced her as Melody Paget, a track trainer. "I'm leaving you in really good hands. Mel is one of our best. Stop by on your way out—the list will be ready."

> > >

"It's a real mess out here." Melody was picking her way around piles of debris stacked outside the door to the building that housed the office, kennels, and several prep rooms. The acrid smell of smoke still hung in the air. Dan did a quick inventory—an overstuffed couch with two matching chairs water-soaked and barely recognizable, a charred heavy wooden desk and metal chair, a couple file cabinets, and a metal frame half melted that could have been from a cot, Dan thought. Not a lot.

"Is this everything from the office?"

"Yeah, pretty much. Firemen gave orders for it to be dragged outside—didn't want any flare-ups."

"Why don't we go see what's left inside?" Dan couldn't see anything that needed his attention out here.

"Don't get your hopes up. It's just a charred, soggy mess."

And she wasn't kidding. The building was cement block so this wing was still standing, but that was about all. Window casings had melted away, doors had disappeared, a large molten lump just inside the door had probably been a file cabinet. A couple of slender twisted pieces of metal resting against the wall suggested a picture frame. Must have been something poster-sized. He stepped into the room.

Dan's shoes squished as he walked and after taking about a half dozen steps forward, there didn't seem to be any point in going further. It must have been a hot fire which right up front suggested arson. He dragged out his trusty Nikon and snapped pictures—floor, ceiling, windows or lack thereof, doorway leading to the hall—this was more perfunctory than noticing something suspect. Soot, water stains, and charred wood supports obscured possible clues. It looked like arson and everyone supposed it was, but he made a mental note to check with the Volusia County FD and walked back through the door.

He paused in the hallway to record his notes. A dictaphone app...who could have guessed at how quickly technology would progress. But he wasn't complaining, the saved time was a boon. He turned slowly, pausing at each potential point of interest, and voiced his comments watching them miraculously pop up in print. Would he be giving away his age if he admitted to how impressed he always was by this technology? Yeah, probably.

"Ready to take a look at the kennels?" Melody had been standing quietly beside the doorway.

"Sure." He slipped the mini iPad into his briefcase and started to follow. "What the...?" He'd obviously stepped on something. He leaned against an outer wall, slipped off his right loafer and checked the crepe sole. Wedged into the rubbery grooves on the base of the shoe was a small die—the number 9.

"Any idea what this is?" He held out the blackened number in the palm of his hand.

"Part of an old tattoo kit. All racing greyhounds have tattoos."

Dan tried to get his mind around every dog having a heart on its chest with maybe MOM or a flag in the middle. "I don't think I'm following you."

"Oh, sorry, every dog has an identifying tattoo—one in each ear. In the right ear is the NGA registration number. That's National Greyhound Association. In the left you'll find a combination of letters and numbers. The first is a digit depicting month of birth, second digit is the year, and the third die is a letter which tells you what litter order the dog was tattooed in."

"Give me an example."

"Well, the five numbers in the right ear are self-explanatory. It's the left ear that gets tricky. If you have an 119B, the dog was born in November of 2009 and was the second dog in the litter to be tattooed. There will never be more than three numbers and a single letter in the left ear. Try this one: 88C."

"August of 2008 and the third dog in a particular litter to be tattooed."

"Perfect."

"Would tattoo kits have been kept in the office?"

"Not really. I don't know why any would even be at the track. The kennel owners tattoo their dogs long before we see them here. All a part of puppy preparedness. And the tattoos are usually done with a pretty sophisticated kit—or a pen nowadays if you have the money. That's the old-fashioned way." She pointed to the number 9 in his palm then bent forward for a better look. "Boy, this is from a really old set. It's some sort of pot metal, not even cast aluminum."

Dan turned the relic over. It appeared to be made of lead. He knew Melody was right; he doubted that this material was used anymore. He dropped it in his jacket pocket.

"Guess the kennel is next?" He fell in beside Melody and noted that the closer they got to the kennel area, the fewer the signs of a fire. Walls were still coated with a scummy gray over yellow utility paint, but other than evidence of water damage along the floor—ceramic tiles were broken and popping up—the kennel area had missed the brunt of a very hot fire.

"Where would the five dogs have been crated?"

"Right here by the door."

Dan stepped into the room and looked at row after row of large crates. Three deep, they covered every wall. And they weren't small but long enough and tall enough to allow even the biggest greyhound to move around comfortably.

"Where is this turn-out area—the place where most of the dogs were found?"

"Right across the hall. Fucher did an heroic job of corralling forty-five dogs and getting them to safety."

"Weren't some found in the hallway?"

"Only three."

"Any idea why they were separated from the rest?"

"Probably the last to leave their crates. One, I know for sure, was housed on the back wall—a young dog who may have been at the track only a couple times before. He would have been disoriented. I don't know about the others."

That made sense. Dan made a couple of notes. "I'm still not sure I understand how five dogs were lost."

"You're not alone." Melody's voice dropped to a whisper. "They were the closest to the smoke and Fucher says they just disappeared—he kept saying that he looked for them and they just weren't there. I think he was busy with all the others and he lost track of them. But why they'd head toward the fire and not away from it…well, goes without saying, that's a puzzle."

"What with the fire and the noise and the utter panic…it would be easy to become disoriented—even for a dog, don't you think?"

"Maybe, but their instincts are stronger than humans'—danger signs are built into their DNA. But it makes Fucher sound guilty. Like he didn't do enough—even with forty-five saved."

"Do you know how the dogs died?"

"Smoke inhalation, I think. They were only inches from safety, frantically trying to get out the side door."

Dan made a note to see if the track vet corroborated the story. "I guess I'm wondering why all five stayed together, didn't split up, follow the other dogs across the hall to safety."

"They were raised together, housed together—one of the dogs was a pretty dominant male—they probably just followed the wrong leader."

Dan stepped across the hall and opened the doors to the exercise area. The doors were in pretty good shape, some rubber insulation crinkled from heat but otherwise intact. The area was about four hundred square feet in size. He tried to imagine forty-five dogs in the space. Probably every one reacting to the smoke and fire—jumping around, howling, picking fights… how could anyone stay calm in that situation? He had new respect for Fucher.

"Anything else I should see?"

"I was going to point out the exits. The chain-link gate there leads to the track and that one," she pointed to her right, "goes to another closed-in area that extends to the maintenance barn."

"Maintenance for the track or grounds in general?"

"Mostly the track. It's pretty labor-intensive—it's dragged before every race. It's sand so it needs to be smoothed and leveled. Eight dogs per race means thirty-two paws digging into the surface. It gets torn up quickly."

"Anything else in the barn?"

"Only the usual lawn equipment—riding mowers, that sort of thing. And that's Fred's domain. You might want to get a hold of him for a tour. He doesn't like just anybody poking around."

Dan didn't think he needed to see the barn. Couldn't think of a good reason anyway. Maybe another day. He made a note of Fred's name. As usual, this was a puzzle. A challenged young man sitting in jail possibly without a good reason as to why; five urns on a desk; a hefty insurance payout; and, oh yes, lest he forget, a dead body.

"Do you have time to talk with the track vet? He asked me to bring you by."

Dan jerked back to the present. The vet was on his list, "Sure, now's a good time."

Melody led him down an east hallway and left him at the door to Kevin Elliot's office. A quick knock got him inside the immaculate office/lab/treatment room. Absolutely spotless and without any damage from the fire. The man behind the desk was probably his age, early fifties, salt and pepper hair, receding hairline, but crisply decked out in a freshly starched, white lab coat over faded jeans.

Kevin Elliott motioned him in. "Have a seat. I'd like to help in any way that I can."

Dan settled into a chair opposite the vet and took out the iPad. "I appreciate the time. I'd like to clear up a few things for starters."

"Fire away."

"Were you the first on the scene? That is, after Fucher Crumm and Jackson Sanchez."

"Yes, I was on my way into the office that morning. About five. Working early in the day is about the only time I can get paperwork done. It gets pretty crazy during race time. I'm more or less 24/7 around here and I'd just finished inoculating about thirty dogs for kennel cough—didn't get out of here until around eight in the evening. I decided to go home, get something to eat and a little rest before finishing up the files."

"Maintenance crew wasn't in yet?"

"Their day usually starts around six or six-thirty."

"Did you call in the fire?"

"Yeah. I thought I saw smoke from over this way coming down Williamson Boulevard. I called it in the minute I turned into the back lot. Flames were through the roof by then. Volusia FD got here in under ten minutes."

"But by that time you'd already found the five dogs that had died?"

"They were stacked up against the side door. It took a little muscle to just get the door open a couple inches—ended up breaking a window and crawling in. That's when I found them. I bagged up each of them and carried them out to my truck."

"About how long had they been dead?"

"Not long. Maybe only a matter of minutes. The fire was hot—blistering the paint on the walls in that end of the corridor. And any escape had been cut off—the fire closed in behind them. If I'd only been ten minutes earlier…These were dogs I'd cared for since they were whelped." Kevin reached across the desk for a couple Kleenex and blew his nose. "They weren't pretty to look at."

"I can understand. I'm a dog owner and it would be very difficult to lose my pet under these circumstances. When was Ms. Halifax alerted to the severity of the situation?"

"I'm afraid not until somewhat later when I was on my way to the crematorium. By the time I had the bodies in the truck, the fire department was here and things went from barely controlled craziness to all-out chaos."

"Did you check on the other dogs at this time?"

"I made sure they were safe, of course. Fucher did a hell of a job keeping forty-five dogs out of harm's way."

"If he was able to save forty-five, how could five have been lost?"

"I wonder the same thing. I would have expected the five to follow the others—go out the double doors across the hall. They were probably disoriented because they were released from their crates first. To be honest? I would not have expected them to go toward the fire—back into the building. That goes against natural instinct."

"Melody was saying the same thing. Do you think they had help?"

"Enticed to go against their instincts? That's interesting. But who?"

"I think we can assume Fucher already had his hands full. Jackson Sanchez was on the premises."

"Assuming he was alive."

"Has there been a time of death established?" Dan didn't remember any mention of one.

"Well, actually I have no idea. I'm sure an autopsy's been done. But then you'd have to come up with a reason for Jackson to even be here."

"It was unusual for him to be at the kennels at this hour of the morning?"

"Let's just say not the usual. If there was something that could be handled by an assistant, Jackson would be long gone. I think it's fair to say he wasn't very hands-on."

"Sounds like you might not have been too surprised by his death?"

"Hey, don't go putting words in my mouth. Jackson was an okay guy—liked the bottle a little too much and would go running off at the mouth when he shouldn't, but, you know, he was a fixture around here. I don't think anyone took him too seriously. I certainly never thought he had any enemies."

"You didn't hear that he'd threatened to fire Fucher?"

"Oh, that was a heat of the moment sort of thing—Jackson came close to losing a dog and he looked for someone to blame."

"Did he set things straight with Fucher? Apologize, maybe?"

"Not that I know of. Doesn't sound like Jackson—he didn't make many mistakes, if you know what I mean."

He didn't sound like a guy without enemies, Dan thought. "Oh, before I forget, when were the dogs cremated?"

"The night they died. I didn't see a reason to even take them out of the truck. As I said, I gave Dixie a call and got the go ahead. I use the facilities here in Daytona—out on Bellevue. I drove out there that morning and she met me. I have a folder of paperwork here somewhere." Dan waited as Kevin opened a couple of drawers before putting a manila envelope on the desk. "This has everything you'll need—dates, causes of death, cremation certificates."

Dan stood. "I won't keep you any longer. Thanks for this." He reached down and picked up the envelope. One more interview and he'd call it a day.

>>>

Because this was a "business" meeting, he'd called ahead to the county jail to state time and intent of his visit and to give the facility the opportunity to check his credentials. He also stated that he'd have a recorder. He doubted he'd use it but that depended upon Fucher. The visit was basically a trust-building one. County jails were usually more relaxed about rules—more relaxed than a state pen—but there was still protocol. They were used as a holding facility only, with long-term incarceration coming after a trial, when a move to permanent housing was made. Dan liked dealing with county facilities. If the jail followed normal procedures, Fucher would already be out of his cell and waiting on him.

And Dan wasn't disappointed. Fucher was much calmer today, Dan noted. He had been put in a small conference room with one ankle shackled to the chair he was sitting in and someone had given him a soda.

"Where's Sadie?"

"She's waiting in the car. I'll walk her after we're finished and you can see her." Thank God the end of October meant cooler weather. He'd found some shade and with a bowl of water and every window opened four inches, she would be fine. He didn't expect this to take long. He reminded himself to watch for signs of stress—he didn't want any answers skewed. He'd decided to take notes and not use a recorder. The less obtrusive, the better.

"You want a Coke?" Fucher pushed the red can his way.

"No, but thanks anyway."

"Can I see Sadie now?"

"I've got some questions I need to ask you first."

"Okay." Fucher sat forward elbows on the table. "Questions about Sadie?"

"These are questions about the fire."

"I answered lots of questions already."

"I'm sure you've had to." Dan sat down across from Fucher and opened his briefcase taking out the iPad. "Here are some pictures I took today of the office area. Can you show me where you slept?"

"In the corner on a cot. It's not there now."

"No, it burned in the fire. Was Sadie in the office with you?"

"Yeah. She slept on the cot, too."

A little crowded, Dan thought. "When you woke up that night, Sadie was gone?"

Vigorous nodding, "I called and called and then went out to find her."

"What time did you go to bed?"

"Maybe ten. There used to be a TV there but somebody took it home. So I don't know for sure."

"Did you wake up before you noticed the fire? I mean like to go to the bathroom or maybe if you heard something?" Leading the witness, Dan admonished himself, but it didn't seem to lead anywhere as he noted Fucher shaking his head.

"I just woke up when the fire made the office all orange. And the smoke, that was bad. I ran out the door but that's when I fell over Jackson."

"Jackson Sanchez? A kennel owner at the track."

"Yeah."

"Where was Jackson?"

"Right there." Fucher pulled the screen closer and pointed to the doorway of the office. "There was a puddle of blood all over here"—again his index finger swept the doorway area—"and I stepped right in it. He was in the middle."

"What did you do when you found him?"

"He was on his stomach with a big knife handle sticking straight up right in the middle of his back. Well, I pulled the knife out. That's the first thing." And left a good set of prints for the police, Dan was certain.

"Can you show me where the knife was?" Dan walked around to the other side of the table, stopped by Fucher and turned around. "Touch my back where the knife was sticking out."

Fucher stood and poked his finger to the right of Dan's spine directly between his shoulder blades and sat down. "Right there."

"Thank you, Fucher." Dan walked back around the table to his chair. It wouldn't have taken more than a man of average height, Dan noted. "Can you describe the knife?"

"My momma would have called it a butcher knife."

"You mean a kitchen knife of some sort?"

"Yeah, like for cutting up a chicken."

Dan paused. Butcher knife? That didn't exactly scream "premeditation." More like grab what's handy—a spur-of-the-moment, in the heat of anger sort of thing.

"Is there a kitchen close to the office?"

"Right next door." Fucher pointed to the left of the now non-existent office. Convenient. Made spur-of-the-moment even more likely. And it did make Fucher look guilty. Someone had to know where to find a knife.

"Do you remember what you did after you took the knife out?"

"Yeah, I turned him over. Then I had to go let the dogs out."

"Did you take the knife with you?"

"No, it fell on the floor. I never saw it again, even after I came back."

"You came back?"

"I needed to get Jackson out of the fire. I know his momma— well, I seen her here at the track. If Jackson had burned it wouldn't have shown respect for his family."

"Are you saying you moved the body?"

"Didn't have to. Jackson was gone. I thought he maybe crawled away. I thought he was dead but maybe I was wrong. Then the police said they found him where I found him—the first time when I fell over him in the doorway to the office. Only I don't think he crawled back."

"Let me get this straight—you first fell over Jackson in the doorway, here," Dan pointed to the iPad screen. "You pulled the knife out of his back and turned him over?" Vigorous nodding. "Then you ran to let the dogs out and when you came back to the office, Jackson's body was gone?"

More nodding. "Just like those dogs."

"What dogs?"

"Max and Mellow Yellow and Sandy—"

"Wait. Slow down a little here. I don't know these dogs."

"The ones that died. Only I never saw them. When I went to open those crates? They were empty."

"Which crates were these?"

"Right inside the door. I went to let them out first but every crate was open and no dog."

No wonder he told Mel he hadn't seen them. He meant that they never existed—that they weren't there. Literal thinking always threw people a curve. "Did you tell the police this?"

"They said I forgot. They said the fire and smoke mixed me up. But Mister Mahoney, I know better. I know what I didn't see. All them crates were empty. They were in their crates when I fed them—that would have been about six. Then at seven-thirty they were put up in their crates again after they were exercised. But they weren't in those crates once the fire started." Fucher's breath came in short bursts, "I never hurt them dogs. I loved them. I didn't start that fire. I didn't kill Jackson Sanchez. I want to go home. I want to see Sadie." His voice now was a wail and the rocking was picking up in intensity.

Dan reached across and put his hand on Fucher's arm and left it there until the sobs subsided and he quieted. Then Dan took a deep breath and slowly exhaled. This put a wrinkle in things. He should probably just go ahead and extend the lease on the townhouse because something told him the young man sitting beside him wasn't capable of lying. And if he were telling the truth, UL&C would want more answers. Dan simply had to prove that the fire wasn't started by or at the bidding of someone who stood to gain from the killing of five greyhounds.

He hadn't planned on it but after walking Sadie around the parking lot and waving a few times to Fucher, Dan went back inside the building. He needed to pick up the copy of the police report he'd requested, and he might as well see if the arresting cop was available to answer a couple questions as long as he was here.

"You're in luck. Officer Bartlett is just getting off duty." The girl at the desk presumably buzzed the locker room because a young man in street clothes stuck his head through the door to the reception area.

"You needed to see me?"

"Officer Bartlett? Dan Mahoney here. I'd like a couple minutes of your time—I have a few questions concerning the fire at the greyhound track this week." Dan handed him a card.

"Sure. Is the conference room empty?" With a nod from the receptionist, Officer Bartlett picked up a key from her desk and indicated Dan follow him down a short hallway. "Not the most comfortable but it'll work." He opened the door to roughly a

five-hundred-square-foot space with a huge carved oak table that
would seat at least fifteen, Dan thought. Metal folding chairs
screamed tight budget and made him think the table was probably donated. And, no, it wasn't really comfortable—the table
was way too high for the chairs, but Dan took a seat. He briefly
explained who he was and why he was there—five dead dogs
whose deaths needed to be investigated.

"Now, how can I help?" Officer Bartlett pulled up a chair
opposite.

"You were the first on the scene at the track fire, correct?"
Dan continued after a nod from the officer. "What were your
reasons for arresting Mr. Crumm?"

"Well, other than he had blood all over him and we'd found
a body and a knife. We figured we had a pretty good reason to
detain him. He admitted he'd handled the knife but tried to tell
us the body had disappeared and then showed up again. Some
kind of screwy story. Same thing with those dogs that died."

"Did you see the dogs?"

"The bodies? No, the vet had bagged them and already had
them loaded in his truck by the time we got there. Only body
we dealt with was this Jackson Sanchez."

"Why do you think Fucher said the body moved?"

"Who knows? The guy's not right—you know, a couple
bricks shy."

Dan ignored the ill-timed attempt at humor. Bad taste, to
say the least, and maybe hinted at a preconceived prejudice.
Slapping cuffs on Fucher made his life easier. Solved a problem
without a lot of work.

"Didn't you wonder why if he was the murderer he'd still be
hanging around working—feeding and taking care of forty-five
dogs?"

"Like I said you can't count on this guy to make much sense. I
think he got confused, turned around by all the noise and smoke.
Do I think he could have killed Mr. Sanchez and started a fire
to cover it up? Yeah, I do. In my line of work you learn to never
underestimate the handicapped. The call I hate to take most?

When someone mentally impaired is holding a family hostage. Or doing anything threatening, for that matter. It's like walking into a minefield. You just never know what's going to happen."

"And you think he would have knowingly endangered the lives of the dogs he cared for by starting a fire? I've talked to Fucher. He may be a bit challenged, but I think he pretty much knows right from wrong and recognizes danger when he sees it."

"When it comes to all those dogs in the kennel that night, I don't think he thought things through. I don't think he's capable of following a thought to its logical conclusion."

"But this same individual was able to save the lives of forty-five dogs—that seems to take some deductive reasoning."

"He lost five—didn't you just say that's your interest in the case? Five insured animals? Hey, I don't think I can help you any so if you don't have any more questions, I'm a little behind in some end-of-the-day R & R. By the way, it turns out this Fucher had a pretty good reason to be angry at Jackson Sanchez. Guess the guy was trying to get him fired. That's reason enough in my books to do him in."

Dan stood. This was a dead end and a little unnerving. He hated closed minds and the man in front of him certainly seemed to have one. He thanked the officer, picked up the incident report from the receptionist, and walked out to the SUV. Slipping behind the wheel he instantly got a wet kiss on the ear and didn't reprimand Sadie as she crawled over the console into the passenger-side front seat. He liked this dog and he really liked the dog's owner. Dan was beginning to think of Fucher as having been framed. Dangerous thinking. He had no evidence and was letting emotions push in. Yet that cop left a bad taste in his mouth. Maybe he shouldn't read more into it. It was probably just what he said, he was in a hurry to get away from work and unwind. Still…a lack of feeling and a bit too quick to finger-point. No, not enough to judge someone on. Dan admonished himself to keep an open mind.

Chapter Five

"Mom's moving to Florida." Dan folded the letter and slipped it back into its lilac-scented envelope. Even his tech-savvy mother reverted to some time-honored Emily Post tradition of only the written word would do in matters of importance. He would have thought an email would have sufficed. Not the guaranteed to get there within twenty-four hours delivery that cost her an arm and a leg. He'd sent their new address via email. Had that been a mistake? He hadn't lived in the same state as his mother in over twenty years. He hadn't counted on starting now.

"She's coming here? Are you joking?" Elaine took a toaster out of the box marked "kitchen." Joan hadn't been kidding, her garage held all the comforts of home. And their new home was shaping up—furniture in place, dishes in cupboards—they'd spent the weekend acting like newlyweds. Putting the finishing touches on the first "place" they'd lived in together. Granted, it was a rental and destined to be short-lived, but still they were having more than a little fun fixing things up.

"I may wish I was."

"She's not moving in—"

"With us? No. Mom would be the first to nix that."

"So where in Florida is she moving? I presume with Stanley?"

"Someplace called The Villages and, yes, Stanley seems to be very much in the picture."

"I really like your mother. I'd be the first to say dear sister Carolyn can be a pain in the ass, but your mom seems to really have it together—you know, confident of what she wants and goes for it. This could be a good thing."

"True. She wants us to help with their house-hunt."

"So it's close to here?"

"About an hour and a half away. Seventy-five miles, to be exact, on the other side of Orlando."

"Tell her we'll do it. We have a little 'wait and see' time. You still have some interviewing to do but didn't you say the track's not due to reopen for another couple days? It'll be fun."

Fun probably wouldn't be his descriptive term, but like Carolyn, he felt his mother in small doses could be…interesting. Stanley, he wasn't sure about. The only time he'd been around him, Dan had listened to an hour's diatribe on the need to unionize college ball and quit screwing over the players. That, a sadly overdone smoked turkey, and warm beer just about summed up the afternoon. How often could he put himself through that?

"Oh no. Look at this." Elaine had flipped open her laptop and placed it on the kitchen counter. "Maggie Mahoney may want to consider running drugs in her new community. One little blue pill can go as high as fourteen dollars."

"Viagra? Isn't this a senior community?"

"Don't be naive. It's not supposed to wear out." The gesture, index-finger extended, appeared to be aimed at his crotch.

"Right." Dan didn't need an explanation of what "it" was; he just willed himself to tune back into what she was saying and stop figuring out how many good years his "it" had left.

"Listen to this—The Villages is a hot bed…literally…for STDs and the human papilloma virus."

"Seriously? What about golf courses, lakes, clubs…you know, regular amenities?"

"I am being serious. Sex seems to be the amenity. A little value-added. Couples have been picked up for doing it in golf carts, poolside, in the sauna—"

"You're making this up."

"Take a look." Elaine turned her laptop toward him.

Dan leaned forward and scanned the article. Then he pulled up another. This wasn't some shock-factor writing by a reporter seeking his or her fifteen minutes of fame; there were a number of articles from several newspapers including the *Times*. Even a gynecologist warning women to insist upon protection. To not take for granted that just because they might be too old to get pregnant that there weren't some other worries out there.

Still it was a little tough to accept…his mother and all. The caption under the picture of a golf cart heading away from the photographer, the woman's arms around the driver—"sex on wheels." Another article, presumably more of a sales pitch, head-lined—"If you weren't 'lucky' in high school, get 'lucky' now!"

Dan closed the laptop.

"Do you think she has any idea?" Elaine was placing the toaster next to a coffee grinder on the counter.

"I would doubt it. I think we need to check it out first. I can't believe the articles were telling the truth. Just more sensational-ism, I hope."

"Are you suggesting a road trip?"

"Why not? I'd feel better if I could talk about the place objec-tively. I'm sure there are other places in Florida to live. We could look into one of those seaside communities. A condo in Ormond Beach, maybe—they're advertised everywhere."

"I think we should. I don't see the attraction of a community that's landlocked. Unless Stanley plays golf?"

"Don't ask me but I'd guess he does. The word 'duffer' comes to mind when I think of him."

"Dan, be nice. This is your mother's life and if she's happy with Stanley, then we should be, too."

Dan wasn't sure about that line of reasoning but he had to hand it to his mother; at seventy-four (or was she only admitting to seventy-two?), she was out having fun. How many cruises had she taken last year alone? He should be thankful he wasn't visiting or supporting her in a nursing home. And Stanley? Well, he just wouldn't spend a lot of time thinking about that.

"Do we have a date of arrival?"

"Mom said they were hoping to be here this week."

"So soon?"

"I think they've been planning this for awhile. Our being here just seems to have hastened the decision."

"How sweet. You should be flattered."

Maggie Mahoney had never struck him as "sweet" and had never needed backup to make up her mind. There was something odd about wanting him involved. Guess he'd find out why quickly enough.

>>>

"You know what? This is Disneyland for adults." Dan braked quickly for a golf cart that careened into his path. "The area is beautiful—I have to give it that. Lake Sumter, inland canals…" He'd turned onto the main boulevard that led to the center of the "town." So this was the infamous Villages. He kept looking but he didn't see a bicycle or anyone walking and he didn't see an animal on a leash—no one out for a stroll with the family Yorkie or French Bulldog. In fact, there weren't *any* animals, on a leash or off. No errant squirrel or rabbit dashing across the road in front of him, and he hadn't seen a bird in five miles. Roadkill? What was that? The place was clean. Amend that, sterile would be a better word. God forbid he should see a little graffiti. That was probably a hanging offense.

They seemed to have arrived at Lake Sumter Landing Market Square. That alone was a mouthful. Brightly colored storefronts, hanging pots of flowers, scrubbed sidewalks, and not one place to park. Some parking spots held three golf carts all lined up. He continued driving block after block, thinking that the public parking lots would have room—but no. Frustrating. And all the time he had to be on the lookout for golf carts. They were everywhere.

Dan idly wondered if they held recreational events with the ubiquitous carts—some form of chariot racing in a coliseum on weekends, maybe. Okay, now he was just letting his imagination run wild, but the generation he was looking at had driven some souped-up cars in their day. He tried to conjure up what a turbocharged golf cart would look like.

"Dan, quick, a parking place." Elaine pointed to her left. The last spot in a public lot. "It'll be fun to walk around a little."

A stroll in The Villages wasn't Dan's idea of fun, still he would like some lunch and there was a feeling of relief that he wouldn't be circling the rest of the afternoon just trying to land.

The main street seemed to have all the usual stores and restaurants. Italian sounded good and the Red Sauce looked inviting. With a population of over sixty thousand in mostly an over-sixty demographic, eating out was a way of life. He quickly noticed that the twenty- and thirty-something wait people stood out in stark contrast. He wondered where they lived. On the periphery outside city limits, he guessed. He was tempted to say outside "the dome" because that's what it reminded him of—a special, sterile living bubble that dropped over a certain few acres and kept an homogenous way of life intact.

He remembered reading that there was a fifty-five-year-old requirement for residency and no one under nineteen could visit longer than thirty days in any calendar year. Wow. He never thought he'd long for kids on skateboards, but he was getting close.

"Mr. Mahoney, how nice to see you again." Dixie Halifax stepped out from a booth. "I'd like you to meet my mother, Agnes Halifax, and my father, John. I wouldn't have expected to see you here." A sweet half-smile from Agnes, a nod from John.

Dan introduced Elaine and explained they were on a check-it-out sort of trip for his mother and her partner. He hoped he was being correct that "partner" didn't denote only same-sex arrangements. But what did you call "live-ins"? You couldn't use the word "lover" in polite company, not that he even associated that word with his mother, and "mate" seemed dated and at the very least gave him an Aussie accent. Significant other? He remembered picking up a popular magazine recently that had an article on "Sig-Os." No, "partner" was the best choice.

"My parents moved here last year and love it." Dixie had sat back down. "Good to see you make use of a little track downtime.

Things will get busy once we open up again." She passed the breadbasket to her mother.

Dismissed. Apparently allotted small-talk time was over and Dan and Elaine followed the hostess to a booth at the back of the dining area.

"A shame Dixie's parents aren't able to speak for themselves." Elaine was being a little snide, but those were his sentiments exactly. The lady seemed to have real control issues. "I can see why Melody didn't want to cross her."

"Me, too. I'm glad we took Sadie in."

"So what do you think? Is the place a thumbs-up for Maggie and Stanley?" The entrees of pasta and sauces were excellent, salads crisp, bread fresh...crème brulee, a perfect touch with coffee. With the dishes removed and only the coffee left, it felt good to just relax and talk. Based on the last few months, this was a luxury. Elaine leaned against the cushioned seatback.

"I have to look at things through their eyes. I'd hate it but I'm not in my seventies and not a golfer. It's probably fine for them. Maybe they could rent for awhile—not make a decision to buy until they were sure."

"I'd agree to that." Now if he could only convince his mother.

"Your mom still has an apartment in Chicago but spends a lot of her time visiting Carolyn in New Mexico. Do we know where Stanley is from?"

"She met him on a cruise—I've forgotten which one. I think it was the Arthur Murray cruise—billed as a dance camp on the waves."

"That sounds so romantic."

"Yeah, I guess." Okay, he needed a little work in the romance department but he knew without a shadow of a doubt that if he lived to be a hundred, he wouldn't be tripping the light fantastic on the deck of a cruise ship. Nope. Not today. Not tomorrow. Not ever.

"Let's go look at some houses." Elaine pushed out of the booth and stood. The sideways glance made him think she'd read his mind.

Chapter Six

Their townhouse looked pretty good. A trip to the World Market on International Speedway Boulevard for a few throw pillows and cloth napkins, a set of Mexican, hand-blown margarita glasses and pitcher, little hand-carved end tables from Africa, a framed seascape poster for the upstairs bath, and the place was becoming a home. Granted, some of these were things she'd have to donate to Joan's garage when the time came to move, but in the meantime, they would enjoy them. She had dropped Dan off at the track and the day was hers to putter away. Well, do laundry, grocery shop, and give Sadie a nice long walk.

One of the first things she intended to do was wash Sadie's bed. There was every indication that it had never been washed. A little too much dog hair and doggy odor to be living with it in such a small space. And poor Fucher probably didn't even notice.

The bed's flannel outer case had a zipper. She only hoped washing the casing would do the trick and that the stuffing wasn't too "doggy." She wasn't sure what she'd do then, maybe buy some cheap towels and fill the bag. Getting Sadie to relinquish her favorite spot took some coaxing. And a hotdog. But finally Sadie was closed in the kitchen with her treat, and Elaine was sitting on the floor with the dog bed.

The first thing she realized was that the flannel case was just a covering for a heavy canvas-like material that was really the bag itself. This was not a cheap bed. Elaine peeled off the first cover and set it aside. The canvas covering had a heavy-duty zipper that was rusted and probably reflected its age. Or was maybe just another victim of the salt air this close to the ocean. But there was no doubt that it needed a washing, too.

The zipper took a little work and a trip to Joan's garage to borrow some WD-40. Finally she'd inched the zipper back about a foot but needed more light to continue. Grabbing one end of the bed she jerked it upright and pulled it after her toward the nearest window. Turning back to sit down she sucked in her breath and dropped the bed. Trailing after her across the floor were several neatly bound stacks of twenties with more peeking out of the unzipped hole.

"Oh my God…" She'd found Fucher's bank. And it made sense that he wouldn't trust a real bank or maybe just didn't know how to open an account. So, a dog bed worked just as well. Gave new meaning to keeping one's savings under the mattress. But now what to do? Count it? It was beginning to bother her to even look at what promised to be quite a sum. It raised all kinds of questions—who should be notified? Was Fucher really responsible enough to make decisions? But maybe more importantly, could they, or even *should* they use it to make his bail?

〉〉〉

"Two hundred and ninety thousand dollars." The stacks of twenties covering the dining room table were impressive. Dan had counted it twice, yet it was still difficult to believe. In a dog bed and who knew how long it had been there. Amazing that it hadn't been stolen but then who would look in a dog bed? Quite possibly Fucher had found one of the best kept secrets for safeguarding valuables at home. Made him think of a certain Barbasol can that had held a five-hundred-thousand-dollar necklace in Wagon Mound, New Mexico. People could be pretty inventive when it came to hiding valuables. But then so could thieves when it came to finding them. Fucher had been lucky his "bank" hadn't been discovered.

"What should we do? This amount of money makes me really nervous." Elaine was just staring at the table. "I don't think I could sleep tonight knowing it was here."

"I'm with you. We need to get it somewhere for safekeeping—preferably a bank. Didn't Joan say her brother was a lawyer and had helped Fucher with money matters before? That's probably the best place to start."

> > >

Roger Carter didn't ask questions but came to the townhouse at his sister's insistence. And simply kept shaking his head as he looked at the piles of twenties.

"I wondered where the rest of the settlement was. Fucher had made so many handouts and loans that I just supposed it had all trickled away. He was pretty close-mouthed. I knew I probably didn't have a record of all of them. And collecting was going to be a nightmare even with contracts."

"Has there been a hearing?" Dan knew that that would determine bail.

"Interestingly enough, set for tomorrow morning. I'll be representing Fucher. I hate to think my degree in criminal law is coming in handy for a friend. I know you don't know him but I'd like to think you concur with me that an innocent man is being charged."

"I think we both agree with you," Elaine added.

"I'm going to re-count this and draw up papers as to when and how it was found, and then we'll take it to the bank. I know the charge is murder but I think under the circumstances, and knowing Fucher's limitations, the judge won't see him as a flight risk. I think we'll get a reasonable bail."

"Any guess as to what the sum might be?" Dan was hoping the two hundred and ninety would cover it.

"Probably two hundred and fifty. It's a little high only because the charge is murder. Why don't you join me at the courthouse in the morning? Nine sharp. I've got a judge that doesn't like his time wasted waiting.

> > >

Fucher looked almost handsome in a sports jacket and tie. Even his jeans looked neatly pressed, the cuffs covering the shackles.

He excitedly waved to all his friends until Roger made him turn around. Mel sat two rows up beside a rather dapper look-ing older man in a somewhat dated suit, white shirt, and tie. His short white beard looked neatly trimmed for the occasion and white hair curled away from his face in a cherubic halo of fluff. The way his lower jaw sort of slanted backwards tucking in just slightly under his upper lip, Dan guessed the man wasn't wearing his lower dentures. Must be Fred, Fucher's friend, the maintenance guy.

The judge was punctual but the surprise came when it was determined that Dixie Halifax, the Daytona Dog Track, *and* the family of Jackson Sanchez would be represented by joint counsel. Being some ten minutes late didn't endear them to the judge. But finally, two lawyers, a man and a woman, took their seats at a table in front of the dais. Dan's sixth sense put him on alert but he wasn't sure why. They wouldn't interfere with his investigation, but he was just curious as to why Ms. Halifax and the track felt they needed representation.

It didn't take long to figure out—after the two lawyers pre-sented an overview of the supposed losses. Ms. Halifax and the track were looking for compensation for downtime including lost wages for employees, and the Sanchez family expected to pursue a wrongful death suit, hoping to recoup half a lifetime of unreal-ized earning power—lost salary and support of two children.

Wow. Someone must think Fucher had deep pockets, Dan thought. But then the lead lawyer on the opposing team argued against bail. They did not want Fucher Crumm released. Char-acterized him as a threat to humanity—not in control of his own emotions. It was difficult to sit and listen to the character assigna-tion of someone so trusting. Fucher had to be hushed several times.

Roger asked to approach the bench and, finally, both lawyers left the courtroom to meet in the judge's chambers. Coming back into the room some fifteen minutes later, Roger caught Dan's eye and gave him the briefest of nods. The opposing attorney looked disgruntled and quickly pushed papers into his briefcase all the while whispering to the woman beside him at the table.

But bail was set at two hundred and fifty thousand and after Roger explained to Fucher what had happened, there was much jumping up and down—even in shackles. Followed by Mel and Fred hugging each other and then coming down front to hug Fucher.

It took a moment for Roger to get everyone's attention. "I'll pick him up at the jail later after I withdraw the bail money and sign a few papers. I'm relieved it's turned out this way. How 'bout dinner on me tonight? I'm thinking Bonefish Grill, Atlantic Boulevard in Ormond. Let's say around seven?"

Chapter Seven

Dan could not stop smiling as Fucher tried first one appetizer and then another—the verdict written clearly on his face after usually one bite or a loud, "This one's yummy." A generous mound of fried calamari had just disappeared into his mouth and a thin trail of dipping oil left a shiny streak down his chin. But Fucher was oblivious—Sadie was in a car outside in the parking lot, he was snuggly back in his house, and all was right with his world. Joan Carter had set him up with several odd jobs—maybe more busy work than much-needed repairs—and Mel had promised to get him involved in preparing Nero for the track. Life was good again. Dan certainly hoped it would stay that way.

He looked around the table—Roger, Joan, Mel, Fred, Elaine, himself—this was Fucher's family. And he could certainly do worse. Mel and Roger were going to petition the judge to allow Fucher to cross county lines to travel to Miami. Next weekend would be Nero's debut at a Class A track. There was a lot of clinking of iced tea and water glasses and toasting to well-deserved success. Dan thought he'd never forget the look of utter joy on Fucher's face.

For the first time in almost a week, Dan felt he'd accomplished something. But he knew UL&C would want more than a gut feeling that the accused was innocent and he wasn't sure how he was going to go about that. He needed to prove that Fucher not only didn't start the fire that killed the greyhounds but he didn't do it at the request of Dixie Halifax. Accidental death, the result of criminal intent—someone wanted to cover a murder? That's what it looked like. But Fucher just didn't fit the bill. And, yeah, it wasn't Dan's job to prove Fucher's innocence. But the guy could use a little help. What he did have to prove was that the one insured had no hand in setting up the circumstances that gave him or her the payoff. But Dixie killing her own dogs? Tough to get his mind around. Still, for the moment he just wanted to bask in the glow of a small victory. Fucher Crumm was not incarcerated.

〉〉〉

"So what's the plan of action?" He knew Elaine was genuinely curious and the ride back to Daytona gave them time to talk.

"I need a break. A break in the case."

"What would that break look like?"

"Not sure, but I think I'd recognize it." A rueful smile. He was always suspicious when things were too neatly wrapped up—especially before he got there. There were a lot of people jumping to conclusions in this case. And not enough people asking questions.

"See, it's just this kind of dead end, too-neatly-wrapped-up kind of investigation that makes me second-guess my wanting to be a PI. If the authorities are just accepting the easy way out and don't seem to be trying to uncover other possibilities, then what chance do you have?"

"Good point, but I have a two-hundred-fifty-thousand-dollar payout that better go to the right person."

"So, if it's proved that Fucher started the fire that caused the losses, Dixie stands to gain? She gets the full two-fifty?"

"Yeah. Dixie's name is the only one on the policy. And I don't see any breaks in sight. If Fucher is innocent, he's the perfect fall guy. His explanation of what happened is easy to discount because of his challenges and, before we came along, it didn't seem anyone was looking out for his interests. All in all, he'd be a good choice to take the brunt of a murder and cover-up. Did Dixie have any part in all this? I just don't think things happened the way they're being presented. And I'm not sure my gut feelings have ever been wrong."

"Do you think you were born with 'gut feelings' or are they more of a skill that can be learned?"

"Really good question. I think any PI needs to have a healthy natural curiosity and a sixth sense that keeps him from accepting everything at face value. But the rest of it comes from exposure—by the fifteen-hundredth surveillance case you work on, your instincts will be honed to perfection."

"I hope so. To even get started I need to align myself with a local PI—someone with a license in Florida."

"Leaves me out. Are you sure you want to start now? We could be here two weeks, a month…I have no idea."

"All the courses are online so I could be anywhere, but the very first assignment involves actual fieldwork. Real hands-on. I kinda like that—jump right in, get exposure to surveillance work outside of a textbook. I guess I don't see why I shouldn't be doing something more than washing dog beds."

"Hey, don't knock it. That was pretty lucrative for a little homemaker." He ducked the blow to his shoulder. "But when it comes to working with a local PI, there need to be some ground rules."

"Such as?"

"For starters, do not team up with anyone under the age of seventy. Do not agree to any overnight surveillance. Do not—" This time Elaine's fist connected soundly with his shoulder.

›››

The online yellow pages for the area listed five private investigators—only three appeared to have actual offices. Elaine started with those. The first almost laughed in the phone barely covering the receiver before a chortle of disgust. A university professor in the humanities, no less, wanted to start a career in private investigation? That was a good one.

The second one's receptionist put her through to an individual who seemed to feel it was his express reason for living to tell her how little money she'd make and how very dangerous the job was. Another strikeout. And, oh my goodness, she'd never shot a gun? And didn't even own one? She probably imagined the barely discernible "poor thing" before hanging up, then again, maybe not.

There had to be an easier way. Of course, she should have thought of this first—she called the college. Yes, of course, the department had a list of several PIs they could recommend. But if the receptionist were doing the choosing, it would be Scott Ramsey. Elaine took his number and email address and hung up. She looked him up online. He'd been in the business for twenty-seven years. Would that make him closer to seventy? Probably not, but definitely out of his thirties. And he didn't want to discuss particulars over the phone; he wanted a personal interview. Could she meet with him in the morning at his office in Palm Coast? Yes. Absolutely. She preferred it, too. She'd see him at eleven.

The office was easy to find. She dropped Dan off at the track and headed north on Highway 1. Palm Coast was a mere thirty-five minutes away. She took the Palm Coast Parkway exit to Pine Lakes Blvd. and just as the GPS promised, her destination was on the left.

If she'd expected some rundown rickety storefront, she would have been wrong. This small, two-room office around the corner from a veterinarian had space for a receptionist, ample storage, a wall of local maps, another office, *and* a conference room that probably only seated four comfortably, but still offered space to meet and work. The magazines were not only up-to-date but offered a wide range of choices—from *Money* to *US* to *Car And Driver*. The wait wasn't long, the leather chair was comfortable, and if customer satisfaction could be gauged by the looks of adoration from the woman coming out of the PI's office, he'd just earned five stars.

"Ms. Linden? Give me another minute or two and then we can talk. Linda would be happy to get you coffee or a soft drink."

"I'm fine, thank you." Well, he certainly wasn't going to pass the "close to seventy" test. And he'd probably never seen a gym he didn't like. This man was forty-something and looked thirty-five. Shaved head, dark tan, a bodybuilder's physique… he could be a poster boy for the PI industry. Definitely not what Dan had in mind.

But he asked the right questions, wasn't in a rush, and didn't seem to have any preconceived notion of what a PI needed to look like or what kind of background might be a prerequisite. He wasn't put off by a PhD in English Lit—thought it meant she had solid research skills; in fact, he had a master's in exercise physiology. Which, as he put it, only meant he could probably win a footrace if called for. He was more than familiar with the coursework from Daytona State College's online certification and licensing program—he'd helped design it. He continued to be on their roster as a guest lecturer and curriculum advisor. He appreciated their referrals because he enjoyed mentoring so much.

Elaine felt herself relax. Scott Ramsey was perfect. He just wouldn't pass Dan Mahoney's stringent requirements. Or were those restrictions? Scott took an hour to go through his syllabus—all on-the-ground training exercises involving real-life, hands-on cases and all approved by the college. She would need to apply for a permit to carry. He had the paperwork handy and could recommend the gun-safety school in Daytona. Good material and good instructors with a practice range adjacent. He suggested getting the paperwork in right away. She could get the required passport-sized picture taken at the local library for a nominal fee, and do the fingerprinting at the sheriff's office. He assumed she had no felonies and hadn't recently escaped from any type of mental institution. Elaine thought this was a form of PI humor but assured him the answer was "no" on both accounts.

He'd like them to start on their first assignment Friday and maybe work through the weekend if called for. Uh oh. Wasn't this a planned getaway weekend? A couple days at the beach? She hadn't expected going to school to meld easily with Dan's schedule, still to give up the first free weekend ….

"Not a good time?" He was watching her closely. "I'm hoping we won't need any extra time but just in case."

"It's fine." She hoped her smile supported that statement. How perceptive, but then "reading people" was certainly a part of his job. She left his office with a quick-read book designed to give her a thorough overview, *The Complete Idiot's Guide To Private Investigating*, 3rd edition. She was going to ignore the title but, then, it was rather apropos. Still, she had over a page of notes and an appointment time of four p.m. on Friday. And she might as well sign up for that class in gun-safety training, too. She reached for her phone and felt a little blip of excitement—it looked like she was on her way.

〉〉〉

The car in the driveway outside the townhouse wasn't familiar. A white Chrysler or Buick sedan. Elaine wasn't supposed to pick up Dan for another hour, and she didn't think they were expecting guests. She parked in front, gathered up her class materials and got out of the SUV.

"Oh, wait. I didn't mean to block the garage. I'll move my car." The woman's bright red bob was partially hidden by a narrow-brimmed, black fedora. Maggie Mahoney stood on the porch, waving and gesturing toward the car in the drive.

"Please, don't bother. I have to pick up Dan in an hour, so I won't be putting the car in."

"I hate to see you leave it on the street." Dan's mother leaned in with a loud, smacking air-kiss just as Elaine reached the top step of the porch. "I couldn't have planned this better. An hour of girl-talk before we're interrupted. I've so looked forward to getting to know you better."

"Me, too." And that wasn't a fib. One lunch with Mom and sister, Carolyn, in Santa Fe a month or so ago wasn't really enough to get to know her future mother-in-law. She unlocked the door and held the screen open. "I don't think Dan knew you were in Florida. When did you get here?"

"Only a couple days ago. Stanley considers this area home and has his heart set on finding something in The Villages as I told Dan. A condo, probably—I don't think either one of us wants to get tied down to a big place with an equally big yard."

"It's an interesting area." Elaine was trying to be circumspect, that is, trying to keep visions of the fakey looking main street out of her head. "Is Stan a golfer?"

"As he lives and breathes."

"Then you're probably looking in the right place. Can I get you a latte or cappuccino?" The machine she'd found in the garage wasn't exactly from Starbucks but it wasn't half bad.

"A latte sounds perfect."

Once coffees were in hand, Elaine moved to the dining room table. "Anything else? Sugar? Cream?"

"No, thank you. This is great."

Elaine was beginning to get the distinct feeling that Maggie might have known that Dan was working—that maybe she had hoped to catch Elaine alone. After exclaiming over the ring and commenting again how lucky Dan was to have escaped serious injury in the rollover in Wagon Mound, she paused and seemed reluctant to continue the conversation.

"Maggie, is there something we need to talk about?"

The look of relief said it all. Elaine knew she'd guessed correctly and now just needed to wait.

"I'm not really sure where to start. I'm a little afraid of what you might think of me…but in this day and age a person just can't be too careful."

Elaine still didn't know anything but it was a start.

"Dan mentioned in his email that you were considering becoming a PI—that you would start school down here. I just couldn't be more enthusiastic. The two of you are just made for each other and to share the same vocation, well, that will just be frosting on the cake." Maggie sat beaming.

"Thank you for the vote of confidence. I admit I'm looking forward to a change in career."

"How would you like me for your first client?"

Elaine hoped the shock didn't show. "That would be great. How can I help you? You know I'm just starting my coursework, I'm not sure I would be the best person—"

"You would be the most discreet person and surely if things were over your head, you have instructors who could help?"

"Yes, of course."

"And I'd like to think this might be simple. Frankly, I just need to know if Stanley Evers is who he says he is."

"Has he given you reason to think otherwise?"

"Yes, and no. We met on a cruise—an Arthur Murray dance cruise where a number of single men of a certain age are invited to join the group in order to give everyone a partner. All expenses paid, of course. It's a shame that at my age women far outnumber eligible men." She paused for a sip of coffee. "A lot of these toe-tapping gigolos are just that—gigolos—looking for the next meal ticket. Or, and I know this sounds macabre, looking to be made next of kin before the aging lovely kicks. So I knew what I was up against. And then one night on deck a man takes me by the arm and suggests a drink and late-night supper with a stroll in the moonlight instead of dessert. We talked until dawn. I cannot tell you how romantic that was. Dan's father has been gone for fifteen years. To be paid this sort of attention…it was heady, intoxicating."

"How long ago was this?"

"Six months. And in that time we've been on four cruises. It's like that joke where the woman calculates what it would cost her to be in a nursing home and she concludes it's cheaper to just cruise all year. This will be the first extended stay on land that we've had since we met. It just seems odd. I know he's retired and has discretionary money and loves to sail…still I'd love to have my things around me and be in one place for awhile."

"Won't living in The Villages give you that?"

"Yes. But I'm not comfortable investing in property with him. He'd like us to find a house and share costs. But he wants me to put the house in my name. He'll pay me his part in cash— something to do with his wife's children from another marriage. It sounds complicated and a little contentious. I don't mind pulling my own weight, but I don't want to get into something that would be too much for me to handle on my own if Stanley decided to go back to sea. Or just disappeared."

"Valid point. Let me take a few notes." Elaine grabbed a tablet and pen from the kitchen counter and sat back down. "Is there anything else that makes you think he's keeping something from you?"

He's secretive—leaves the room to take phone calls, stops the car and walks a block away to make a call. One of his prerequisites for a house? It must have closet doors in the bedroom that lock. Can you imagine? I'm not the snooping type but that just screams out for me to take a look."

Elaine wanted to ask her if she'd given into temptation, but didn't. "There could be a simple explanation." Even though nothing was coming to mind.

"He lived in Palm Coast for at least five years. I know he dated after his wife died, and I've certainly suspected he's kept in touch with a lady or two. I think it's healthy to maintain a friendship with former spouses or lovers, don't you?"

Would she keep in touch with her former husband, Eric? Maybe because of Jason. Without a shared child it would be difficult. "Yes, I suppose I do, too. Under most circumstances…"

"My sixth sense is usually spot-on—most women can be very intuitive—they just don't trust it. So I don't think you'll laugh when I say my alarms are going off. Let me give you an example. Shortly after we met I was telling him about a case that Dan had solved, and Stanley assumed he was a cop. Seemed agitated, threatened, asked me all kinds of questions; I finally got through to him that he worked for an insurance company. That was okay, somehow, it made what Dan does inconsequential."

"You're doing the right thing by letting me help. Let's start with the obvious, full name, middle name if there is one."

"Stanley Richardson Evers."

"Age?"

Hesitation. "Ummm, sixty next month. He's a year or two younger than I am."

A year or two? At that rate she would have been ten when she gave birth to Dan. Elaine thought twelve to fourteen years difference might be more like it. "You know I'm too old to be a cougar—so I prefer being called a lioness." A coquettish smile and a little shrug of the shoulders.

Elaine smiled but wisely chose not to comment. "Do you have a date of birth for Stanley?"

"November 27, 1955."

"Place of birth?"

"Ackley, Iowa. That's in Hardin County, I believe."

"Family members?"

"I have no idea."

"Last known address?"

"As I mentioned, Palm Coast, Florida. But he didn't live there for very long—less than five years. I think he retired there and then his wife died and he took off."

"Do you have a specific address?"

"I think I could get one."

"Good. And his Social Security number would be good, too."

"I'll have to work on that one. But I could get a copy of his driver's license. Maybe his passport, too. And I do know he's a Republican. More TP than moderate."

"TP?"

"Tea Party."

"Of course. Oh, I almost forgot, wife's name and date of birth?"

"Patricia, but I don't know her age."

"What did he do before he retired?"

"Owned a small business in Ames—he made specialized hinges and hardware for doors. A lot of his business was online."

"Name of business?"

"I've only seen a screen shot…the banner read, "See EVERs for EVERything!"

"This should be enough to get started. I'll give you a call if I need something else."

After another cup of coffee and catching up on Carolyn and Philip, Maggie begged off waiting around to see Dan. Elaine walked her to her car and swore she wouldn't utter a peep. This was their secret and would stay that way. Another air-kiss and Maggie backed out of the driveway. The car had Florida tags so it must be Stanley's. On a whim Elaine jotted down the license plate. Motor Vehicle Departments were good for basic stats. What an unexpected afternoon.

Yet, Elaine couldn't help but feel elated over her very first assignment. How tough could it be to find information on someone from Ackley, Iowa? She was sure Stanley was who he said he was but still how smart of Maggie to check. And even though she was certain that Maggie didn't really need her help—not in today's world of computers and easy online research—it was still easier to have someone do the legwork for you. She had three days before she met with Scott. It would be nice to show him a tidy research project completed all on her own.

Chapter Eight

Elaine decided there were a number of things she could find out locally. At least double-check Maggie's information as to full name and date of birth. Death certificate for the wife, voters registration, home ownership, car registration—all would either give credence to Maggie's story or throw up a red flag. Dan was busy with interviews at the track; Sadie was happily back with Fucher; and Elaine's time was her own. Dan didn't question her working on an assignment. He was really supportive about her going back to school. She didn't have to divulge for whom she was working. And she didn't have to fib about her whereabouts. Conscience-free snooping—she could learn to like this.

She was getting good at buzzing up Highway 1 to Palm Coast. An old highway but without the push and shove of I-95. The tax collection office and voter registration were housed in the same place—in a strip mall off of Old King's in the Staples Plaza. GPS made things easy to find but this commuters' village of seventy-six thousand was a dream to navigate. Thirty-five minutes door-to-door from Daytona and she didn't even have to take a number and wait for service.

But how disappointing. For all of his supposed staunch Republican leanings, Stanley was not a registered voter. Available as public record, the voter registration office would have been a source for name and date of birth. But then maybe not being a voter wasn't too unusual, but he did come from the group age-wise that AARP claimed had the most people active in their government. The voting record was unknown to start with so maybe it would work better to check on known facts—deaths recorded in the last five years. Patricia Evers, wife to Stanley Richardson Evers of Palm Coast, Florida. Off to the public library and the obituaries for the last five years.

Nothing. No Evers, Patricia or otherwise, had died in Palm Coast in that timeframe. Had he even been married? A trip to the clerk of the court's office would give marriages—the original if the couple divorced, as well as, possible others. No one with the last name of Evers divorced a Patricia or married anyone else. But then he was probably married to Patricia in Iowa and was telling the truth about only being married once. That was positive anyway. No divorces or remarriages. Yet this felt like another dead end. She was beginning to feel foolish. She'd spent a morning running around with absolutely nothing to show for it. So, what now?

Driver's license information wouldn't be handed out to just anyone, so Elaine could only hope Maggie would be able to get a copy. But what could she tell Maggie as the result of a morning's sleuthing? One last avenue—surely he'd owned a house if he lived in the area for up to five years. Off to check the real property tax rolls—again public record and available. She ended up searching the local property appraiser's records just to double-check the lack of info uncovered by a look at the tax rolls. Maybe if he lived in the area, he rented, and that probably meant paying utilities. Another lead.

She looked up the address of Palm Coast Water and Sewer and headed toward Utility Drive. Maybe if she told them that the family had lost track of her uncle and they feared he had Alzheimer's, and all she wanted was a "yes" or "no" as to whether he'd lived in the community, she could get information. And it worked. Only the answer was "no." No record of a Stanly Evers paying a water/sewer bill in the last five years. Or ever, for that matter. The clerk was absolutely certain. So, still nothing. For all intent and purposes, the man never existed—at least not in this part of the world.

She couldn't just give up. Think. Maybe it would make sense to just start at the source. How big could Ackley, Iowa, be? Would the hospital have records of births from 1955? She thought they probably would. And wouldn't there be other Evers in the town? Brothers, sisters, maybe? At least aunts, uncles, or cousins. She needed to go home, pick up a phone and do some calling. The one area that she was avoiding was anything having to do with criminal activity. Many counties put their criminal records online. She could take a look at Flagler County, and stop wasting gas.

〉〉〉

She made a pot of coffee and lost the battle to ignore the last cheese Danish in the fridge. She had to wait until Beverly Simpson in the Ackley, Iowa, courthouse got back from lunch, so she might as well use her time to fortify herself. Eastern Standard Time meant Ms. Simpson was an hour behind and had just left. Elaine requested voicemail and hoped the woman would check her messages first thing. And she wasn't disappointed.

Elaine started to explain that she was trying to track the family of one Stanley Richardson Evers, born in Ackley in 1955 and later moved to Ames, when she was interrupted.

"There are no Evers in this community."

Elaine, afraid she was going to hang up, asked her to check the record of births for that year.

"Ms. Linden, this is a town of thirty-nine hundred and three people. To say we're a close-knit community doesn't even begin to capture it. One hospital is shared with two other towns within a twenty-mile radius and a high school is also shared. In 1973 fifty-four students graduated from that high school. I was one of them. Don't you think I'd remember if I'd gone to school with someone named Evers?"

Elaine felt the click as well as heard it. Ms. Simpson had hung up. Elaine was completely without direction—other than checking county criminal records, she had no other places to go. Instead of having answers for Maggie and a star report for Scott Ramsey, she had nothing. How could she have flunked her very first assignment? Then again, maybe no news *was* good news. If Stanley didn't exist, there must be a reason. He had something to hide. Maybe her fruitless morning had really saved Maggie from making a big mistake. She was starting to feel better.

Chapter Nine

Dan was nursing a third cup of coffee at the track's restaurant while waiting for his fourth interview of the morning. Was he sabotaging himself? So convinced that Fucher was innocent that he heard only what he wanted to hear? UL&C was getting a little antsy without a concrete reason for continuing to bankroll the investigation. His email updates were leaving a little to be desired. But they trusted him. He'd asked for one more week with a final report due Friday a week from today. And if he didn't have the info that his gut told him was out there…Well, he had a week didn't he?

He used the first half hour to get better acquainted with Fucher's mentor and supposed guardian, Fred Manson. He made this more of a friendly unofficial chat, no recorder, no note-taking. Dan motioned for him to take a chair across the table from him. He took in the fluffy white hair, graying beard, and hard, squinty brown eyes that looked up through shaggy brows—an odd little, muscular man somewhere in his fifties who took his work home with him if the dirty fingernails were any indication. And how odd a pinky ring so mud-encrusted that Dan couldn't name the stone but a hefty amount of gold peeked through the grime. The diamond stud in his left ear fared better—it was sparkly clean—a diamond a little too big to be real, Dan thought. A little ostentatious none the less even for a Zircon.

"Coffee?" Dan had ordered a carafe and several set-ups.

"Tea man myself this early in the morning." A pleasant smile. At least his bottom denture was in place, Dan noticed.

"Have you worked for the track long?"

"A few years now. I did some work for Dixie Halifax and she steered me in this direction."

"Maintenance always been your line of work?"

"No. I've been a Master Gardener most of my life. Orchids are my specialty. Put ninety-six points on the dendrobium, Andree Millar, in '97. Beautiful plant over one hundred buds or fully open blooms the day of judging."

"That's impressive. Do you still raise orchids?" Dan had no idea where this was leading; he needed to get back to information about Fucher.

"No, nothing on a big scale anymore. Ms. Halifax hired me to bring the track up to snuff—I'd done some work in the area—that and the grounds here keep me busy. I have a crew of twenty including those doing track maintenance."

"So you've known Fucher for three years? Or longer?"

"More like five. I used to date his mother. God rest her soul. Beautiful lady, just devoted her life to her son. That boy wouldn't read or write today if it hadn't been for her. She schooled him all at home—never sent him away."

"That's commendable."

"I'll say it is. Women don't put family first anymore. Out traipsing around, working full time—home takes second fiddle nowadays."

Dan wasn't going to comment on that. "Give me your take on Fucher. His ethics, his ability to do his job here at the track. And anything else you want to share."

Fred reiterated more of the same. Honest, natural with the dogs, didn't have any enemies—none that were worthwhile mentioning, anyway. He'd trust Fucher with his life.

That seemed to be about it. Once again, Dan thought how lucky Fucher was to have friends like Mel and Fred. Dan thanked the man and accepted an invitation to take a look at the maintenance barn one of these days. Fred was pretty proud of his state-of-the-art grounds equipment. Dan stood and shook hands, then motioned the next interviewee over and turned his attention to the young man pulling up a chair opposite him. Dirty jeans, unwashed hair, fingernails chewed to the quick…he was down to running grunt labor through the interviewing process, that was for sure. But who knew where and when he'd get the break he knew was coming. Convinced himself was coming.

"Pete Ellis?" Dan got a nod, switched on the recorder and established location, those involved, and procedure before he began. The initial questions were all the same—date of hire, job description, name of supervisor. Answers all rattled off without hesitation. Then for the good stuff…

"Would you consider Fucher Crumm a friend?"

"Well, yeah, I guess so."

"Define friend. What do you mean by the word?"

"Uh, you know, someone you can trust, someone who helps you out."

"Can you give me an example that proved you could trust Fucher?"

"Well, when my mom needed implants, he gave us the money."

Dan didn't blink but quietly prayed that Fucher hadn't invested in chest enhancement. "She needed dental work?"

"Yeah, she'd broken her jaw when she was a kid—got kicked by a horse—so dentures were out. It was implants or nothing. She was pretty sick. Infections and stuff."

"Did Fucher pay for everything?"

"Came in with a wad of cash. Forty thousand worth and just gave it to my mom."

"How's your mom doing?"

"Great! She just got the crowns on and they look better than her real teeth ever did."

"That's good to hear. Will you repay Fucher?"

"He doesn't want money. Mom works the front desk here and she sort of takes care of him. She brings him food and looks after Sadie if he has to go out of town."

"Did you know Jackson Sanchez?"

"Yeah, everyone did." Dan made a mental note of the slight wrinkle of the nose—in distaste?

"Describe him for me."

"For starters no one liked him. He always wanted something for nothing. He'd get you to stay overtime to do some shit-work and then not even offer to pay."

"What kinds of things did he ask you to do?"

"A couple months ago, he brought in two pups from The Farm—that's his kennel over by Palatka—these were young but someone had screwed up the ear tats. Took me two hours of my own time with a pen to correct them. He didn't even say thank you."

Something was trying to surface in Dan's brain—correct mistakes done to ear tats…"How often did something like that happen? I mean where someone would have to go back and redo a tat?"

"Hardly ever. You got a good litter of runners you're not going to screw 'em up by trusting their ears to just anybody. Unless you're too cheap to pay for someone who could do it right the first time. I used to do tat art so I get called on a lot."

"Did Fucher kill Jackson Sanchez?" Dan always tried for the element of surprise. Get the witness to talk about one topic and then change mid-stream. Don't give them time to formulate an answer. Go for "off the cuff" or nothing.

"No way. Fucher didn't want anything to do with him. One time he had Fucher wash down some cages and then blamed Fucher for breaking a latch. That latch had been broken for months—we all knew it."

"What did Fucher do?"

"Nothing. He just laughed it off. Even if he'd threatened to fire him like people are saying, Fucher wouldn't have taken Jackson seriously. Nobody did. The guy drank like a fish."

Dan turned off the recorder, thanked Pete, gave him a card and asked him to call him if he thought of anything that might have something to do with the case—anything—even if it seemed inconsequential. He'd be the judge of that.

Boy, if he had a template for interviews that would be what he'd used for the last eleven people. Cookie-cutter stamp-outs. They all sounded alike. Most had gotten handouts from Fucher but everyone seemed to accept him. All talked about what a good worker he was. And the word, "honest" came up over and over.

He'd read the fire chief's report—arson—someone had emptied a can of gasoline along the back of the building. So, was the death of the five most heavily insured dogs just an accident? Wrong place, wrong time? Even though no other dogs were even seriously injured? Just seemed far too coincidental to Dan. He needed that break more than ever.

〉〉〉

A call at the last minute from the class sponsor at the shooting range and conference facility in Daytona—there had been a dropout and a spot was open in the gun-safety class starting at nine. Yes, she could make it—if she hurried. Jeans, a bright coral linen shirt with a few more wrinkles than even linen was supposed to have, and she was out the door. Joan could drop Dan off at the track and Elaine would pick him up. All set.

Twenty-two people ranging in age from twenty to seventy-five packed the small classroom. Folding chairs arranged in a horseshoe pattern all faced the VCR. For some reason she hadn't thought getting a permit to carry would be this popular. And women in attendance? Over half. There were just too many news stories about car-jackings at filling stations, or break-ins in the middle of the night. Most of the women listed living alone as the reason they were seeking extra protection.

The instructors were two FBI agents and two ex-policemen. Classroom instruction in the morning and an hour on the range right after lunch. The sheriff's department even had someone there to do fingerprinting. Because she, as well as six others in the class, were unfamiliar with firearms, there was a brief lecture and discussion after the general workshop ended. How to load and unload a revolver, how to safely pick up a handgun, and carry it was practiced before each individual was assigned a mentor to continue the hands-on training outside at the range. Elaine was impressed. The courses were well planned and seemed to basically cover everything she would need to know.

Target practice, however, was another story. The .38 felt clunky and heavy. The instructor suggested larger grips if she chose a .38 to carry. Hitting the target was a real challenge—anticipating the recoil threw her off and she was pulling her shots to the right but the instructor had patience and tips and by the end of the hour, she was pretty much dead on. Impressive enough that she asked if she could have the paper target. Dan would want to see. And she needed some evidence for bragging rights.

A certificate of class completion included a sign-off on gun handling. She knew Dan would scoff at that and give her a teensy lecture on how important it was going to be to practice. And she agreed. She still had to work on being comfortable carrying.

>>>

Having only one car was the pits. Elaine picked up Dan at three-thirty and dropped him off at the townhouse, then took off for Palm Coast and her Friday afternoon meeting with Scott Ramsey. She'd give Dan a call when she'd finished and maybe pick up takeout on the way home. The community seemed to have a number of Thai restaurants. Thai by Thai had gotten great reviews online; maybe she'd try that one. She tried not to dwell on what she knew or actually didn't know about Stanley. It was becoming crazy-making, a burden even. She'd never kept secrets from Dan and this was fast becoming one. Throw his mother into the mix and the guilt was mounting.

The receptionist was on the phone when she got there, but waved her toward the conference room.

"Did you have time to get some reading done?" Scott indicated she take a chair on the other side of the small conference table.

"Better than that. I took the gun-safety class and completed the requirements for a permit to carry. And I tackled my first job."

"First job? That's great but why do I detect a less than enthu-siastic response?"

Elaine filled him in, showed him her notes, the list of con-tacts, the results…the dead end. How this was all for her future mother-in-law and could have serious consequences. And even though the book warned about taking cases for family members, it had seemed so simple—not one warning that she might have stepped in over her head. But how, now, she wasn't sure.

Scott pushed back from the table and didn't say anything, then got up and closed the door to the conference room. The receptionist was gone by quarter to five; the office was empty. Closing the door put her on her guard. What could be so omi-nous as to require this kind of precaution?

"I'm going to give you my best guess. Until we prove some-thing, please remember it's just that—a guess. And let me com-pliment you—good work!" A pause, pursed lips, slight frown, fingers tapping on the edge of the table…"My *guess* is that Stanley, or whoever he is, is in the Witness Protection Program."

"You mean like the FBI's attempt to keep someone from being killed because they've testified against some high-profile criminal?"

"Exactly."

"Oh, my God."

"I don't want to sound callous but this area has been known to be a dumping ground for older candidates in the program—it's a favorite with the government."

"I find this so surreal. I mean you read about it but to know it really happens…"

"I'll give you an example. How long have you been in this area?"

"One week."

"I'm kinda surprised that you haven't heard about Palm Coast's one claim to fame already. It happened a couple years ago when the program placed Joey Calco in the area. You know who he is? A killer for the Bonanno crime family—the Beth Avenue crew? He helped the feds take down the clan's one-time boss—the Feds owed him big-time. They brought him here, bought him a pizzeria, Goomba's pizza joint, and there wouldn't have been a problem if Joey hadn't pistol-whipped a customer over a calzone."

"Come on, you're just making this up to give me a laugh. I mean, seriously, Goombas? A pistol-whipping over food?"

"I kid you not. They gave him a new name, Joseph Milano, a new social security number, the business I mentioned, a house, and a car. When the calzone story broke—Joey had not only accosted the customer with the calzone but had also been turned in for sexual harassment that same week—the *Daytona News-Journal* did some checking. Seems Milano shared the same birthdate with Calco and "both" men had a mother named Giuseppina. How's that for coincidence? Think that might throw up a red flag?"

"What happened?"

"Well, the Sicilian-trained henchman known as crazy Joe had pretty much escaped any life sentence when he ratted on Bonanno *consigliere* Anthony Spero. It came down to deciding what to do with him. Joe public will probably never know if he was thrown back into prison or relocated. Supposedly he got a few more years behind bars."

"What do you think? Did he go to prison?"

A shrug, a half-smile. "Just depends on how you want to look at things. I guess my message is if you don't want a little excitement in your life, be careful of the calzones—there are a lot of pizza joints in this town."

Elaine laughed. A good story but hard to believe. "Why Palm Coast? What makes this an ideal hiding place?"

"All the New Yorkers. Throw in more than a couple from New Jersey and the Feds' guys can hide in plain sight. Easy cover. All I know is you don't hear of any federal transplants setting up house in Alabama."

"True. But it's still hard to believe that Stanley could be… well…possibly involved with the mob."

"Another rule of this business? Don't assume and don't make people what you want them to be. Open mind means just that."

"If what you suspect is true, what do I tell Dan's mother? Do you think she's in danger?"

"I've been thinking about that. If it were my mother? I think I'd want her to first of all be safe. Feel safe. For starters, why don't you encourage her to take the gun-safety class?"

"Great idea. I think she'd enjoy it." Elaine shared a thumbs-up review of the class she'd just taken. Yet there was simply no way she could sell that to Dan. His mother with a gun? She knew him—that was out of his realm of thinking.

"So I should tell her your suspicions?"

"You know her better than I do. Would she panic? Dissolve into hysteria? Confront him?"

"My guess is none of those. The woman seems pretty together and careful. I may be more worried about what her son might do." Elaine could only imagine Dan's reaction.

"I wasn't thinking of that. Let's make certain this isn't just conjecture—that we're really onto something with Stanley. As much as I'd like to be wrong, I'd hate to share my suspicions and then be wrong—if that makes sense. I have some friends who might be able to help—at least tell us for certain if our suspicions are well founded. Why don't you tell your fiancé what you know and give him my phone number? In the meantime I'll make sure we're telling the truth."

>>>

The Panang curry and Thai fried rice with pineapple were both delicious. Elaine wasn't certain a Dos XXs beer was the best compliment, but it sort of made an international meal out of it. Dessert was mango sorbet—Haagan Dazs, of course. And it took the time to finish dinner for her to decide exactly what to say to Dan. She'd started out by giving him a rundown on the gun-safety class and showing him her very first target. He was impressed and immediately reiterated about buying her a handgun and continuing target practice. He seemed genuinely pleased to be sharing an interest in shooting.

Finally, she couldn't put off talking about the rest of her day any longer. She decided to keep it simple and stick to the facts. State what she'd found but also share Scott Ramsey's suspicions. No hypotheses, no conclusions.

"I had no idea that mom was worried. She never said anything."

"I think she knew how busy you were and, honestly, I think she wanted to help me. Neither one of us had any idea that it would lead in this direction."

Dan twisted the cap off of a second beer. "What would you say to my having Mom fly into New Mexico, spend a couple days with Carolyn, and then drive back down here with Simon?"

"I think that's a terrific idea."

"It'd buy us a week or so to sort through things here—maybe even wrap things up on my side. And keep Mom out of harm's way a little longer."

"I miss Simon and I'm sure he misses us."

"Yeah, we'll have to figure out some beach-time for the guy."

Dan didn't mention the swimming pool and the game of doggy water polo he'd witnessed. But he'd even admit to missing Sadie, let alone Simon. He liked having a dog around. "I'll text Mom and see if she'll do it." *And I'll have to get used to Mom carrying a handgun in her purse.* Dan sighed.

Chapter Ten

It's funny how you never forget where you were when something big happens. Dan was trying to think through getting his mother out of town long enough to get some answers about Stanley, and wrap up a case in a way that he knew was all wrong, when the call came. Sometime after the mango sorbet and halfway through an episode of *Foyle's War*, his cell rang. Not recognizing the number and thinking it was an interviewee with new information, Dan went out on the porch before answering.

"Mr. Mahoney, a dead dog just won the fifth race at the Mardi Gras Casino outside Miami." Click.

A fist-pump in the air. "Yes." The break. The one he knew was out there. The voice was, no doubt, Mel Paget. She'd taken Nero to the track in that area for Nero's maiden race. And she, above and beyond anyone else, would recognize the five "dead" dogs supposedly killed in the fire. She'd been their trainer—this was ironclad information. Stuff he could take to the bank or use to reopen an almost shut case.

And then reality set in. He met Mel at the track late Sunday when she got back. The fifth race winner might as well have been a ghost. She'd gotten pictures of the dog winning and had a program giving the dog's stats, but that was it. Dog and handler disappeared directly following the race. They seemingly evaporated. The trainer listed was someone Mel had never heard of; the kennel supposedly in Kansas never existed. The dog's registration number didn't match any on the list of insured dogs. Even Mel might have missed the dog had it not gone crazy wagging his tail and whining to reach her when they were at the weigh-in station before being led to the box.

"I know I spooked the handler who obviously told the trainer that the dog knew me. It was Mellow Yellow. They won the fifth race and were out of there. I'm so sorry I didn't follow them to the parking lot, get a license number or something. I was just so taken by surprise. This really makes a lot of things different, doesn't it?"

"If we can prove it. I'm afraid it doesn't exactly exonerate Fucher. He could still be charged with the murder of Sanchez and a cover-up fire."

"Oh, I wasn't thinking of that. But doesn't it make sense that someone was trying to steal the dogs? Like maybe Jackson?"

"Maybe and maybe not. We have nothing to tie the dogs to Jackson Sanchez. The events could be totally unrelated."

"But at least the dogs didn't die."

"Well, one dog didn't." Dan suddenly realized how dejected Mel looked—like someone had just poked her with a pin letting all the air out and, well, hadn't he done just that? "Mel, I hate to keep bringing you back to reality. I really appreciate your help—that was a, solid, heads-up find. I can stay on the case now. Even the suggestion of one insured dog being alive and UL&C isn't about to pay out. It's not a solution but it suggests that there *are* four other dogs out there. Very much alive. But now we have to wonder why Keith Elliott lied about putting five bags of dog remains in the back of his truck."

"It's like I've caused you more work."

Dan put an arm around her shoulders. "More work? Yes, but you've helped me ask the right questions now. Where there was a pretty ironclad case before, we now have one with a few holes. Mel, believe me, you've been a big help."

But on the way back to the townhouse, he had to admit things still looked bleak. He could, however, keep the case open. If they hadn't driven Mellow Yellow and his trainer underground, there might be another race. That old sixth sense said there would be—no doubt about it. Money and the arrogance of the criminal always won out. Hadn't he seen it over and over? But whether they would continue to race the dog in Florida or move to out-of-state tracks, there was no knowing. He just had to figure out how to find them. And the other four? They could be anywhere. For the first time he felt certain they were not in little dog-shaped ceramic urns on Ms. Halifax's desk.

And then it came to him. Dan slapped the steering wheel, glanced in the rearview, and pulled a U-turn. Back to the track. Why hadn't he thought of this before? It was right there under his nose or stuck in his shoe as the case might be. The ear tattoos—if they could be redefined to make them clearer and clean up shoddy work, why couldn't they be altered to indicate an entirely different dog? And who would know? One Pete Ellis, tat artist extraordinaire. Dan could kick himself. He just hadn't asked the right questions when he had the kid in front of him.

Dan didn't have Pete paged. He knew the kennel cleanup crews traded off Sundays and if luck was with him, this would be Pete's time on. He parked by the kennels and went in the back to the part of the building untouched by the fire. Pete was cleaning cages and didn't seem too happy to see him.

"Got a minute? I thought of a couple more things I think you can help me with."

"I got a tight schedule. I need to be out of here in a half hour."

"This won't take long. Let's step out back." Dan held the back door open and a somewhat reluctant Pete followed.

"Are you familiar with this ear tat number?" Dan held out the back of his card where he'd written Mellow Yellow's registration number—111B. Good grief, even as he looked at it now the number in the program that Mel brought back would be the easiest to alter—411B. Dan had a feeling and he knew he was right. He just had to have this man in front of him confirm it.

"Um, I see a lot of numbers—"

"Pete, I'll come right to the point. I think 111B became 411B, thanks to your talent with a pen. I think Jackson Sanchez maybe even paid you to alter the original number."

Nothing. But no eye contact either just a nervous tick in his left eye.

"We can talk or I can go to the commission."

"Look, I need this job. I got in a little trouble last year. Got caught with an ounce and some pills. I'm on probation and something like your saying? Well, that'd go really hard on me."

"You're ducking the question, Pete. Were you asked to alter this number?" Dan pointed to the card. "And if you did it, when was it done?"

"What are you going to do about it?"

"I'm not going to do anything. My company just needs to know that at least one dog is still alive."

"You're not going to turn me in?"

"No." Dan wouldn't do anything, but he couldn't guarantee that other law enforcement wouldn't ask questions. Subpoena him if things came to court. In the meantime it was enough for UL&C to withhold payout. "Did you alter this number?"

A nod.

"Who asked you to do it?"

"Jackson."

"When?"

"The afternoon of the fire."

⟩⟩⟩

"Coffee?" The last of the mango sorbet and time alone. Usually a couple things Elaine cherished but Dan was deep in thought. Not the best of company but he'd share when he was ready. She was getting to know him—including all the quirks.

"Who would know the five dogs in question as well as Mel does?"

"Fucher, of course." She wasn't sure where this was going but she sensed Dan's excitement.

"Exactly. I could subpoena race videos from tracks in Florida and set up Fucher to watch them—look for signs of the three dogs that might be racing. I could show him how to stop and start, do frame captures—"

"Dan, that would be hours and hours of tedious work."

"It's called 'research.' UL&C would pay for his time. How do you think insurance investigators catch workman's comp cheaters? Set up cameras and monitor them. You know, catch the guy with the bad back hoisting hundred-pound bags of cement. I'd put money on your first case being either an errant spouse or someone feigning injury in order to stay on the payroll."

"I'm sure you're right. And when I think about it, Fucher will love to be involved—be helping you solve a case."

"It may help UL&C more than it will help him, but there is the chance we'll uncover something tied to the murder."

>>>

UL&C didn't question Dan's request and put Fucher on a temporary payroll as a "research assistant." Chalk it up to too much TV but Fucher seemed to think he needed to be in costume. Seemed to fancy himself in some kind of undercover NCIS drama—started wearing dark glasses and a baseball cap turned backwards—even in the house. Oh yes, grew one of those in-vogue, seemingly pencil-drawn thin beards that outlined the jaw. But most importantly Dan could see that Fucher was thrilled to be asked to help. This was the next best thing to working at the track.

Dan rented equipment, had Roger Carter secure the necessary subpoenas, served them to all Class A tracks in the state and had each track download a full week's races onto disks and overnight them to Fucher's home. Fucher would, however, continue to get race results on disks from some seven tracks on a daily basis. FedEx'd every afternoon at two. Only a couple things kept the project from being totally overwhelming—they were checking only "A" tracks and only a week had passed since the fire. Still, a more than daunting task for most. Dan was thankful for Fucher's dedication.

Fucher started his day at six a.m. and if Dan saw his lights on much after ten, he went over and under the pretext of discussing his day, made certain he went to bed. Finally, he explained to Fucher how he really needed "fresh" eyes—how easy it was to miss something if he'd been looking at a screen all day. Dan shortened Fucher's workday to six hours, made him sign a make-believe contract, and that seemed to work. Dan wouldn't have ruining Fucher's health on his conscience. And if they were lucky, a couple supposedly dead dogs might be out there running races and they'd have proof. He had to have absolute proof that a dog—any one of the five—was alive. And that meant having the dog in hand, so to speak. Conclusive evidence that would rely on DNA and not the owner's say so.

If he was feeling good about one problem he was facing, he was at a loss as to what to tell his mother about Stanley. Because he really didn't have any definitive information, he chose to say nothing. It was too much like horning in on Elaine's territory anyway. She'd probably hear from Scott Ramsey in the next day or two. He'd let her get the skinny and then they'd decide together how much or how little to share with Mom. But in the meantime getting Mom to New Mexico for a visit and help with transporting Simon to Florida made sense. A week or two of not worrying about her meant one less potential problem.

But convincing Maggie Mahoney proved difficult. She was driving when he caught up with her and it seemed Stanley's Chrysler didn't have a built-in car phone so he had to wait until she got home and could call him back.

"Darling, of course, I'd love to help. Simon may be the closest thing to a grandchild I ever get from you. I got your text but just didn't know how to answer. I have sort of committed to Stanley—at least to help him find some place for us to stay. He's counting on me to stick around, not run off."

"You're looking at rentals, right?"

"Well, we're trying to but there aren't very many. Stanley has a lead on something we're supposed to look at this afternoon. It sounds perfect. Swimming pool, backs up to the fifth green…I'll keep you posted."

"So is it a yea or nay on rescuing Simon?"

"Oh, an absolute 'yea'…I just don't know when I can get away."

"Okay, let me know when you do."

Damn. If he admitted it, he'd have to say he was afraid for Maggie Mahoney. On top of everything else, he felt responsible...wasn't there some kind of irony in worrying about keeping your *mother* out of trouble? But the Witness Protection Program? What was it that one columnist called Palm Coast? The "mob slob dump"? Something like that.

Just thinking about her being hooked up with some wannabe Godfather...well, made his blood run cold. She was way too naïve to play games—especially when they were the kind that could kill you. He could only hope Scott Ramsey was wrong.

Chapter Eleven

Elaine had left Dan at the townhouse. Paperwork would keep him busy. She had to run by the college annex in Palm Coast, grocery shop, pick up Dan's dry cleaning, and meet with Scott Ramsey. Dry cleaning? Wasn't that from some other era? There was a "spray and press" cycle on the dryer that did a pretty good job on linen and knits but didn't seem good enough for dressier shirts. The cost was staggering. An already pricy hundred-dollar shirt could rack up another thirty-five dollars in dry cleaning bills before it was six months old. She looked at the ring on her finger. It was his money—his life and way of doing things. Had she been alone too long? She needed to give a little. But hadn't he heard of permanent press?

To get pissy over laundry wasn't like her but she guessed she was feeling the pressure of moving—and not just logistically. A job change as drastic as the one she was considering was monumental. From a lot of angles—type of work, salary, location. But wasn't she already committed? The paperwork was in the mail for the permit to carry—passport picture, written application, a check for one hundred seventeen dollars, certification from the class, and a copy of her fingerprints. Dan was on board with the PI training—maybe more than a little excited to have her in the field.

But now to find out Dan's mother was involved…the added stress wasn't something she'd bargained for. And she needed to buy a car. The check from the insurance company for the

Mercedes that was burned in New Mexico had finally come through. But car shopping was one of her five least favorite activities, somewhere on the list after ridding the attic of rats.

Mid-afternoon and she was dragging. A double shot latte was called for…no, needed. She pulled off of Palm Coast Parkway and drove through the Starbucks parking lot. When Scott Ramsey had called and asked her to stop by—three o'clock would work for him—he indicated that he might have information and an assignment. He felt they needed to get started on her school work. Ugh. Could she really do this? Start back to school at forty-six? Or was she just smarting over flunking her first assignment? She really hadn't found out anything concrete for Dan's mother. Stanley Evers remained an enigma.

Damn. There wasn't a drive-through at this Starbucks and not one parking spot available in the lot out front. No surprise; the coffeehouse was popular. She parked across the street in back, at the end of a large grocery-store parking lot, and walked back to the shop, got the latte, and returned to her car. Total time gone? Maybe five minutes. So, who put the sheet of paper under the wiper blade? The one addressed to her. Who had been watching her? She couldn't control a shiver.

She pulled out the paper, and looked around. There wasn't another car near her. There wasn't a soul in sight—no walkers, no cyclists just a single sheet of white paper with her name at the top and the typed words:

I am not here to hurt you. Stand beside the car and do not get in. I have the information that you want.

"Do as it says." A gloved hand shot out from under the car and grabbed her ankle. She screamed, jerked her foot back but the hand tethering it didn't let go, and the *venti* latte hit the pavement, cup-top separating and bouncing to the side, steaming liquid splashing on her and the car before rolling underneath. If the cursing was any indication, the coffee had also doused her assailant.

"Who are you?" False bravado but the hand held her anchored.

"You don't need to know. Take your phone out and conduct this conversation as if you were talking on it."

Elaine reached in her pocket, pulled out the iPhone, and held it to her ear.

"Ready?"

"Yes."

"It's been reported that you have been seeking information concerning Stanley Evers. Is this correct?"

"Yes."

"I believe the woman he's living with is a relative?"

"The mother of my fiancé."

"Have you told her of your findings to date?"

"No."

"It has to remain that way."

"Is she in danger?"

"Only if she knows the truth."

"Which is?"

"I think Scott Ramsey has shared a pretty accurate picture with you. Trust him. He'll give you the particulars."

"How do you know Mr. Ramsey?"

"He used to work for the Bureau."

FBI. Was that what he was insinuating? Since when did agents hide under cars to share information? Well, she guessed it wasn't too far-fetched.

"What am I supposed to do?"

"I'm leaving an envelope of material for you with the results of your 'supposed' research. I want you to give this to Ms. Mahoney. I believe it will answer any questions that she might have."

"Lies." It wasn't even a question. Of course, it was a fabrication.

"At this point we need to protect the truth."

"And my fiancé? What do I tell him?"

"As much or as little as you want. You are in a position to protect his mother—I think he'll see the necessity of that. You might encourage him not to be a hero."

"That might be difficult."

"I think you can manage." A pause, "I'm going to exit on the opposite side of the car. Continue to address your phone. Allow me thirty seconds from the time I release your ankle, then pick up the envelope, unlock the car and get in. It's been a pleasure."

"Likewise." Yeah, right. Anger wouldn't get her anywhere and if she was having a problem with cat and mouse tactics now, what would it be like when she was a PI? She was afraid this was just a part of what she'd signed on for. Melodramatics…or maybe it wasn't. The edge of a manila envelope peeked out from under the car. She picked it up, got into the SUV, and locked all the doors. Maybe she needed to rethink her new career choice.

She didn't go back for another latte but looked through the envelope of Stanley Evers facts. Wow, they'd thought of everything—driver's license, passport, utility bills, deed of trust on a house in Palm Coast, death certificate for a Patricia Evers, copy of a 1955 birth certificate…and everything an absolute lie. She was anxious to hear what Scott Ramsey would have to say—former *Agent Ramsey*, that is. Would he own up to having some part in this charade? She started the car; there was only one way to find out.

He met her at the door to his office. Had someone tipped him off that she'd been contacted? He nodded toward the conference room and held the door open for her to go in first. He shut the door, pulled out a chair and took one opposite her.

"I understand that you've had a…um, little encounter?"

"Yes." She put the envelope on the table and slid it across to him, watched as he removed every piece of paper and then rifled through the stack stopping at the birth certificate and the passport.

"They do a good job."

"I understand you were a part of that 'they' at one time?"

"Who told you that? No, let me guess, the same person who handed you this." He did a sweeping motion over the scattered papers.

"I'd amend that to read the same person who crawled under my car and had me tethered by the ankle."

Scott looked up sharply, eyes squinting, seemingly to read her face, then a sigh and he slumped against the chair-back. "Yeah, tactics sometimes lack a little in civility."

"They don't seem to lack in originality and the scare quotient is pretty high."

"Let me apologize. I've never seen the merit in scaring the innocent. Yes, I was a member of the Bureau—I'll amend that—I'm still a member. I retired, came to Florida, opened shop, and was invited back into service about a year ago. They've let me continue with my business because it's good cover. They needed an extra agent down here and it's worked out. I don't have to tell you that this information is confidential."

Elaine nodded. "Of course."

"Are you okay with everything? I mean can you give this info to your mother-in-law and not let it bother your conscience?"

"I think so. I don't suppose I can get a real name—what Stanley Evers is covering up?"

A shake of the head. "It's safer this way."

"Spare me the 'it's for the good of your country' lecture."

"I think you know the importance of pretense here." He wasn't smiling.

She met his stare and again simply nodded.

"Good girl. You're going to be great at this job." Finally, an approving smile. "I'd like to make copies." He indicated the papers in front of him.

"Go ahead." Elaine was just going to turn everything over to Maggie. Well, after a quick read by her son. She waited while Scott took the packet out to the receptionist.

"There. Now as to why I wanted to meet today. Your first assignment needs to include surveillance. I've just been hired to track the comings and goings of a suspected two-timing wife. I'm sure you realize that this is the type of assignment that makes up over fifty percent of a PI's business."

"I've been warned."

"Friday is this woman's mah-jongg night. The husband suspects she's leaving early and meeting someone. Can you be available Friday?"

"Yes."

"Then meet me here at the office by six."

"Do I get to know where we're going?"

"The Villages. Remember, nondescript dark clothing, night lens binoculars, and a zoom lens-equipped camera."

Chapter Twelve

Without physical evidence—that is, the dog in hand—Dan was reluctant to approach Kevin Elliott. He had nothing more concrete than Mel's observation of the fifth race winner at a southern Florida track. A dog acted like it recognized her. Jumped around and wagged its tail. And he had Pete Ellis' word that he'd been asked to tamper with the registration number on one of the five dogs presumed dead, but as Mel had discovered, was still being raced. Of course, he'd promised not to use Pete's name and he'd just bet Pete would deny everything if asked. So, the vet could still laugh in his face and probably would. And if he *were* guilty, then he'd be on the defensive. And Dan didn't need to spook any more possible players. He needed the people behind the theft to continue to race the dogs while not suspecting a thing. He needed to catch people in the act—confiscate a dog with an altered ear tat.

However, this was the third day without Fucher finding any evidence of a dead dog being entered in a race at a Florida track. Had they gone out of state? Possibly. And almost impossible to find out for sure. Collecting recorded races from tracks outside of Florida would require the kind of clout that Dan didn't have. And even if he *could* get disks, who would watch them? The sheer number would be prohibitive. It would take more than a research team of one.

The only upside to his morning was a call from his mother. She and Stanley had found a perfect rental in The Villages—on the golf course like the realtor promised—even some indication that the bungalow-style house might be available for sale at some future date. She was leaving for Chicago at one to close out her apartment, meet with movers, and "make the leap." Her words, not his. And it would be a "leap." How long had she been in Chicago? Most of her (however many years she was admitting to) adult life.

And, yes, she'd come back via New Mexico, a couple days with Carolyn, rent a car, pick up Simon, and she'd be home. Calling Florida "home" wasn't lost on Dan. That seemed quick and obviously had a lot to do with moving in with Stanley. He sure hoped Elaine hadn't found out anything definitive to burst Mom's bubble. Stanley better be who he said he was and not who this Scott Ramsey thought he was. Difficult to estimate how long everything would take—too many variables—but Mom was planning to be gone a week, maybe more. Still, Dan was silently relieved to have one fewer woman in his life to worry about.

His day looked relatively easy. He had some odds and ends that need checking—cause of Jackson's death for one; he needed to speak with the coroner. The stab wound seemed self-explanatory but time and cause were pretty basic to the entire investigation. Then there was corroboration of the supposed cremation of the five greyhounds at the animal crematorium in Daytona. Dan had the paperwork. Supposedly Kevin Elliott cremated five dogs. Was he there alone? Was someone in cahoots with him? In fact, was he there at all?

Somehow, and this was really a long shot, he needed samples of the ashes from those five urns on Dixie Halifax's desk. Were the contents, in fact, dog remains? Or just some leftover charred hickory chips from last month's bar-b-que? Important? Yes, Dan would say so. Those ashes, if they could be proved to be from the insured dogs, would be the key to any payout. And could tell them just how many dogs UL&C would need to pay for. Four? Three? None? And he had no idea how he was going to get samples.

>>>

Dan called ahead and requested an appointment with Dr. Marie Hunt, chief medical examiner, Volusia County Medical Center.

He dropped the address of 1360 Indian Lake Road, Daytona, into the Rover's GPS and headed out.

Dr. Hunt was direct, to the point of being abrupt, and let him know that meeting with him was somewhat of an imposition. After a tepid handshake, she turned and motioned for him to follow her.

"Let's go back to the lab. We're holding the body until the toxicology report is back, but, between us? I expect levels to far exceed BAC legal limits. And I would guess that based on other physical characteristics, Mr. Sanchez was not new to…what is it kids say? Partying down."

"That's the rumor, anyway."

Dr. Hunt stepped to the side of the gurney, unzipped the body bag and pulled back the flap covering the face. "Here he is. There were a few anomalies. Such as this one." She pointed to the corpse's forehead.

Dan moved to the head of the table. "I don't understand. What in the world…is that a word?" He pointed to a series of cuts starting in the hairline above the left ear and ending just above the right. Edema and clotting blood had erased any crispness to the penmanship.

"Those scratchings formed the word 'thief.' Misspelled, I might add—e before i. But still a message for someone."

"Was the etching done before or after he was stabbed?"

"Oh, definitely before the stabbing but well after he was dead."

"Wait. The stabbing wasn't the cause of death?"

"No. I thought you knew. Cause of death was alcohol poisoning. And I don't think we're talking accidental ingestion, like I'll bet someone wants us to believe. There is every indication that Mr. Sanchez either willingly, or more probably unwillingly, took part in what I believe is called "butt chugging.""

"Do I even want to know what that is?"

"Probably not. Do you have children, Mr. Mahoney? Perhaps, college-aged?"

"No."

"I thought that you might have heard of an incident at a popular Southern college a couple years back. Frat house shenanigans that turned lethal. Or perhaps the sherry enema murder—wife in Texas does in her husband—I think that was in 2004."

"This all comes under 'fact is stranger than fiction,' right?"

"So true. I believe Mr. Sanchez could have been 'murdered' by two different people—one who got the job done, and one who only thought he or she had succeeded. There is evidence in the rectal area to suggest the tubing of alcohol directly into the colon. Alcohol ingested in this manner has nowhere to go other than directly into the intestines. An overdose can be administered in a short period of time. The body is then left where it will look like an accidental death. In this case with a known history of drinking to excess, the murderer thought he or she would easily get away with it. I doubt the murderer thought someone would use the deceased's face as a billboard. For some reason the murderer returned and found the defaced corpse and decided to use a knife and hope to implicate someone else. Or yet a third person decided to get in on the act."

"You think *at least* two people were involved—but maybe three? One to orchestrate the perfect murder and then another person marked the body—yet maybe a third stuck a knife in his back."

"I do."

That would explain the moving of the body. Hadn't Fucher claimed that he'd first stumbled over the body in the doorway, removed the knife, left it beside the body and went to corral the dogs only to return to an empty space sans body and knife? Was the murderer the one who started a fire? Or did the fire cover up something else? Was he being wrong linking the two? Obviously if Fucher was going to be implicated, the body couldn't burn. It had to be removed and then brought back. Someone carving "thief" on Jackson's forehead caused a lot of extra work for his murderer.

"It's my opinion because of the angle of the knife as it entered the body that someone standing over him when he was on the floor did the stabbing."

"You're saying that someone found him lying facedown in the hallway, assumed he was drunk, and took the opportunity to do what he or she thought would kill him." Dan wasn't prepared for any of this. What happened to cut and dried, plain ol' straightforward gunshot or stabbing?

"Precisely, but the deed had already been done. I do have pictures. You can see from these that the word is meant to be 'thief.'" Dr. Hunt picked up a manila envelope from a desk in the corner, pulled out a couple eight and a half by eleven, black-and-white glossies and handed them to Dan.

The lopsided "THEif," mostly in caps, stood out sharply against the pale skin of the corpse. Truly a kindergarten level of penmanship, but writing something on human flesh couldn't be easy. "May I?" Dr. Hunt nodded and Dan slipped the rest of the photos from the envelope, pulled one from the pile, and studied it. "So this is the knife." Fucher was correct; it was a kitchen knife, actually more like a carving knife—wide blade, pointed end, solid handle—too big and unwieldy to carry around. Not the tool of a professional killer. But didn't that only further implicate Fucher?

"But this may be just as important. See these bruises? Here and here? Our Mr. Sanchez suffered quite a beating before he died. Badly bruised ribs and another discoloration in the groin. Not something that would kill him but would probably render him helpless. It's even possible his assailant attacked him while he was dying."

"Any idea how these were administered? Blunt instrument? Bare knuckles?"

"I believe they were received while he was on the floor. Boots, possibly steel-toed, would be my educated guess."

"Time of death?"

"Somewhere around one a.m."

More surprises. Wouldn't be the first time that what looked like one thing turned out to be another. But could Fucher have slept through a beating like this? Wouldn't Sanchez have yelled bloody murder? A person just didn't acquiesce to being carved up and stomped on. But maybe more importantly, did he think Fucher could have done something like this? Know enough about administering alcohol to poison a person, let alone carve up his forehead, ferociously beat him, and *then* stab him? This whole scenario was slipping into the realm of complete make-believe.

"Do you think he was killed on the premises or killed somewhere else and brought to the track?"

"Difficult to know. The fire erased any evidence that could help us there."

"Anything else I should know?" Might as well get all the surprises out on the table at the same time.

"This, possibly." Dr. Hunt unzipped the bag and with latex gloves firmly in place, brought the left leg out from its covering. "See the markings on the ankle? He had been rather tightly bound and tethered to something. And the toes on both feet…" She pulled the left foot out and held it next to the right, "Crushed."

Dan leaned in to look at the mangled toes, blue-black now, nails broken and split and the surrounding flesh more like pulp. "Any idea…?"

"Consistent with being run over by a car, but just the toes doesn't make sense. Of course, I've seen the bodies of drunks come through here with amazing injuries."

"This could mean that he'd been held somewhere for some indefinite period of time—probably not at the track." No wonder Fucher didn't hear anything. "Was the carving on the forehead done with the same knife as the one that had been stuck in his back?"

"No, the knife wound to the back was done by something large, a kitchen instrument, meat carver's tool—wide blade, ornate guard at the end of the handle. Obviously expensive." Dr. Hunt pointed to the photo that Dan had separated from the pile. "This is the knife found beside the body. It matches the entry wound and was rammed into the body with such force that the guard"—she indicated two brass knobs at the base of the blade—"left bruises."

"And your best guess as to what kind of instrument was used on his forehead?"

"Something as simple as a pocketknife or the sharpened point of a nail."

"Any ideas as to why the corpse was marked in this way?"

"Almost always it's meant to be seen—a message sent. The Mafia and gangs are known for this sort of thing—it's a warning to others. In this case it would seem to indicate Mr. Sanchez took something that wasn't his. I saw more of this up north when I interned in New Jersey."

"I can imagine. I may be naïve, but I don't see Palm Coast or even Daytona as a hotbed for organized crime."

"It's not Vegas. Still, any sort of gambling seems to invite that element."

Hmmm. Dan stood corrected. This was food for thought and certainly broadened the spectrum of reasons for wanting Jackson dead—more or less ruled out a crime of passion just because he'd threatened to fire someone. The "thief" said it all and it made no sense that Fucher would have needed to broadcast that accusation…unless Jackson had borrowed money from Fucher and hadn't paid it back. Damn. Someone could make a case out of that. It didn't exonerate Fucher—it tightened the noose if Jackson was on the list of recipients. He needed to check with Roger Carter. Still, if Fucher only *thought* he was killing Jackson…how did that change his case?

"One last question. Both Fucher, the man who was arrested for his murder, and the cop who arrested him talked about there being blood. I think it was referred to as a 'pool' with some mention of blood on Fucher's clothes. This picture of the knife appears to only show traces on the blade. I don't see anything that would have caused a pool or any spatter unless it was the stab wound. Yet, if your time of death is correct, the blood would have already settled away from the knife entry."

"Exactly. There would not have been any large amounts of blood, a spray or even scattered droplets."

"When will your report be completed?"

"As I said, I'm just waiting on the toxicology report."

Dan walked back to his car and decided to give Roger Carter a heads-up. Could a good lawyer get the charges against Fucher thrown out based on the evidence Dan had just seen? He sure hoped so. But just when he was feeling good about Fucher's chances of beating a false rap, evidence that might exonerate him appeared to indict him. Roger Carter burst his bubble. Sure enough, Jackson Sanchez had borrowed twenty-five thousand dollars. The debt was eighteen months old and even though the contract had been drawn up for payments of one hundred dollars to begin immediately on a monthly basis, no payments had been made. Ever. Not one cent paid back. Lawyers for the opposing team would have a field day with that. And on the surface it looked like a good reason for murder—complete with a carved out warning for others. And the misspelling of "thief." Dan could only imagine that Fucher's spelling skills might not be the best.

Maybe this was a major defeat but he couldn't get sidetracked. He needed to continue to look for evidence that would clear Fucher. Because Fucher, the murder, and the fire had everything to do with five greyhounds—five alive or five dead greyhounds. And he had to trust his gut. He'd go by the crematorium, but first a trip to the track kennel area was in order. The "pool of blood" bothered him. Both Fucher and the cop mentioned substantial blood—first on the floor and then on clothing—and there wasn't any reason to lie about it. Yet, there was no indication that it had come from Jackson Sanchez' body. Dan hoped that the hallway hadn't been torn out or scrubbed clean.

He parked along the side of the building next to a flatbed truck loaded with a few hundred cement blocks. Dan knew it was the building material of choice in an area that boasts of termites. Rumor had it the winged insects could eat the wooden studs right out of a house, leaving it a shell. St. Augustine was famous for ornate wood Victorians that were now only held together by plaster board on a rock foundation. You could poke a pencil into a wall and see nothing but sawdust. No, cement block made a lot of sense.

The kennel and track office had a blue plastic tarp draped over the roofline and it looked like they were expanding—adding an extra room or two along the back. The place was eerily quiet without dogs. A young workman let him into the roped-off general area but wasn't certain that the area of flooring that Dan was interested in was still intact. They were getting ready to pour a solid concrete pad that would tie the old office together with the two new ones, and much of the hallway had been torn up.

"Shoot, looks like it's gone." His guide had rounded the corner first. "You know the cops were here. They took pictures and samples of everything. Looks like they took most of the floor."

"I may be wasting our time." Dan looked around. Not only were the walls to the office now nonexistent, the floor was a pile of cement and tile chips—nothing much larger than three by four inches—and the entire floor was in three, three-foot piles.

"Tell me exactly what you're looking for and I'll help."

Dan explained that there had supposedly been a puddle of blood right outside the door and he needed to find stained tiles to support the story. He thought the kid looked a little queasy and was probably second-guessing his offer of help, but any reluctance was short-lived.

"Let's try that pile closest to where the old office door was." Immediately his helper was down on his knees digging through the pile with two hands, discards tossed to the side.

"What do you think? Could this be a piece of what you're looking for?" He held up a remnant of tile still attached to a piece of concrete.

Dan took the chunk the size of his fist, bigger than the rest, with a blackened coating thick enough to flake off. "I think you've found it. Any more?"

"Two more pieces but they aren't as big. Most of the flooring is gone, though."

"These'll do. I appreciate your help." Dan bagged them separately in the zip-lock bags he'd remembered to tuck in his pocket. He'd get the chunks tested. He hoped Dr. Hunt might suggest a lab, or because the samples are related to her work with Jackson, she'd do it at the County facility herself. Fingers crossed. It'd save him a lot of running around and he just wasn't sure he trusted the police lab. Something about Officer Bartlett still bothered him.

He'd drop them by the coroner's office in the morning. But for now he needed to get to the pet crematorium on the other side of town.

〉〉〉

The building was at the edge of a residential area. An older house-turned-office with bright red geraniums flanking the walk to the front steps. He presented his card and explained briefly the need to verify the cremation of five greyhounds killed in last week's fire at the track. The receptionist had no record of cremating any dogs on the morning in question, but she hastened to explain that that wasn't unusual.

"Dr. Elliot often uses the facilities without anyone being here. He has a key to the crematorium out back."

"I'd like to see the area, if I could."

"Oh, I don't think—"

"Nonsense, Rachel, I'll be glad to show our guest around… uh, Mahoney, was it?" A tall elderly man emerged from an office to his right. According to the nameplate on the door, this was Paul Fenwick, owner.

"Yes, Dan Mahoney, United Life and Casualty." Dan took out another card. "I appreciate your help."

"Not a problem."

Dan waited while Mr. Fenwick took a set of keys off a peg on the wall behind the receptionist and then followed him down a hallway to the back door. Dan tried not to stare at the case of pet cremation jewelry. Small vials to hold ashes, some in the shape of hearts, stainless steel, silver or gold, with or without rhinestones, but all with an area for inscription—a pet's name or just a declaration of love. Something was terribly sad about all this, and Dan was suddenly very happy he was seeing Simon soon.

Then, in the last case before the door, he saw shelf after shelf of urns—all different sizes and all different breeds. The greyhound ones? Exactly like the five on Dixie Halifax's desk. A sign directed anyone interested in purchasing to check with the receptionist. Apparently she could also take care of any engraving.

"We sell a lot of those. We have the exclusive rights. Almost every breed is represented except for a few of the new ones. We even carry some of what they're calling 'designer breeds.' In my day that meant you'd left the back gate open when your dog was in season." A chortle. "For ceramics I think the likenesses are pretty damned good." Mr. Fenwick paused by the door, "We played hell getting the right colored ribbons for Ms. Halifax's set. Such a shame. I understand those dogs were top-notch."

"Yes, they were. Just out of curiosity, how do you know what size urn a particular dog will need?"

"Good question. Everything's figured mathematically. A sixty-pound dog—by the way, that's average for the greyhound breed—would produce sixty cubic inches of cremains. Or one pound of dog is equal to one cubic inch of ash. Dogs weighing between fifty and seventy pounds would produce three to five cups of ash."

After some fiddling with both a deadbolt and a padlock, he led Dan into a metal building the size of a single-car garage. Inside, brick flooring had been laid wall-to-wall and yellow fire-brick lined the wall behind three stainless steel ovens. State-of-the-art. Dan knew he was looking at a sophisticated setup. He listened to an explanation of how everything worked—temperatures, times it took to cremate varying sized animals, how many grateful families he'd served this past year; yes, families could stay with their beloved pet and then there was a room where they could compose themselves back in the main house, meet with the veterinarian—Mr. Fenwick handled this part of the event. Hand-holding. Not pleasant but of so much comfort to the owners. He'd helped Dr. Elliot with that terrible burden last week, sat with Ms. Halifax and all. He just oozed caring and sincerity. Dan thanked him for the tour and walked back to his car.

Had Mel been wrong? The dog she thought was Mellow Yellow really wasn't? But Pete Ellis? He admitted to altering the dog's registration number. There was no reason that he would have shared information that would incriminate himself. But why would Paul Fenwick lie? The truth was somewhere in all this—but it sure seemed to involve a lot of people stretching it.

Chapter Thirteen

"I'm hoping your day was better than mine." Dan finished opening a classic Chianti and poured two glasses. Elaine had picked up peppers-and-sausage dinners freshly prepared by Massimo's Italian deli on Palm Coast Parkway and dinner was on the table.

"Don't bet on it." Elaine passed Dan a green salad followed by warm ciabatta bread, then went back to the kitchen for butter.

"I don't think real Italians put butter on their ciabatta."

"I'm not real, then." She laughed, it was a long-standing joke between them. She could probably prove three-quarters Italian blood but that was pretty far removed from the old country. And as for the Irish, well, she didn't think the Mahoneys were any closer to their origins.

"You first." Dan looked up from loading his plate with penne pasta and a generous topping of sausage and peppers.

"What?"

"Your day. Are you trying to duck sharing the excitement of an afternoon in Palm Coast?"

Actually, if the truth were known, she probably was. She was reluctant to discuss the contents of the envelope of false information that implied his mother lived with a criminal and by the time she told how she'd gotten it, she could only imagine Dan's reaction. But there was no way out of it. Scott Ramsey had been right.

When she'd finished—complete with the agent hiding under the car—Dan didn't say anything.

Finally, he said, "I'm glad Mom's out of town for a week or so." Elaine breathed a sigh of relief—nothing about her being tethered by the ankle by an unknown assailant who was supposedly an FBI agent. She was afraid she might have to defend her choice of career.

"She can't know. I mean I think it would be dangerous to tell her the truth."

"I'm sure it would be."

"She's already suspicious. You've met him. Did you get the idea that Stanley might be a criminal?"

"No. In retrospect, if I'd thought about it, I would have suspected he wasn't from Iowa. Iowans don't put an 'r' in saw. That was the worst. He was just boring, not threatening."

"So, we give her the packet of information and what? Hope for the best?"

Dan shrugged. There was no winning this one. "At the moment we don't have a choice—we just have a little time before we have to do it."

Over coffee and Elaine's favorite decadent Italian tarts with orange peel and cream centers, he shared his day. When he got to Jackson Sanchez' possible multiple killers, Elaine interrupted.

"You've got to be kidding. A gang killing? Or maybe the Mafia? But who did the initial killing—with the alcohol overdose?"

"Not a clue."

"But you think the carving wasn't done by the same person? And maybe the stabbing was done by yet another? The police should be looking for up to three people instead of pointing a finger at one?"

"If someone goes to the trouble of making the murder look like an accidental alcohol overdose, he's not going to deface the body. That screams for an autopsy and the medical examiner. No, I think someone came along, found Jackson dead, and used him to send a message. Then, possibly a third person not seeing the etched warning, stabs him thinking he or she's killed him. Remember Jackson was lying facedown in the hallway."

"You know there's no way that Fucher could have killed Jackson via tubed ingestion. He wouldn't know there was such a thing, let alone do it. What a disgusting way to commit murder."

"I agree. I've given Roger a heads-up. As soon as the coroner's report is released, he'll be able to approach the judge. Of course, given the warning message, the knife, and Sanchez owing him money, it might not change things that much. Intent to kill is still a serious charge. In the meantime I hope to have answers as to the 'puddle' of blood under the body."

〉〉〉

They didn't get to bed before one. He liked running things by Elaine—this sharing a career interest was working out just fine. As long as he didn't dwell on the possible dangers. Like maybe her needing to carry a gun. He was pretty proud of himself for not reacting to a guy hiding under the car and grabbing her ankle. And the grabber was one of the good guys.

They'd divided up the last of the Chianti and carried glasses upstairs. Alone time. It had been a long day and a little cuddling and whatever that led to sounded just about perfect to Dan. And it was. Funny how little it took to push Mom and Stanley and five greyhounds to a back burner and let him just enjoy the moment. He loved this beautiful woman with his ring on her finger.

What he didn't love was his cell phone going off at two thirty.

"Mr. Mahoney? You gotta come quick. They're gonna shoot me."

"Fucher?" Dan's feet were on the floor and he was already reaching for jeans and tee-shirt. "Where are you?"

"Here."

"At home?"

"Yeah."

Dan hung up and told Elaine to call 911—someone was threatening Fucher's life.

By the time Dan had reached the front door, he could hear angry voices coming from the parking lot in front of Fucher's townhouse. Fucher's porch light was on and about six people crowded together on the steps and stoop. Two people had guns.

Uh oh. Not good. Dan broke into a jog.

"Hey, what's going on here?" He pushed through the group to stand by Fucher and Sadie.

"This crazy son of a bitch kills my brother and the father of these girls here and he's loose." The woman talking held up the hands of two teenaged girls. Her black hair was piled loosely on top of her head, and bright red lipstick had found the creases around her mouth as well as the filter on the cigarette dangling to one side. There was a strong smell of alcohol and the most inebriated of the bunch also had a gun—a man slouched against the railing at the bottom of the steps.

"We live in a country where you're innocent until proven otherwise and no—"

"That's just so much bullshit." The man with the gun started up the steps, then lost his balance and fell against the man next to him. "You deserve to die." He waved the gun in the air in the general direction of Fucher. "Nobody gets away with killing my compadre."

As if on cue the sirens of three cop cars drowned out any more dialogue. The group abruptly scrambled to their cars and, making U-turns, headed for the exit. Dan hoped the cars would be stopped. There were a couple potential DUIs in the group.

"Are you okay?" Dan realized that Fucher was shaking.

"Yeah. Sadie's okay, too. She was pretty scared, though. I had to give her lots of pets."

"Good for you. Sadie's a very lucky dog. I'll wait here until the police leave. They might have some questions."

The cops didn't take long and promised to put an extra car in the area to patrol at night. Maybe nothing more than an occasional drive-by, but it was something. Finally, Dan could say "good night" and admonish Fucher to lock the door after he left and keep it locked while he was inside. He got a promise and was feeling relieved as he took off down the steps. Nothing worse had happened than just a good scare. They were lucky—then he heard Fucher's door open behind him.

"Mr. Mahoney? I forgot to tell you. This evening? I saw Maximillian take second at Tampa in the first race."

Dan turned around, surprised by the rush of adrenalin. Wow. He hadn't realized how much he wanted those dogs to be alive.

"Were you able to get a screen shot?"

"Uh uh. You want to come see?"

"Yes, I'd like to take a look." Could wild horses keep him away? Dan doubted it and took the steps in two leaps.

He waited while Fucher put Sadie back to bed—this entailed straightening her blankets and giving her a dog biscuit once she laid down. If a dog could look smug then that was the expression on Sadie's face. She knew when she had it good.

"Over here."

Dan followed Fucher to a table set up with viewing equipment, a computer, and printer. Actually, Fucher was good with electronics and quickly isolated the screen shot and blew it up for viewing.

Dan leaned in. He just wished these damned dogs didn't all look alike. But then he was more than sure that someone could put Rottweilers in the same boat. He studied the yellowish gray brindle with reddish-brown stripes. Maximillian was a big dog—over seventy pounds, he'd guess—long and lean with superior rear angulation. You didn't have to be an expert to see that this animal was special.

"What makes you so sure this is Maximillian?"

"His eyeliner."

"I'm not following."

"See his eyes? He's got thick black lines, like makeup."

Funny, once he mentioned it, there did appear to be heavy pigmentation around the eyes.

"See here, it's at the end of the race? The trainers give them treats. I don't know that guy." Fucher pointed to a blurred image of what was probably a man snapping a lead on Maximillian.

Dan was trying not to feel too excited. But still, instinct told him someone who knew the dog well couldn't be wrong. Mellow Yellow was out there racing and so was Maximillian. He had Fucher email the screen print to him. He'd keep Fucher working on the tapes; if surveillance had paid off once, maybe it would again. There were still three other dogs unaccounted for. But, for now, he felt like there'd been a small victory.

〉〉〉

Elaine borrowed night-lens binoculars and the zoom-lens camera from Dan and showed up promptly at six p.m. at Scott's office. She'd opted for a black baseball cap instead of a scarf, but thought the black linen shirt and slacks were exactly what was called for. And she'd traded in sandals for gray cross-trainers. The uniform of her new career. No killer heels, silk blouses, or pencil skirts… not a bad trade-off.

The ride to The Villages was uneventful. Once again Elaine was taken with the beautiful farms—most replete with sleek, thoroughbreds frolicking in green fields. A winter training area in preparation for spring racing. It reminded her of New Mexico—the farms outside Carrizozo, just to the south of where she grew up. She would never tire of open spaces.

"A penny."

"Sorry. I'm not very good company. I was just thinking of home."

"Well, enjoy the scenery. It gets a little congested in The Villages."

Scott reviewed the drill one more time as they passed the entrance to the right of Lake Sumter. This was surveillance, pure and simple. The husband had first contacted him early in the summer. The man's wife had admitted to having an affair, but he cancelled any surveillance when she apparently had a change of heart and came home—only to rekindle his suspicions now. Scott reiterated how the husband thought his wife was lying about playing mah-jongg and was really sneaking off to meet someone. They were to follow her to the recreational hall and record any comings or goings. She would leave home around seven-thirty and was supposed to be back by eleven. Scott had a description of her car and the license number. Elaine stifled a yawn. Her first case seemed boringly straightforward, but hadn't Dan warned her that surveillance would make up the bulk of any PI work?

"Cactus Jack and the Cadillacs are playing tonight." Elaine read the activities board to the right of the stop sign.

"Wouldn't have guessed you to be a Cactus Jack groupie."

"I'm not, but I am trying to imagine living here in another twenty years. And I don't think I could do it."

"I'm with you. A little too regimented. Still, if you like everything planned and play a lot of golf—it's paradise."

He passed five gated individual communities and pulled through the first set of wrought-iron gates in number six. He punched in the security code and they followed the road as it curved to the right.

"We're looking for 1168 Sleepy Hollow. We'll pull past the house and then circle back but stay a safe distance away. Usually a half block is sufficient. When no one is looking to be tailed, they're usually blind to what's going on around them."

The houses were incredibly close together. Elaine couldn't imagine living with just a few feet separating you from your neighbor on either side. A sneeze and half the block would reach for a box of Kleenex. And people were standing in line to buy these? And the golf carts…was there one in every driveway? She thought so. Once they spotted 1168, Scott executed a U-turn and pulled to the opposite side of the street, cut the engine, and picked up his binoculars.

"Two cars in the driveway, can barely see a cart from here. Uh oh, looks like we got here just in time."

Elaine focused her binoculars on the house just as a female exited and, walking between the parked cars, opened the door on what appeared to be a late-model, black Cadillac and got behind the wheel. Elaine's view was somewhat hampered by the car being on the far-side of the drive, but the shoulder-length bob of platinum hair acted like a beacon. Elaine watched her as she backed slowly out of the driveway and seemed to hesitate at the edge of the street.

Scott leaned forward to start the car just as the garage door started to rise on the house directly north. A car exited with what appeared to be a single male driver. "This is interesting." Scott had picked up his binoculars. "Coincidence that a male is exiting the house on their right? Guess we need to wait a minute to see."

"Won't we lose our subject?"

"Not at the rate she's driving."

Elaine watched as the Cadillac rolled to the corner stop sign where she seemed to be taking overly long to assess traffic and pull across the intersection. In the meantime the white Chrysler sedan backed to the edge of the driveway and turned in the direction of the Cadillac before slowly falling in behind and following it through the intersection.

Scott put his car in gear and moved forward. "Might be a good idea to jot down the license number. We don't know if there's a connection but we might be ahead of the game if there is. Here, let me get you a little closer." He maneuvered his car to within twenty feet and Elaine opened her iPad and added the number on a clean "notes" page.

"Oh, wait. I have this number already. I thought it looked familiar." She explained how when Maggie Mahoney had first asked her to check Stanley's info, she had been driving his car. Elaine had taken down the plate thinking it might help trace him.

"Good going. It'll be interesting if he's the other party."

Their progress was painstakingly slow. Scott allowed two other vehicles to separate them from the white Chrysler. And the Chrysler was about four car-lengths behind the Cadillac. Approximately two miles from where she started, the driver of the Cadillac pulled into a large parking lot in front of a recreational center. The driver hesitated, then drove around the side of the building and disappeared. Scott signaled and deftly parallel-parked across the street. The Chrysler continued on by.

"Oh no, have we lost her?"

"Just finding a parking place, I think."

As if on cue, their subject walked back around the side of the building, up the steps, and went inside. The Chrysler had made a U-turn and slowly came back in the opposite direction. If it hadn't been for the furtive wave as the Chrysler drove by, it would have been easy to think they'd guessed wrong. But there it was. A connection of sorts. Now they just had to see if the two subjects made actual contact.

The wait wasn't long. The blond bob reappeared at the door of the building and walked down the steps. The Chrysler had accelerated, turned around once again, and was now waiting at the curb. Scott's camera was clicking away and he waited until she had entered the car to get his final shots. Elaine did the same zooming in on Stanley.

"Great. Timing was perfect."

Elaine couldn't help but notice his enthusiasm—here was a man who loved his job. Could she ever be that upbeat about tracking down and proving people's foibles?

Scott waited until the Chrysler was stopped for a stoplight at the end of the block before pulling out, making a U-turn and being careful to slip back into traffic two cars behind. The Chrysler accelerated, continued straight for two blocks, then signaled, and turned left onto a wide boulevard—a long stretch of paved road with few turnoffs. Scott let the Chrysler stay a few car-lengths ahead and didn't try to close the gap.

"Where do you think they're going?" Elaine was intrigued.

"Living side by side they can't sneak off to each others' houses. Gotta find another place to rendezvous."

It soon became clear that any tryst wasn't going to happen within city limits. The Chrysler continued out the main entrance and turned to follow the east shoreline of Lake Sumter. Now it became trickier to fall behind and still keep them in sight as the road twisted and turned back upon itself.

"Are we on a golf course?"

"I think you're right. Looks like it ends at the edge of that wooded area. Too many courses in this area to keep track of. This one looks new."

Suddenly the lights ahead of them blinked, then disappeared in the outcropping of trees that formed a boundary to the mani- cured greens. Scott slowed, "I think they just pulled off. I'm going to continue but look to your left. Unless they're driving without lights, you should be able to see them."

Elaine squinted into the almost pitch black evening. Then around the second turn, she spotted it—what must be their destination. About a quarter mile off the main road, several yard lights illuminated a large metal building. It could even be some kind of hanger. A person could certainly store an RV in it.

"Looks like that's where they're headed. I don't see the car. They could have already pulled over."

"I'm pretty sure they did—parked along the road and are going to hoof it in. We need to check it out." Scott pulled off the road at the edge of a turn-around and got out of the car.

A tingle of excitement—this was certainly no longer boring. Elaine straightened the strap on the binoculars and placed them around her neck. She opened her car door. October—and there was just the hint of coolness once the sun went down. She pulled on the field jacket she'd borrowed from Scott and pushed the camera deep into a front pocket. Ready. She fell in behind him as he crossed the road.

"From this point on, no talking."

She nodded. There was no comparison between this and teaching Lit 101 or even a master's level course. She smugly wondered if Dan still felt this kind of excitement. She could certainly understand how he'd made investigation his career.

The cross-trainers had been a good choice. Elaine slipped on wet leaves and felt her shoes sink into a sandy loam that caked the soles. Not the place for a pair of Jimmy Choos, that was for sure. And low hanging branches on palmetto palms snagged her jacket and tugged at her cap. So much of Florida reverted to a jungle status if not hacked back on a regular basis.

They were close enough now to hear voices ahead of them. One male, one female. Then a trill of laughter. The two of them certainly seemed to enjoy one another. Scott put out a hand to stop her and motioned toward a thicket. From this vantage point they could see the big double-doors of the building about forty feet ahead.

The couple paused while the man dug into his jacket pocket for what was probably keys and, then, as if they just realized that they were alone, they kissed. And not some chaste peck on the cheek. For all the world this looked like a warm-up to tearing each other's clothes off.

Elaine already had her camera ready and had snapped a shot after zooming in for a close-up. Pretty chummy—especially his two hands placed squarely on the backside of his partner. And speaking of that backside, the tight, rounded bottom hinted of a little "tucking." At this stage in life, gravity would have taken a toll. Elaine was sure of it. And there certainly didn't seem to be any resistance from the blonde. If this was Stanley Evers, maybe this photo alone would discourage Maggie Mahoney from continuing the relationship and Elaine wouldn't have to divulge the bogus personal information—and run the risk that the lying would be discovered. It certainly would be the safest to have her just walk away.

The doors swung open and the man produced a flashlight pointing it into the building before they entered. Then, they both stepped inside and the doors closed. A faint light could be detected under the door like the flashlight was on the floor pointed toward the interior.

"I'm going to try to get closer." Scott eased out of the thicket and mouthed, "This way."

Scott stayed in the sandy ditch to the side of the road that led directly to the double-doors. Quieter that way, she knew. They were just at the edge of the building when that quiet was shattered by the siren from a cruiser barreling down the main highway, abruptly turning and bouncing along the overgrown, two tire-track trail that led to the oversized barn.

"Here, quick." Scott grabbed her arm and sprinted for cover. Back to the bushes—good protection and a great vantage point.

"You okay?" She nodded. "Then listen and learn; this could get interesting."

And it did. Rapidly. First the man opened the door and stepped out craning his neck to see where the siren was coming from. The fact that he was putting on his slacks at the same time was pretty impressive, Elaine thought, as she snapped a picture. Someone had switched on big oversized, loft ceiling lights in the barn and now his companion appeared with his shirt. The man seemed to be really upset—yelling and punching his fist in the air for emphasis.

"If that son of a bitch had us followed, I'm not going to promise I won't hurt him."

"Stanley, control yourself. Nothing has been compromised."

There it was—"Stanley." Dan's mother's boyfriend. The lead cruiser skidding to a halt a bare thirty feet in front of her interrupted her thoughts. *Now what?*

"Hands in the air." Two uniforms, both with guns drawn stepped out of the cruiser and walked toward Stanley and the girlfriend.

"Listen, Officer, I can explain—"

"Ron, let's make sure we don't have any surprises." The younger officer stepped forward and not so gently turned Stanley toward the side of the building, pressed him forward, kicked his legs apart and patted him down.

"Clean." This time he was gentler in helping Stanley regain his balance and turn around. Meanwhile the older cop had instructed the girlfriend to hold her arms straight out and he also did a quick pat-down.

"Likewise, no problems, but I need to know what you're doing on private property."

"I just rented a corner of this building for my bass boat and a few odds and ends left over from moving. I got a key to the padlock, for God's sake."

"And I'm just here to help him retrieve his garden elf."

"I'm not going to touch that one," Scott muttered under his breath.

The blonde pointed behind her and sure enough in the doorway, spotlighted by both cop's flashlights, was a molded cement troll crossed with a leprechaun holding a lantern.

The officers seemed satisfied after looking at drivers' licenses, checking addresses, and asking questions as to length of residency.

"Sorry about the inconvenience but there's been some break-ins over this way. We saw the car parked off the road back there and thought we better check." Elaine couldn't hear the rest of the conversation but it was handshakes all around before the officers walked back to their cruiser.

Stan and the girlfriend watched them go, then went back into the storage barn and closed the door. Scott checked his watch and made a note of the time.

"You think they're going to finish what they started?"

"Looks that way. Now comes the tough part of our job—wait and see." Scott took a picture of the Chrysler. "Need a time stamp on this photo and then another time-stamped photo when they leave. Indisputable evidence."

Two hours later, broken only by Stanley returning to his car to get a bottle of wine and paper cups after the first hour, both emerged and walked arm in arm to the car. Another kiss—far less rambunctious this time, Elaine noted—and they took off.

"It's ten fifteen. Looks like she's going to make curfew."

"That's right, home by eleven. So, what happens now? Will tonight be enough to convince the husband of hanky-panky?"

"Should be. The kissing, amount of time spent alone, remote hideaway…not sure retrieving a garden elf should take a bottle of wine and two-and-a-half hours. And I'll bet my client agrees. I'd like you to write the report as part of your class assignment. Let's get together tomorrow, compare pictures, pick the best ones, and finish this up."

Chapter Fourteen

"Dan, she's in Chicago, closing out her apartment and moving to Florida. I'd think under the circumstances, you'd want her to know about Stanley—before she commits to a move and all that expense."

Elaine poured each of them a second cup of coffee. Breakfast had been sour cream blintzes with fresh strawberries—Dan's favorite. Well, one of his favorites. She suspected things hit the favorite list pretty easily just to keep her doing the cooking and saving him the agony. Actually, that was saving them both the agony. She remembered his story about having to buy a second freezer just to keep all the frozen dinners. Did that qualify as hoarding? Maybe a reality TV show—never met a potpie I didn't want to take home. That might even be too much plot for the shows she'd seen. But you had to love a guy who thought boiling water took special talent.

"Guess I'm thinking that a move down here might not be a bad idea—with or without Stanley in the picture."

"How can you say that? She doesn't have friends here, no doctors, dentists—no base...we have no idea how long we'll be here."

"What if that were to change?"

The look was more than a little part Cheshire cat. "Why do I think you know something I don't?"

"Elaine, I'm not keeping anything from you. Honest. The home office emailed last night."

"And?"

"There's an offer of a permanent position in Florida. Not that I wouldn't have some travel, I would. But I'd spend some time in the office, too. For one thing, I'd be doing some training. You know, get recruits off to the right start. The Orlando office would be home-base. You could get your license. There seems to be plenty of work down here. And it's pretty wide open as to where we could live. Ocean-side, gulf-side—"

"Ocean-side."

"So, you're in?" The sigh was almost palpable. "You know that means giving your resignation? A tenured, faculty position doesn't grow on trees. Are you sure you're ready?" He waited a second before he saw the nod.

"More than ready." There simply comes a time in life when embracing the unknown and leaving the known was the only thing to do. Elaine had always thought this. No better way to lose unwanted baggage than to just leave it stacked somewhere, walk away, and start over. She'd still have that heart-to-heart with Dan's mom—that was only fair—and she hoped Maggie would move to Florida. And Jason—would she have a tough time luring him to the beach for spring breaks and holidays? She doubted it. This just felt right. A family in the making. And home, Roswell, New Mexico, in the dust.

"What if I wanted to have that second cup of coffee in bed… among other things."

"Hey, those blintzes were pretty filling. Don't I have to wait an hour before any strenuous exercise?" There was that grin she was in love with.

"I think that used to pertain to swimming and that's even been proved wrong. No excuses, pal—especially if I volunteer to do most of the work." That caught his attention. She picked up both mugs and started up the stairs.

〉〉〉

It was lunchtime in Chicago, and Elaine wasn't sure she'd catch up with Maggie but she answered on the second ring. Elaine quickly filled her in on Scott Ramsey's surveillance assignment and her shock when she realized it was Stanley Evers being tailed. Elaine offered her condolences and said she was so sorry to have to tell her but hoped she would want to know. There was silence and the sound of a sigh.

"First of all, never be sorry about giving me the truth. I can take it and in this case it'll probably save me a lot of anguish. You know that adage about old dogs and new tricks? Well, it applies to smarts, too. Wouldn't you think seventy-two years would have improved the gray matter?"

"There are no guarantees as they say."

"I knew something just wasn't right. He seemed to have a lot of friends in Florida. I understood that—he'd lived in Florida for a few years. But I think I told you that some calls always necessitated taking them out of earshot. I should have known there was another woman—probably some old girlfriend. He's Italian on his mother's side, you know."

Elaine didn't know what being half Italian had to do with anything, but she couldn't help thinking secretive calls could pertain to his undercover status and not necessarily his extra-curricular activities. But she couldn't say anything .

"Of course, Dan and I would love to have you move to Florida." Elaine explained UL&C's job offer and their acceptance and how excited they both were to be starting out together—new place, new life.

"You know, I don't rule out going ahead with my own plans to move to Florida. The realtor in The Villages had found a darling townhouse that I liked, and Stan thought was too small. I'm going to give her a call. If it's available, I'll take it. I like the concept of a planned community. I'll let you know what happens. I feel a symbolic burning of snow shovels coming on."

Elaine laughed, offered her help with anything that Maggie might need. With a big feeling of relief, she hung up.

"I take it Mom was okay with the news?"

"She even seemed relieved. She's calling the realtor from The Villages. I'm a little surprised that she'd move somewhere close to Stanley, but I truly hope the townhouse that she liked hasn't been taken. I'd love to have her in Florida. I can't imagine her enduring another Chicago winter."

"Me either. Last year was brutal. Do you have the car keys?" Dan held up her shoulder bag.

"Look in the front pocket."

"Did that, not there."

"Just dump everything on the table. They're probably at the very bottom. Here, let me do it." She took the purse from him and upended it over the dining room table. A jumble of lipgloss, coin purse, billfold, Kleenex packets, paperback, comb and…she hesitated…the zip-lock bag holding a latex glove with brown stains.

"Oh no. You're not going to believe what I did." She reiterated how Sadie had presented her with this "present" the day she'd found her hiding in the bushes. She'd carefully preserved it only to promptly forget about it. "And no comments about how anything could get lost in there or my diminished mental capabilities. I'm not an Alzheimer's candidate quite yet."

"No jokes. It's interesting that Sadie would have had it—that she had obviously hung onto it. Could be garbage from the area or something else. I'll ask the lab to take a look when I pick up the floor samples."

>>>

"Well, you were right about a couple things—it's blood and it's human." Marie Hunt met him at the door to her office, a bag with the samples of tile flooring in hand. "Let's talk." She motioned toward a chair in front of her desk. "The surprise is that it's not from Jackson Sanchez."

"That's interesting. Fucher reported slipping in 'a pool of blood' in front of the office door. And he found the body there—*in* the blood. We know the blood was fresh the night of the fire."

"And let me add that, based on the depth of the blood caked on these pieces of tile, the victim lost a lot of it. I'd venture to say that you have more than one dead body to worry about."

"And only one found." Dan leaned back in the chair. This was not what he expected to find out.

"You seem to believe this Fucher."

"I don't think he's capable of lying. Yes, I believe he stumbled over the body of Jackson Sanchez, but he didn't kill him. There's no way he could have force-ingested Jackson with the alcohol."

"I've been meaning to ask if there is some reason you haven't used the police labs for testing? I'm not complaining, just curious."

"Haven't gotten a warm fuzzy feeling from them. They seem overworked and set on closing this case out as quickly as they can. Looking at only the obvious. And speaking of labs, what are my chances of having this checked?" Dan placed the plastic bag with the stained latex glove on the desk and explained how he got it. "This is a real long shot. I sort of suspect the dog was going through garbage nearby and this was appealing for one reason or another."

"I'll get the results to you by close of business."

〉〉〉

The call came quicker than he'd expected. Dr. Hunt was succinct—the blood was human and, no, it didn't match Mr. Sanchez, but it did match the phantom body which had left blood on the tile chips she'd analyzed.

Another surprise. But just who was missing? It would seem someone from the track. A grounds worker? Handler? Driver/delivery person? No one had been reported missing. There had to be a reason for that and suggested some peripheral worker—maybe not even on the track's payroll. Might be a good idea to just stop by the track—unannounced.

Rebuilding was in full swing. Dan parked in back beside the six-foot chain-link fence separating the track and casino's property from the flea market. He was amazed to see the progress in just a couple days. One section was ready for stucco. The silver BMW K 1600 motorcycle caught his eye. One of the workers had good taste. Something like the BMW had always been on his bucket list. Wasn't there a part of him that hoped partnering up wouldn't mean taming down? He was about to find out.

He continued through the restaurant area to the casino's front desk and asked to have Mel paged. He wanted to tell her about

the sighting of Maximillian and ask a favor. He needed samples
of the ashes from the urns on Dixie Halifax's desk. Could she
help him? He thought she was his best bet.

"You've got to be kidding," wasn't the response he'd hoped
for. Mel seemed absolutely scared to death. "You don't know the
woman. If I got caught…"

"Okay, point well taken. Do you know of anyone who might
be persuaded?"

"Maybe. There's a guy on the custodial night crew who used
to skydive."

Dan didn't see the correlation between helping himself to a
tablespoon of ashes from each urn and falling out of a plane,
other than the risk element.

"Is he here today?"

"Let's see, it's four. He should be coming to work just about
now. Give me a minute, I'll check."

In scarcely five minutes Mel was back with a young man in
tow. Coveralls, a baseball cap, and shoe coverings over a pair of
biker boots.

"I'm getting ready to do some waxing." Not hello, not I am
Tom, Dick, or Harry, just a reference to the blue paper pull-ons
covering his shoes. The kid had the sullen look of the street—too
many pills, too many lines—too many times busted. And his
teeth screamed meth addiction. Could he trust this kid? Did
he have a choice?

Dan quickly explained what he needed and pulled five zip-
lock bags from his jacket pocket. Each bore the name of one of
the five dogs in indelible ink.

"What's in it for me?" Hard eyes, lowered head, slightly curled
lip—all the posturing of a wannabe bad-ass.

"Look, uh, I didn't catch your name."

"Roddy."

"Okay, Roddy…am I correct to assume that you'll do it if
the price is right?"

A nod. "You the one with the cheese?"

Dan's turn to nod.

"Then let's say five Bens."

Dan would be damned if he'd ask how much that was. Benjamin Franklin was pictured on a hundred-dollar bill and he believed he'd just been asked for five of them.

"One hundred dollars per urn—five total." Dan looked up to catch the slight nod. "It's a deal." No shaking of hands—did that even mean anything anymore? Dan simply handed the bags to Roddy. "I need these as soon as you can get them. At least a rounded tablespoon of ashes from each urn put into a bag with the matching name. Payment on delivery."

"Not a problem, Pops."

Dan started to correct him—demand the use of his proper name. But did it matter? He doubted he'd see much of Roddy. And there was no doubt that Roddy was cut out for this type of work. Dan considered himself lucky. If he'd had to get a subpoena, it would have tipped his hand and he wasn't quite ready to do that until a few more pieces of the puzzle fell into place. It was always better when people didn't think you smelled a rat.

He thanked Mel and got directions to the manager's office. He was hoping to pick up a list of workers—everyone, even part-timers, who had anything to do with the running of the track and casino. The phantom body that had left a puddle of blood in the hallway intrigued him. Had to be connected with everything...but then, maybe not. Hadn't he learned it was better to not assume? Yeah, only a few hundred times.

The office door was open and Carol Taichert, according to her name plate, just oozed efficiency behind the desk. Or maybe it was the large, round, black plastic-framed glasses. Gray hair, severe bun at the base of her neck, muted paisley patterned dress in tones of black and white. Very much in charge. He stepped through the door.

"Can I help you?"

Dan handed her a card, explained his involvement in the investigation and asked for a list of employees under the pretext of possibly needing to conduct interviews.

"Let me print out what we have. Each contractor, kennel owner, even the custodial company, adds and deletes workers all the time. I honestly don't think we could keep a list that was correct every second. There are over a hundred people here at any given time. We ask for updates on a monthly basis." She reached to pull three sheets out of the printer beside her desk. "But this one is already three weeks old."

Wow. This complicated things. The owner of the pool of blood had just become a needle in the haystack.

"I know Mr. Warren would be of more help. I expect him back Monday. I don't know how he does it, but he keeps tabs on everyone."

"I'm sorry, Mr. Warren is…?"

"Head honcho around here. Well, that's a shared position. I like to say he's Ms. Halifax's alter ego. This is, after all, the Daytona Beach Kennel Club and Poker Room. A staple in this community." Her surprise at his lack of knowledge exhibited itself in raised eyebrows and a barely concealed, derisive snort. "We have a fifty-five-table card room, private betting carrels, three hundred flat-screen monitors displaying simulcast races. We feature thoroughbred, harness, and greyhound racing—most of the dog racing is live. We have an absolutely superb track out back. And, in addition, we have jai alai."

"Jai alai?" Dan was drawing a total blank.

"Very popular in Florida. Teams with a ball in a closed room?"

Dan shook his head. "Like racquetball?"

"Somewhat. Mr. Warren was the one to introduce jai alai to central Florida. It's very popular in pari-mutuel betting. He has almost single-handedly built this complex. Built it and made it a lucrative part of the community. We have a complete betting venue for the sportsman. Or woman."

"And you expect Mr. Warren back on Monday?"

"Yes. October is his time to take a couple weeks to tour the Southwest. He's an amateur photographer. The Albuquerque International Balloon Fiesta is always a draw." She pointed to poster-sized, framed pictures of the event on the walls.

"Pencil me in for nine on Monday if he has that available."

"Done." She looked up with a pasted-on smile and a nod of dismissal.

Dan turned to go. "Oh, I almost forgot. I'd like to view any footage from your outside cameras the day of the fire. I assume you keep digital records?"

"For one month and then we destroy. Just let me know what you need."

"I'll get back to you."

>>>

A beer on the porch. That was all he could think of. Some downtime. Maybe a weekend at the beach. But the minute he turned into the complex of townhouses and saw the three police cars, lights blazing, sitting in front of Fucher's place, the beer was forgotten.

He didn't spot Joan Carter with a subdued Sadie beside her until after he'd gotten out of the car.

"Where's Fucher?"

"They took him. Back to jail, I'd guess. Oh, Mr. Mahoney, this is so awful. What did that poor boy do now?"

"Probably nothing," Dan muttered under his breath. He knew harassment when he saw it and this as clear a case as any. Nothing was happening, so stirring things up made people think you were busy solving the crime. Sometimes it did scare up new evidence—and the operative word there was "scare." But these tactics usually made a person of interest just shut down.

"They loaded up all the track disks and equipment. I'm so glad you got here. I've called Roger but he was in a deposition. He'll get here as quickly as he can."

Joan was right behind him when he reached Fucher's front steps just as Officer Bartlett stepped through the living room door.

"Just collecting a little evidence." He held up a two-gallon gas can complete with spout. "Not sure what our boy would be doing with this but I can guess." That smirky half-smile that Dan hated played around his mouth.

"Oh, for God's sake, he mows the lawns for me. Put that back where you found it." Joan Carter stepped forward. "That happens to belong to me."

"Sorry, ma'am, you'll be able to pick up the gas can downtown when we're through with it."

He made an elaborate gesture of putting it in a black plastic garbage bag another officer held open, then taped the bag shut and handed it off.

"You know I'm going to ask to see the warrant." Dan held out his hand.

"And I'm happy to oblige." Officer Bartlett brought out a folded paper from an inside jacket pocket.

A quick scan and Dan knew it was in order—reason for search? Certain reported incendiary materials on the premises, copies of syndicated races and viewing equipment without proper authorization...damn, Dan had the authorization from UL&C plus copies of the subpoenas at his place. He should have left a copy with Fucher but there was no reason to think anyone would be interested. And that was the puzzle. He certainly didn't keep track of Fucher's friends—who might have visited—but it smacked of someone being able to tell authorities exactly what to find and where it was located. Odd. What would someone get from confiscating the viewing equipment and disks of races?

Shit. Of course. He was being naïve. Someone was able to stop the search for live dogs—stop it or slow it down considerably. Was this proof that he was on the right track? He thought so. But it was also proof that whoever had the dogs wasn't going to stand by and let them be found easily. By the time Roger Carter could get all this straightened out, Fucher would be at least several days—and probably more like a week—behind in viewing. And like it or not, Dan's hand had been tipped. Now the person behind the theft of the dogs knew his suspicions.

Chapter Fifteen

Roger Carter brought Fucher home. He, too, was angry at the blatant disruption and falsely fabricated reasons for confiscating the disks and the gas can. Apparently, the judge agreed and had Fucher released immediately. Dan would need to supply the UL&C contract and subpoenas for the disks and those would have to go through "channels." Their word, not his, and he had no idea how long it might be before he could get the disks and gas can back. They would call. He'd been there before. It'd probably be up to him to bug them.

It was a weekend so he decided to shelve the case for a day. Nothing was going to happen that couldn't be taken care of on Monday. He was frustrated, yet sitting around being angry wouldn't get the materials released any quicker. They'd been in Daytona a week and a half and hadn't seen the ocean. Well, only from a distance. The Atlantic, no less. Warm and inviting even in October. Dan felt a lazy Saturday coming on—picnic on the beach, a little swimming in the surf, sunbathing…maybe dinner at Bonefish—tough to beat that for a holiday. Elaine was thrilled. This was a good time to take a break. Her first assignment was finished and turned in, and Maggie had called back to say she'd rented the townhouse in The Villages. She'd be coming back their way as quickly as she could with Simon and following a moving van. Great news but if they didn't take some time now, things promised to get hectic between helping Mom settle in and work.

Dan had picked up the five bags of supposed greyhound ashes, paid Roddy, and dropped the bags by the lab. Dr. Hunt reiterated that her testing would determine species but couldn't tell an Afghan from an Affenpinscher. Dan wasn't real sure he even knew the difference in the flesh. But it was a place to start. And that was enough business for the day. He owed Elaine a little one-on-one attention and wouldn't mind a little in return.

They loaded the Land Rover with cooler and picnic basket— more finds in Joan's garage—towels, blankets, sunscreen. Then at Elaine's urging, they stopped and bought a kite. The store was warehouse-big, right on the corner of highway A1A and a dead-end side street. It had everything. All at seventy percent off. The sign was so faded, the sale must have been as old as the building.

The beach was perfect—they parked the Land Rover and unloaded, then swam, flew the three-point Delta kite, dozed on the blankets, hunted shells, talked…both agreed the day should never end. But sooner or later the ham and baby swiss on light rye gave out and at the first grumble from his stomach, Dan suggested gathering up and heading to Bonefish. He couldn't remember feeling so relaxed, so rested and just plain happy. If Elaine's smile was any indication, she felt the same way.

Dan was patting himself on the back for making reservations when he saw the restaurant's packed parking lot. Saturday night and the whole town seemed to need a fish-fix. They had twenty minutes to kill before their table would be ready so Dan suggested a drink in the bar.

He was stopped in the doorway by the crowd of people in front of him who had the same idea. And that's when he saw the two men sitting at the far end of the bar—before they saw him—heads close together, one earnestly seeming to entreat the other to do something? Maybe just agree with him? It didn't seem to be working as the other man turned back to the bar and smacked it sharply. Officer Bartlett and Kevin Elliott. And that was not just a pleasant little chat. Officer Bartlett's face was flushed, mouth pulled back into a thin line, and a nervous tapping against the bar with his left fist indicated some urgency to whatever topic had been under discussion. Dr. Elliott just looked sullen and uncommunicative.

As if he felt his gaze, Officer Bartlett looked up quickly, made eye-contact, then slipped off the bar stool, said something to Dr. Elliott, and walked toward Dan. But the instant transformation of expression was interesting. The man coming his way was smiling broadly and holding out a hand.

"Mahoney, we meet again." The grip was firm.

Dan introduced Elaine but refrained from calling Officer Bartlett the arresting officer in Fucher's case. He'd like her feedback on this man and he didn't want it tainted.

"Anything new on the track fire?" Dan thought he might as well test the waters.

"Naw, nothing you don't know. Still working it but it proved to be arson—a simple gas-fueled blaze. We got your boy's prints on a gas can found in the dumpster. And we lifted a matching set from that gas can he had at his house. Not sure what a boy like that needs with two gas cans, but I bet I could guess. I'd say we're about ready to wrap things up." A barely concealed I-told-you-so smirk.

"Interesting. You might want to take a look at the autopsy on Jackson Sanchez first."

"And just what would I find?" Still that jocular attitude but the voice was just a little tighter and the smile a little forced.

"I'm not really at liberty…best to go through channels." Now it was Dan's turn to smile…a shrug and one of those "aw, shucks" sorry about this little hang-up sort of expressions.

"Thanks for the heads-up. I'll do just that." Then, a look over his shoulder. "I'm trying to talk my pal over there into going to the races tomorrow. He seems to think Sundays are workdays. I'm not making any headway but better get back to it. Ma'am, good to make your acquaintance." A nod to Dan and he was gone.

"You rattled his cage. What's going on?"

"I'm sure you sensed the 'we've already got our man' attitude? I just think he's been hasty in naming a suspect—hasn't looked at all the evidence. It's obvious he hasn't seen the coroner's report."

"I'd hate to work for him." Dan agreed and reminded himself to ask her why later, but at the moment they were being directed to follow their server to a table in the main dining area.

Halfway through a round of Bang-Bang shrimp, beet and goat cheese salad, and a cup of corn and lump crab chowder, Dan's cell rang.

Maria Hunt didn't waste time with niceties as usual.

"I need you to meet me at the lab in the morning."

"Sunday?" Dan thought he'd heard wrong. What could be so urgent?

"Yeah. You have a weekends and holidays off policy?"

He didn't rise to the bait and ignored the obvious pique. "I'll be there. Name a time."

>>>

Dan got up at six. He needed a cup of coffee before his seven o'clock meeting. Seven on a Sunday. He was at a loss. What could be so earth-shattering? He ran through possible scenarios on the way over. And later as he thought about it…never in a million years would he have guessed Dr. Hunt's discovery.

She unlocked the door of the lab and didn't say a word until they were seated in her office. The five bags of ashes sat between them on her desk.

She wagged an index finger up and then back over the bags. "The ashes are human."

No fanfare. No lead-in. Just throw it out there. Wow. He could hear his heart beat and found it difficult to take a breath, "Human?" Dan couldn't believe what he'd just heard.

"All from the same human, I might add." She sat back. "And another tidbit of info? I don't think you're going to find a body to go with the blood sample I just analyzed."

"A match?" His turn to point at the five bags.

"Without a doubt. I'll finish my report and wait until morning to turn all this over to authorities. I'm sure you know I'm going to have to keep these." Again, a reference to the five bags of ashes.

Dan nodded. He needed to confiscate the five urns on Dixie's desk legally, but fat chance doing it now. After this discovery the authorities would have first dibs. It might even be difficult to be kept in the loop. But he needed to prove Roddy hadn't been the one to substitute something a little more sinister than the expected dog remains. And he needed to get it done before there were too many questions about why he might have had suspicions. This was not the time to get slapped with a "with-holding information" citation. He wished he hadn't paid to have the evidence illegally lifted. He'd fully expected to find either the remains of a backyard cookout or roadkill. There was no doubt in his mind that Dixie was one hell of a lawyer. If the finger were pointing at her for possible murder, she wouldn't play nice.

>>>

Morning came after a long Sunday afternoon of bringing his report up-to-date and a sleepless night. Even a movie and pizza hadn't brightened his mood. He'd get backup first, but he'd confront Kevin Elliott. With luck, he'd get there first. There were too many questions and too many incidences of the doc's involvement. And this latest? Five bags of dog cremains that actually proved to be human remains? Dr. Elliott had a lot of explaining to do before his inevitable arrest. It was time to involve local law enforcement.

And he hoped his appointment with Mr. Wayne Warren, track owner, would turn up a name of someone missing. A very dead someone missing. And Dixie Halifax? Did having urns of human remains on your desk mean you *knew* they were human? Was it time to confront her? Again with some backup. Or should he just wait until she came after him? It wouldn't be long. One way or the other, he knew he was dreading the confrontation.

And he had to keep things in perspective. His sole reason for being there was to prove that UL&C was either obligated to pay on a policy, or not. That was it—a clear-cut bottom line. And that meant his finding out how much involvement Dixie Halifax had in the disappearance of her own dogs. He felt like so much had surfaced, yet the connections were fuzzy at best.

He still needed living, physical proof that the supposedly dead dogs were out there racing even if he wasn't any closer to finding them. Mellow Yellow's registration was the only number he was certain had been altered. A blanket request to all tracks both in-state and out to report when a dog matching that number was raced was a starting point. But at the moment it would seem both Maximillian and Mellow Yellow had gone underground. There hadn't been any more sightings. Knowing he or someone was monitoring races had forced the dogs into retirement. It might explain a lot if he knew who had turned Fucher in.

He was early despite the slow traffic. Monday morning commuters. He fiddled with the radio dial and passed up a couple music stations to catch the last of the news. Nothing earth-shattering: several break-ins, two busts for graffiti, a child's escaped parakeet, and a plea to have the false teeth returned that were left at a bus stop on Eighth—then, breaking news. Dr. Kevin Elliott, veterinarian to Daytona Beach Kennel Club and Casino, had died in an early morning motorcycle accident on Highway 40.

Dan pulled to the side of the road. There were not a lot of particulars. Elliott was riding with friends returning from Volusia Raceway; alcohol may have played a part; wet pavement seemed the sure culprit...dead at age fifty-three. Dan tuned out the eulogistic comments but it would seem the vet was well liked—a contributor to Little League events, church-goer, graduate of an in-state school...and Dan smelled a rat.

Chapter Sixteen

The place looked dead. Maybe ten cars in front of the casino at eight-thirty in the morning. It looked like he'd beat the crush of reporters and police. Just barely. Between the vet dying and what promised to be a freshly fueled police investigation of the fire, the track would be the center of attention for a few days. Luckily, people had attention spans the length of a sparrow's tail—another truism from his grandmother—and would be on to some other titillating bit of news by the end of the week. In the meantime he hoped Wayne Warren would have some answers.

He decided to pull around to the kennels. He doubted Roddy was still on duty. Maybe a quick heads-up that the ashes were going to fast become the center of attention would be helpful. And he'd like to see Roddy's reaction to the contents—the kid couldn't be ruled out as a suspect.

He entered the building from the outside door next to the vet's office. Already three small bouquets of flowers and a flickering candle filled the entry to his lab. Thoughtful. He glanced through the glass partition. Funny but he had an eerie feeling that someone had gone through things. The usually meticulously neat room was in disarray—not tossed, just a few things out of place. Subtle things. Three file drawers open an inch or two. A couple papers on the floor...blotter on the desk not squared up. He used the tail of his shirt to cover the doorknob—no use someone finding his prints on anything. But the door was locked. Just as well, he really didn't need the temptation of looking around.

Then again…Dan removed a narrow, thin, metal, saw blade from his billfold. How long had it been since he'd used this? The perfect tool for picking a Kwikset, single-cylinder lock. The blade slipped easily into the keyhole. A quick look up, then down the hallway. All clear. He could hear workers feeding dogs. That ought to give him some privacy for a little while. He slowly turned the blade in an opposite direction every time the tumblers caught. One catch, two…at the third click, he withdrew the blade, and turned the door handle. He was in.

Nothing seemed out of place in either the exam room or adjoining lab. A glass-fronted cold storage unit showed vials stacked in neat rows seemingly untouched. Apparently whoever went through things wasn't interested in drugs. Dan turned back to the office area and stepped behind Kevin's desk. Several pens, a black felt tip marker, two drug pamphlets advertising the latest treatment for kennel cough…a Day-Timer open to last Friday's date. Day-Timer? Somehow Dan thought his calendar would have been electronic. Some habits died hard, he guessed.

He leaned down to take a look at Friday's entries. Slow day. Breakfast meeting with Dixie, phone consult with a vet from the St. Augustine track, vaccinations for an incoming group of dogs after four…nothing out of the ordinary unless the note in the upper right-hand corner meant something. "Call 386 283-1020." The number had been underlined three times. Doodling or done for emphasis? On a whim Dan pulled out his cell and dialed.

"Private Investigator, Scott Ramsey's office. How may I help you?"

Dan almost dropped the phone. That wasn't what he expected. He was barely able to mumble something about a wrong number before he hung up. It probably meant nothing, but under the circumstances, anything and everything could be important. He didn't have a clue as to what someone might have been looking for in Kevin's office. And he'd probably reached the end of any safe timeframe to be snooping. He grabbed a Kleenex from a box on a side table, quickly crossed to the door, covered the inside turn button as he twisted it perpendicular, stepped through and pulled the door shut behind him—locked like he'd found it.

"Can I help you?" The man in coveralls looked like he might work for Fred Manson in maintenance if the grease stains were any clue. Dan was just glad he hadn't jumped because he certainly hadn't heard the man walk up, but there was no indication that he'd seen him coming out of Kevin's office.

"Actually, you can. I'm looking for a kid named Roddy. He works as a custodian, I think."

"You're shit out of luck on that one. Roddy came in last night, worked a half shift, and walked out. Said he'd give Fred a call but he didn't plan on coming back."

"Seems sudden. Any idea why?"

"Kid's a hophead. Fred was giving him a chance to straighten out but I don't think it was working. Even doled out his paychecks—you know, only gave him money for food and gas. Just the necessities. Kid was 'up' on something last night. I don't think he could have finished his shift if he'd wanted to."

No doubt, five hundred "Bens" would buy a fair amount of street dope, Dan thought. He'd had no way of knowing, but he could have been a major contributor to Roddy falling off the wagon. He hoped the kid would be all right but that didn't make the sick feeling in his stomach go away. He walked the long way around the casino to the front entrance, then through the main hallway, past some gaming rooms on his right before stopping in front of Wayne Warren's door. Time to get to work.

At first he thought no one was in the reception area. Ms. Taichert was not at her desk. Then she appeared in the doorway to her boss' inner office—holding a cell phone.

"Mr. Mahoney? Could you help me?" She motioned for him to follow as she stepped back into the room and closed the door. "I don't know what to do. People to contact…" Dan leaned down to catch her last words. It wasn't that she was whispering but more like her voice was shaking. Was the woman going into shock? He quickly pulled out a chair from a small conference table and waited until she was seated before taking a seat himself. Carol

Taichert was distraught—coming apart at the seams (there was his grandmother again)—and he had no idea why.

"Water?" The carafe on the table was full but its contents tepid. He poured a glass anyway and placed it where she could reach it. "Now, tell me what's wrong."

She took a sip of water, then another before setting the glass back down. "This…this is what's wrong." She waved the cell phone more or less in his direction. "I found it under the desk. There." An index finger indicated the large wooden monstrosity in front of them—more collector's item than functional piece of office furniture. "I've called and called. Nothing. He didn't contact me the entire two weeks. He never would just be gone that long without checking in. He ran this office from there…" another gesture toward the desk…"on the road. Then just now I found the phone. It's been here all the time. Oh, Mr. Mahoney, he never left. He wouldn't leave without his phone."

Even though Dan reached out and patted her arm, he knew he could offer no words of encouragement. He knew without putting all the pieces together that Wayne Warren, in fact, didn't leave on vacation—probably didn't leave the casino. The blood in the walkway to the kennel, the ashes in the urns? Dan would bet the farm that he could put a name to the contents.

"I can't believe that something would have happened to him. Not now. Not when he's finally getting ahead. He tried so hard to put this place right."

"I'm not following"

"Well, I guess it was no secret that the club and casino had fallen on hard times. The last six months have been awful. And it wasn't just Mr. Warren's pocket—everyone was suffering. Ms. Halifax had her hauler repossessed."

"Hauler?"

"The eighteen-wheeler that she used to carry dogs back and forth to the track. Two-hundred-seventy-five thousand-worth. It had a few years on it, but it was outfitted beautifully—built-in crates, grooming area, water tanks with shower, sleeping quarters for four, and a bottled gas kitchen. It was state-of-the-art. Such a shame that she had to lose it."

"Where's the casino now? Solvent?"

"Getting there. There were just too many costs—too many I.O.U.s—to breathe easy yet. Thanks to the heavy rain this last summer, reroofing set us back an unanticipated five hundred and fifty thousand. Putting that kind of money back in the bank has been slow. But we're still in business."

The owner of a repossessed hauler could certainly use some money about now—two hundred fifty thousand would come in handy. Dan couldn't help but feel elated—wasn't finding motive over half the game?

"What do you think has made the difference? Between now and six months ago?"

"Mr. Warren and I were just talking about that before he left. For one thing, he expanded the closed-circuit offerings. In addition he added I-don't-know-how-many tables of in-house poker. Plus he said we'd picked up some high-rollers—a group from Miami—actually a sort of traveling club for gamblers. Let me tell you, they brought in big bucks. It was all starting to add up."

A "traveling club for gamblers"? Why did that send up a red flag? He found a box of Kleenex in Wayne Warren's executive bathroom and put it on the table. Then, he placed the call to Chief Cox, left a message, got her a bottle of cold water, and suggested she stay put. Was there anyone she would like to have sit with her? The woman who manned the information desk? He'd bring her over. Dan left to find this Rosy, and decide what his next move should be.

His mind was churning…there had to be a connection between Wayne Warren and Jackson Sanchez—both more than likely killed the same night and just maybe in the same vicinity. By the same person or persons? That was the big question. Then throw in one dead veterinarian and the intrigue had just reached proportions that would seem to negate any involvement of a challenged young man who dedicated his life to taking care of dogs.

Dan found a quiet corner in the track's restaurant and flipped his iPad open. He'd go over his notes, then request an interview with police. And he'd bite the bullet and report to Dixie. But first a quick call to Roger Carter.

〉〉〉

Roger met him at the restaurant. It was a little early, but Dan had just put in an order for a patty melt and fries. Who made the rule that breakfast food had to be cereal or eggs? He used to eat a lot of pizza about this time of day and had lived to tell.

"So, take it from the top. I need to know what you know and how you're involved—in each step of the investigation. Mind if I record this?" At Dan's shake of his head, Roger set the recorder between them. This was for Fucher's sake but Dan didn't rule out asking Roger to go with him when he talked with Dixie.

On the iPad, Dan brought up his outline as a prompt, then backtracked to his first meeting with Fucher and started to work his way forward. When he'd finished, Dan closed the iPad. He'd told Roger everything—from ingested alcohol to altered tattoos to human remains in urns, to the track's recent money problems…"Pretty compelling that Fucher just isn't the killer or even one of the killers."

Roger nodded. "I'm assuming you're willing to turn over any evidence? Testify to what you've just said if it comes to that?"

"Based on what we know already, I don't think it will go that far."

"Me either. Especially based on Dr. Hunt's lab work, I think I can get the charges against Fucher dismissed." Roger pushed back from the table but signaled the waitress for another beer. "Sounds like Officer Bartlett won't be too pleased."

Funny, Dan mused, he could order a little beef before eleven but couldn't have faced anything with hops in it at that hour. Ah, well, different tastes…

"Yeah, you can probably expect a little push-back. Officer Bartlett wants things wrapped up neatly and there isn't anything neat about this one. Add another murder and a few folks are going to be working overtime."

"You've agreed to share everything—exactly what you've told me—so let's get started." Roger snapped the cover on the recorder.

"You mean confront Dixie Halifax?"

"That, too. But let's start with the police chief. I'll give him a call and have him meet us here. He might as well get a warrant to search Dixie's office—that'll go over big." A smile that made Dan think Roger almost relished the idea of upsetting her. The woman didn't seem to have a lot of friends. And a fellow lawyer probably had good reason to want Dixie on the hot seat. Dan knew he wouldn't want to face her in court.

Roger looked up from taking notes. "I forgot to ask if this has been done. If not, it's about time that dog crematory was wiped down. Seems probable that the garbage bags of supposed dog bodies the night of the fire could have been human body parts—parts that were carried out of here right in front of everyone. Don't know if it's too late to detect residue twelve days old, but it needs to be checked."

"While they're at it, I suppose the lab here should be checked for human blood—especially instruments."

"Good suggestion. I wasn't thinking of that."

"There's little doubt that Kevin Elliot could have given us some answers."

›››

Was curiosity a good reason to attend a funeral? Dan didn't think so, but he'd talked Elaine and Fucher both into going with him. Funny but with all the emphasis upon cremation for dogs, Dr. Elliot was in a box. A waste of space and expensive. But nobody had asked Dan. There hadn't been a viewing because of the severity of the accident but there was a tasteful, if short, remembrance ceremony at a non-denominational church in town and a cop-led procession to a cemetery on the outskirts of the community.

The six pallbearers were in biker-leathers and after loading the casket into the hearse, followed behind on Harleys draped in black crepe. Fitting. Officer Bartlett assumed leader-of-the-pack duties and rushed ahead to clear intersections for the entourage.

It was a somber group but Dan recognized most of the track's management. Carol Taichert came with Dixie Halifax, Melody sat with fellow trainers, and Fred Manson came over and asked Fucher to sit with him.

"It's so difficult to think a vet would lie about the death of five dogs. It must have been made very worth his while." Elaine, as ever, looked gorgeous in a little black dress barely above the knee, high-necked, but form-fitting and just plain sexy. And immediately Dan admonished himself for impure thoughts at a funeral—somehow that didn't seem appropriate. Funeral etiquette—no jeans, no loud talking, and no lewd thoughts. Had he read that? He was pretty sure it was written somewhere. Maybe it was his mother talking.

Before the final interment, several friends offered anecdotes, one a prayer. So far, Dan didn't see one thing out of order. Then Officer Bartlett started to walk toward them.

"Uh oh. I think I'll go check on Fucher." Elaine nodded to the officer and retreated.

"I see your boy's out. Wouldn't have thought you'd want to bring him here."

"And just why would that be? I think he considered Kevin Elliott a friend."

"Some friend. For starters, Kev's bike had been tampered with. A new set of Metzelers and the inner wall had been shaved. No way to see it from the outside and no way of knowing when the tire would blow. Poor guy never had a chance."

"Come on, you don't expect me to believe that Fucher would be able to do that? His motor skills can be a little challenged. And he might as well have been under house arrest the last couple weeks. He hasn't gone anywhere since he was let out. He certainly hasn't been back to the track." Dan hoped he was right. He hadn't kept tabs on Fucher, but someone would have had to have given him a ride. He didn't remember seeing any cars there, and Fucher was still hard at work on the surveillance records.

"Just saying. This Fucher knew where the bike was parked. And it wasn't like it was out in the open or anything. Pretty secluded—easy to vandalize something parked behind the kennel. And these? Found 'em stuffed in the saddlebags." Officer Bartlett pulled a half dozen Snickers' wrappers from his pocket. "Pretty much his calling card from what I hear."

"Can I have some candy?" Dan hadn't seen Fucher and Elaine walk up.

"Do I have to say more?" With a sneer Officer Bartlett turned to go, then waving the fistful of wrappers turned back, "If I was a bettin' man, I'd put money on this." He crumpled up the wrappers and stuffed them back in his pocket.

Dan watched him walk back toward the crowd. And if you had more than circumstantial evidence, you'd be able to do something about it, he thought. But you don't. He wondered if those wrappers had been dusted for prints? Or had any other lab work done on them? Were they just for show? Could someone be trying to set Fucher up? Again? Implicate him in one murder and when that didn't pan out, try him for another? But who? It would take some knowledge of Fucher's habits. But then he guessed just about everyone who handled dogs at the track would know that Fucher liked Snickers bars.

"He's not nice." Fucher stood watching Officer Bartlett walk away. "He doesn't like me. I want to leave."

Well said, Dan thought. He wanted to leave too.

Chapter Seventeen

Monday. All the chores she'd put off over the weekend needed attention. First, up to Palm Coast to drop off her client report on Stanley and the garden elf retrieval. Next, groceries and last, a stop for dog food before circling back home. There was every possibility that Simon would be with them this week. She'd rented a car. Just as well, she had no time to shop for something permanent. And, as always, her good, economical angel was having a tussle with her bad, throw-caution-to-the-wind angel. Good common sense told her she could put some of the money paid out for the burned Mercedes—part of the nightmare in Wagon Mound last month—in the bank and not buy another, instead spending the rest on maybe a *used* luxury car. Or not buy luxury at all. She could get a truck or SUV or…possibilities were endless and made her head hurt. A rental would buy a little time.

She was faced with more than one major decision. She'd honestly enjoyed the gun-safety workshop and target practice. Yet, a gun permit still seemed like overkill even though the permit could arrive any day. The real question still was did she really want to carry a firearm? She admitted to being a little squeamish. It would just take practice to get used to it. The more comfortable she became, the easier it would be to accept. Dan promised to help her find a gun and take her to the range. The class on gun safety had allowed her to explore a semi-automatic as well as a revolver. And she'd honestly felt safer with the revolver. It was just the feel of the thing.

Dan had already turned up his nose at a nifty looking Lady Smith and Wesson she'd found online. He was suggesting a revolver, too, but nothing with the name "lady" on it, probably a snub-nosed .38—a revolver versus a semi-automatic because a revolver wouldn't jam. She could carry it in a pocket or her purse and no amount of lint or fuzzies would cause it to misfire. It'd be ready to go when she needed it. Needed it? She still felt a little shiver. Could she really kill another human being? And wasn't that the one question you had to be comfortable with before even carrying a gun? She still had a little soul-searching before all this became routine. No class on Chaucer had ever required her to be armed.

The stop at Scott Ramsey's office wouldn't take long but she did want to hand it off personally. She decided not to just leave the report with his receptionist. She needed some info on their next assignment and would just wait. What a luxury to have time to kill. Elaine took a chair against the wall and picked up a *Car and Driver*. She really needed to get serious about getting another car. Elevated voices said he had someone in the office with him but the receptionist indicated she didn't think the wait would be long.

A particularly good article on "going green" was interrupted by a buzz on the intercom. The receptionist quickly picked up and then went to the file cabinet and pulled out two manila folders. She knocked on the conference room door and stood with it partially open getting directions on yet another project, Elaine thought. Then a male voice chimed in and the magazine slipped from Elaine's grasp. The man in the office was the same man who had tethered her by the ankle. Who had hid under her car to do so. The same agent who had handed off an envelope of lies.

She missed what he was saying and quickly stood to place the magazine on the table and leave. But didn't move fast enough.

"Elaine? I didn't realize you were here." Scott had stepped out of the conference room and walked to the copier. "If you have a minute, I think my colleague has some questions for you."

She waited until Scott had finished copying and followed him back into the room. The man sitting just inside the door stood and offered his hand. Manners. Better late than never, she supposed.

"Scott was telling me your first surveillance job involved Stanley Evers. Interesting coincidence."

"It allowed me to use truthful information to dissuade my fiancé's mother from investing in property with him."

"That was timely." Not a reaction to the word "truthful." The man was older than Scott and just slightly past his prime. Not one she would think enjoyed crawling under vehicles. Thinning hair, a couple extra chins and just the hint of love handles suggested retirement might be getting close.

"Yes, it helped me make a decision."

"Do you think it helped Ms. Mahoney make a decision?"

"I'm assuming you mean to stop seeing Mr. Evers?"

"Yes."

"I'm not positive, she's been out of town, but she has indicated that she won't be moving in with him."

"If the romance is still alive and well, I'd appreciate your letting us know."

Elaine looked at Scott but he was staring out the only window in the room with his back slightly turned her way and didn't seem inclined to enter the conversation.

"May I ask why?" She was still feeling that Dan's mother was lucky to have gotten out of the relationship—it didn't seem a possibility that Stanley would still be around after the little two-hour episode in the storage barn.

"Let's just cross that bridge when we get to it." A smile of dismissal. Elaine slid her report across the table to Scott, turned and left.

>>>

The chief couldn't get there until one and Roger needed to run by his office—that left Dan in the casino restaurant sipping his fifth cup of coffee. This might be a good time to catch up with Fred Manson and tour the maintenance barn. Better than just sitting around. News that Wayne Warren was missing coupled with the death of Kevin Elliot and it was like a somber blanket had been thrown over track personnel. People talked in hushed tones reliving when they had last seen the track manager or conversed with the vet. A lot of conjecture—the dead or missing had a tendency to take on the vestiges of martyrdom in a very short period of time. And as to what had happened? Each man had stories circulating and the rumor mills were just getting geared up.

The tall double doors of the metal barn were wide open and a roller attachment sat between a couple of tractors. Along the back wall was what looked like a king-sized bedspring on wheels. Hoses, water tanks, tool boxes, hanging lights, lights on pedestals, work benches, vices, compressors—the place looked pretty well equipped for repairs, as well as storage.

Dan grabbed a pair of safety goggles from a bin marked "Mandatory Safety Gear" and slipped them on. This was probably a place for steel-toed shoes, too, but his Nike cross-trainers would have to do. Fred Manson was at the back of the barn supervising a welding job, and Dan was doubly thankful he'd slipped the dark-tinted wraparound glasses on before he entered. Photokeratitis or welder's eye wasn't something to mess with.

Fred looked up and motioned to him. A young man was welding a cross-bar support onto what could have been the frame for an awning. He vaguely remembered noticing awnings across the front of the casino. He guessed maintenance went beyond just the track.

"I see you decided to visit the dark side. What can I do for you?"

"I guess the nickel tour if you have the time."

"Sure. Let me finish this up." Fred turned back to the welding project, pointed out a joint and a couple seams in the metal tubing that needed reinforcing then gestured toward an office in the back corner. Dan followed him over.

"All the comforts of home." Dan stepped into a neatly set up space of computers, printers, fax machine, not to mention the mini-fridge, and the hot plate next to a coffee and latte machine.

"Can I get you anything? Latte? Cappuccino? I can't break out the beer until after five."

"No, nothing for me, thanks." He watched as Fred got a small bag of espresso out of the mini-fridge, filled the basket, tamped down the grounds, slipped the "arm" into a slot in the machine and flipped the switch to "on." Even after a morning of coffee, Dan had to admit the espresso smelled good.

"Sure you don't want to change your mind?" Had he read his mind? Dan again shook his head. "Then tell me what you'd like to know about track maintenance."

Dan watched Fred dump the shot of espresso into a paper cup, froth some two percent milk in a metal pitcher, and pour the contents on top. There was something odd about this picture—lattes served in a maintenance barn? Sometimes, just when he thought he'd seen everything…but he reminded himself, he was here to get information, not pass judgment.

"For starters, and maybe more out of curiosity than a need to know, how important is track maintenance? You've got a neophyte here—I don't even know the composition of a dog track."

"Then I could tell you anything. Just kidding, you've tapped into one of my favorite subjects. Why don't we take a walk out to the track—easier to show you and talk about it at the same time."

Fred pointed out that from this vantage point at the south end, Dan could see the boxes where up to eight greyhounds lined up for races eight to ten times a day. Weights and condition were tightly regulated and usually one or two dogs were scratched from each race because they were over or under their racing weight. After the weighing of each dog, handlers lead them out to the starting area along the side of the track. The track was dragged and packed between races and only the dogs touched it first.

Dan couldn't help but think what a perfect job this was for Fucher—repetitive, exacting but not necessarily demanding, and it involved living beings. The dogs would reward him with their affection. He had an easy-to-follow routine of feeding and exercising and general care well within his capacity to perform correctly. Dan promised himself once again that he'd see the young man back at his job as quickly as he could.

Fred stopped in front of an apparatus attached to a single rail that circled the track. "The mechanical 'rabbit' or lure is started about here. Then as it passes the boxes it will continue for about fifteen to twenty feet before the dogs are released. The lure is controlled electronically from a mechanical room up there." Fred pointed to a second story on the main building, above the outdoor viewing area that opened off the restaurant.

"You know they say that you should only bet on those dogs that are consistently in first or second, one-eighth of the way into a race. Fifty-seven percent of the dogs who stay in the lead on this track are the winners. I don't follow strategies myself…I just want to make sure my dog has peed on his way to the boxes." A chuckle, then Fred aimed a nasty looking brown stream of spit into the cup that used to hold a latte. "You a betting man?"

"Not if I can help it." From the look of barely concealed disapproval, Dan knew he'd given the wrong answer. Funny, Dan had never looked at it before, but he wasn't a "betting man." He really didn't enjoy taking chances—sometimes he was forced to for work, but he wasn't comfortable doing it. Did that make him stodgy? Maybe he should wear a diamond stud in his ear like the man in front of him? And was that a gold chain peeking out from under the collar of his coveralls? Under the "ring" around his collar? The man was grubby but Dan knew he was probably looking at a lot of money. If the items were real. Somehow, though, it just screamed poor taste. And chewing tobacco? An ugly, messy, cancer-inviting habit.

"What do you know about greyhound racing?"

"You're seeing it. Just about this close to nothing." Dan held index and thumb about a half inch apart.

"Well, let me impress you with just how important the condition of this track is. Greyhounds are trained to race an oval but they run in 'instinctive reaction.' They react to stimuli—the other dogs, the lure—and no one is riding on their backs to steer them around potholes or slow them down for the corners. See those bumpers?"

Dan looked in the direction that Fred was pointing. The fence set back some twenty feet directly across from the track's curve was covered with heavy, rubberized padding for a distance of fifteen feet or more.

"A seventy-pound dog taking that corner at close to forty miles per hour could take a nasty tumble if he lost his footing—momentum could propel him right into the chain-link. That padding can mean life over death."

"I guess I never thought that there would have to be special safety features."

"An' we haven't even talked about the track itself. Let me show you something." Fred knelt down on one knee at the edge of the track. "A track is to a greyhound as a shoe is to a human being. The track has to cushion and protect the feet of the dogs. But it has to give him traction—think of this as a running shoe, a big Nike for the dog. If the traction isn't there, the track eats up the animal's energy. Three things make up the composition: sand, clay/silt, and water. This formula is concocted based on environment—humidity versus dry air, for example. Water is the crucial element. It's real easy to let a track go soupy. I'm proud to say Daytona has a great reputation for speed and safety."

"How long have you been doing this?" Dan had to admit he was impressed.

"I've been numero uno here for about five years. Did research for the University of Kansas. Lot a tracks back there—Abilene's home to it all. Some of the reasons dog racing has a bad rep is due to the tracks they're running on. A hard surface and you get broken bones, too soft and it's pulled muscles."

Dan remembered the National Greyhound Registry or Association was in Abilene. Fred was quite the specialist. He might not fit Dan's idea of the usual maintenance man, but this took some real know-how.

"Let's take a look at the equipment." Fred started back toward the barn. Just inside the door, he stopped by a wide, open-faced, roller machine. "This here maintains the cushion. A big-o hunk of equipment that has a very delicate task. Even adds moisture, if needed." Fred continued around the barn pointing out a conditioning machine with spike-like tongs, a solid drum-shaped roller used to smooth edges that could flatten a roadrunner if used in a comic setting, and machines that resurfaced, dug up, poured new material—each one looking more forbidding, if not menacing. A rogue's gallery of machinery, so to speak, if one thought in terms of methods of torture.

"I don't think I want you mad at me. Seeing one of these monsters in the rearview would be a little discomforting." Did Fred look startled?

Then a belly-laugh. "I forget how all this looks to someone not used to it. These babies are big all right—two to three tons for some of them."

But Dan barely heard him. Torture. The body of Jackson Sanchez came to mind. Bruising, smashed toes....."Who has access to this area?"

"About twenty workers. Why do you ask?"

"Oh, I just might need to do some interviews. Do you have a list of those twenty?"

"Sure, but I don't see how maintenance can be of interest."

"I've learned that you never know. Just keeping options open." Dan smiled and did a little "who knows?" shrug with his shoulders. And the more you protest, the more I'll make sure I do a little chatting, he decided.

>>>

The chief must have come early. He and Roger were waiting on him when he entered the casino restaurant. The chief was tall, a little stooped but wide-shouldered, his steel-gray thinning hair cut neatly with a side-part.

"Don't think we've had the pleasure. Arnold Cox."

The handshake was firm and the blue eyes absolutely piercing. Dan wasn't sure when he'd seen eyes that clear or that naturally blue.

Two young cops walked up with papers and, after a brief exchange, the chief sent them off. "Time to get those search warrants served."

Dan almost blanched. He wondered if he could hear Dixie Halifax yell all the way from her office to where he was sitting in the restaurant. He didn't rule it out. In the meantime he shared his findings—first as to how they applied to the five insured dogs, then as to how his investigation led him to other areas. The deaths of Jackson Sanchez, and now Wayne Warren.

Dan filled the chief in—down to the newest disappearance and death of the casino manager and how the ashes in the urns coupled with blood samples from the kennel after the fire moved Wayne Warren's status from missing person to probable homicide.

"Your guess is that that all three deaths are related? Jackson Sanchez, Wayne Warren, and the vet?"

"I'm throwing in Dr. Elliott's death simply because it seems odd that it would occur just when damaging evidence surfaced indicating his involvement."

"It is a little suspect." The chief leaned toward Dan. "I'm sorry your investigation hasn't gone smoothly, but it would appear that the dogs are, in fact, alive and didn't end up in the crematory. Is this your conclusion?"

"Yes. I'm guessing that all five are still out there very much alive. And the man who supposedly took them to the crematory could have helped us. Kevin Elliott never denied finding the dogs, bagging up their bodies, and taking them for cremation. Obviously, he didn't count on someone testing the ashes or finding two of the dogs still racing—one with an altered ear number. Did the vet steal the dogs? Has he been behind still racing them? And was Dr. Elliott the one who murdered Wayne Warren, bagged his remains and cremated him? We'll know more about that when we get the labwork back—I'm hoping the ovens give up some answers." Dan ordered a cup of coffee. What the hell. It had been over an hour since the last cup and hadn't he read articles recently that the stuff was good for you? Kept Alzheimer's at bay or something.

A young, out-of-breath policewoman interrupted. "Chief, any chance you could talk with Ms. Halifax? She's pretty upset and demanding that she talk with you."

"What do you think boys? Are you in this one with me? I think I could use a little backup."

Well, he probably did because halfway down the hallway to her office, they could hear things breaking—the sound of glass hitting glass.

Opening the door to Dixie's office was life-threatening. The floor-to-ceiling glass partition beside the door itself shuddered but didn't break as a ceramic urn hit it and burst. Ashes and pieces of pottery literally exploded and the woman standing in the middle of the room was about to lob another urn in their direction.

Using the brief lull in the action, Chief Cox pushed open the door. "Ms. Halifax? What seems to be the problem here?" Dan and Roger followed him into the room.

"A search warrant? You send in your people with a warrant? Just what am I supposed to have in my office that could be of interest? If you want the ashes of my darling dead dogs, help yourself but I can't imagine why."

Dan stepped forward, "I can shed some light on that. Two of your supposedly dead dogs have recently won races here in the state." Maybe he could get by without having to mention that he'd had ashes from the five urns analyzed. Set up someone to steal the ashes. And he sure as hell didn't want to tell her she had the cremated body of Wayne Warren on her desk. But he didn't have to say any of that.

The urn that Dixie was holding slipped from her grasp and shattered against the granite floor tiles. Then Dixie followed. Gracefully, her legs and body seemed to fold accordion-style leaving her slumped in the midst of the mess at her feet, head to one side, eyes half-closed, ragged breathing, hand on her throat…Either all this was for show and an Oscar was up for grabs, or the lady really was shocked at hearing that two of her dogs were alive. Dan couldn't tell which.

"Where are they?" The voice was barely above a whisper.

"I'm afraid only on tape. The dogs were identified as Mellow Yellow and Maximillian."

A gasp, deep breath, the closing of eyes, then opening them, looking up at Dan. Dixie dramatically held out her hand and Dan helped her to her feet. Brushing off her skirt before running both hands through her hair, Dixie walked to her desk. "And those are the only ones recovered?"

"Yes, to date.

"And you are continuing to investigate?"

"Yes. But I need to know if you saw the contents of the bags in Dr. Elliot's possession the night of the fire. There's no guarantee that more than two dogs are alive."

"I met Kevin at the crematory. I parked next to his truck in the parking lot. When I walked around his vehicle to go into the building, the tailgate was down and I saw several large, black plastic bags in the bed of his truck. Five to be exact."

"Did you at this time or any time inspect the contents?"

"I went directly inside the building. I sat in the chapel with the proprietor, Paul Fenwick, while the...the...cremation was executed. I picked out the urns and then we went to the chapel. Paul is very comforting. I was beside myself. I couldn't have looked at my babies. It would never have entered my mind to do so. And certainly the offer was never made."

Dan glanced over his shoulder. The chief was directing his officers to bag the remains separately from each of the three shattered urns by first sweeping the contents into neat piles. There was a part of him that hoped he really was looking at the remains of dogs and not Wayne Warren—there was still that outside chance that Roddy with no last name had switched the contents. Yet it made no sense as to why.

A long day only got longer. A priority, rush-request to the police lab confirmed the ashes from all five urns as Wayne Warren's and the chief took Dixie to his office downtown for questioning and a statement. Dan vaguely wondered if she'd get a lawyer. None of his business now. He was spared the nastiness of having to tell her he'd already pilfered ashes from the urns.

la4 Susan Slater

But that seemed small compensation for how ugly the case had become in general. By the time he got home Elaine's rented Hyundai SUV was in the drive and he was already late for dinner.

Pot roast, a good merlot, a flourless chocolate torte, and he was back among the living but maybe the highlight of the evening was a text from his mother:

Arriving late tomorrow with Simon. Carolyn traveling so driving back straight through.

Chapter Eighteen

Simon didn't seem to be any worse for having been cooped up in doggy paradise for two weeks. He was probably going to miss water aerobics. But Dan thought he could remedy that by finding a quiet stretch of beach. Had Simon ever been in the ocean? A couple of ponds, yes, but never saltwater. Fucher finally had his race monitoring equipment back and a stack of disks from tracks around the state. They'd missed out on a few days but it was still worth doing. However, after almost two weeks time he didn't have a solid lead as to where the dogs were. He just knew where they weren't.

Dan took Simon over to meet Sadie and see how things were going. Not the brightest idea he'd had recently. Fucher seemed reluctant to even let Simon inside.

"Your dog is pretty fat."

"Ah, give him a break, Fucher. You know, he's German." Now what did that mean? That Germans could be fat? He could see that Fucher wasn't buying any of it. Maybe a different tactic. "Simon is solid, look at this bone." Dan put his index finger and thumb around a foreleg, then glanced up at Fucher who was still frowning and shaking his head. "You know, Fucher, I think you're right, Simon is pretty fat." Defeat. But certainly compared to that waif of a dog clinging to Fucher's side, he had a point. But Dan didn't comment on Sadie's physique.

And Sadie herself seemed to want the last word—a curled lip and a non-stop low growl was keeping Simon three feet away. Poor Simon, did he smell bad? This wasn't good for his self-esteem. A check of the equipment and a screen-print just for practice and Dan left.

The day promised some quiet time to get caught up on paperwork. That is until his mother showed up.

"A dog? You bought a dog?" Dan was staring at the golden tan greyhound with a white blaze between the eyes and a snowy white chest. The dog seemed to be hanging on her every word. Slanted hazel eyes followed his mother's every move. It was pure adoration. His mother could have that effect on people as well as dogs. That might explain the rather long list of Stanleys from the last few years.

"*Rescued* a dog. Isn't that right, precious? Her name is Daisy." Maggie bent over Daisy for a quick hug. "There I was innocently walking into Publix to buy groceries and this 'save the greyhound' group was set up in the parking lot. Well, I already missed Simon and this seemed perfect. The woman in charge has spent many years around greyhounds. Actually, her daughter is a manager or maybe the owner of the track here in Daytona. She helped me pick Daisy out."

"Agnes Halifax?"

"Yes, that's her name. Lovely woman. We're looking forward to lunch."

"Mom, are you sure a dog is—?"

"Darling, I just adore this poor baby girl. Who knows what she's gone through. I owe her a great life. In turn she'll be my best friend." Another swift hug that Daisy seemed to enjoy.

"Dan, I think Maggie's right. A dog is great company. You wouldn't want to be without Simon." Elaine also gave Daisy a quick hug. "She's beautiful."

Dan knew when he'd been bested. But not everybody agreed with Daisy being beautiful. Ask Simon, Dan thought as he watched the big Rottweiler start to join them in the dining room. He spotted Daisy and turned back to the couch. No doubt he was remembering Sadie's less than warm welcome from earlier.

"But it's not only that. The group is sponsored by the Grey2K—

you know, the people who are trying to shut down dog tracks? Well, as you can imagine, they are overrun with requests to adopt dogs. But there's a waiting list. Mostly because they just don't let dogs go to new owners before they've been acclimated to life off the track. They first place dogs in prisons for training." Rather dramatically Maggie slipped off her jacket to reveal a teal green tee-shirt: *Prison Greyhounds—a new race, a new life!*

"Wait. I'm not sure I'm following."

"Inmates take responsibility for a dog and have two months to socialize it, do basic obedience training, regulate its diet—prepare it for the outside world. They do a fantastic job. Daisy won several ribbons as a companion dog."

"Sounds like a great program." Elaine offered.

"Oh, I so agree. I've even volunteered to join them—deliver and pick up dogs and oversee their treatment."

"You mean you're going to a prison?"

"Sounds better than saying I'm going to the dogs."

"Don't try to be funny, Mother."

"Yes, I'll be in charge of some paperwork—recording progress, addressing problems—that sort of thing. I'll go with them for the once a month delivery of new dogs and take back already trained ones."

"Just where would this be?" Dan didn't like any of this.

"Oh, only a white-collar place. The one in Pensacola. You know, Fed Meds. That's a play on the old Club Meds that—"

"Yeah, Mom, I get it. I just don't want you cavorting with any Bernie Madoff wannabes. White collar still means crime."

"You have nothing to worry about. Stanley will be with me."

"Stanley?" Elaine and Dan in unison, then Dan added, "I had no idea he was even in the picture anymore."

"Well, yes. I don't expect you to understand, but I think this will give us something to do together—share an interest. Whatever little dalliance occurred while I was gone isn't really an issue. I understand she's an old girlfriend and short of stalking him, just won't leave him alone. He's tried to break it off a number of times. My being on the scene will put a stop to that."

"Mom, I think there's something else you need to know about Stanley."

"That he isn't who he says he is? I've been made aware of that. Federal agents." She dropped her voice to a whisper. "I'm actually working for them. Well, sort of *with* them."

Dan realized his head was beginning to hurt. "You are working with the Feds? And just what does this job entail?"

"You realize I have to swear you to secrecy?"

Visions of a "pinky promise" came to mind—hooking little fingers together à la fifth grade. "Mom, give me a break. Whatever any of us says won't leave this room." He looked at Elaine who nodded solemnly.

"Well, they—the federal agents—just want to know of his activities. And maybe any calls that I overhear. Numbers if I can get them. Names, that sort of thing. Absolutely nothing dangerous. You know he's been relocated, and I'm sort of acting as his truant officer—of course, without his knowing." Her smile was a little too bright, Dan thought. Could there be more? Things she wasn't sharing?

"How did they get in touch with you? I guess my question really is *how* did they know to get in touch with you?"

"Elaine and her instructor. I was her very first client. Remember? Scott Ramsey contacted some of his old buddies trying to get information for Elaine's report."

"You know, I'm sort of involved already. I'd love to help. Let me go with you—to the prisons. One of my assignments for class is to get acquainted with the system."

Now Dan knew his head was really going to hurt—his mother and his fiancée. "I doubt if the school expects you to immerse yourself in the penal system to the point of going inside."

"You're such a worry-wart. She'll be fine. If you're certain you want to do this, Elaine, Grey2K is picking up a group of dogs at the Daytona track this afternoon. They'll be vet-checked here locally, returned to the track overnight, and we take off in the morning."

"Count me in. And I want a tee-shirt."

≻ ≻ ≻

"It's six a.m." Dan squinted at the bedside clock. "You don't have to go this early, do you?"

"I need to be at the track by six-thirty. I think it's a seven-hour drive to Pensacola and I'm going to help load the dogs. I've left coffee in the thermal carafe and there are the muffins that Joan brought over. Just save an apple strudel one for me. I'll text when I get there." A quick kiss and she was closing the bedroom door.

Then the sound of it reopening. "I forgot to mention that I told Maggie she could bring Daisy over. She didn't want to leave her home for the day—doggy anxiety and all that being how this is so new to her. I think Maggie is overreacting but I was sure you wouldn't mind. Love you." The door shut again.

This time when Dan woke up, he was staring into two sets of brown eyes—one light, one dark. But both dogs were sitting beside the bed close enough to touch each other. Interesting. There must have been some kind of bonding that happened because these two were chummy.

"How'd you guys get in here?" Then Dan remembered the bedroom door had a handle, not a knob. Simon had learned to be pretty good at letting his chin rest on a door handle and watching it pop the door open.

"Okay, who's ready for breakfast?" Simon did his butt-wiggle (this in lieu of wagging a measurable tail) and emitted a low "woof." Daisy wasn't sure but followed Simon to the door.

"Gotta give me time to get some clothes on." Dan threw on a pair of jeans and followed the dogs to the kitchen. Two bowls of kibble were fast disappearing and gave Dan time to finish dressing. Clean bowls meant it was time for leashes and a walk around the block.

He had to admit that Daisy was sweet and tractable. Maybe she was the perfect dog for his mother. But this prison thing… well, that didn't sit well. And spying on Stanley? Asking for trouble. Could he persuade his mother to give up the "assignment"? He doubted it. He hadn't even been able to discourage Elaine from tagging along.

The morning went quickly. He was halfway through last week's expense report when Daisy walked over and put her head on his knee. Really a sweet dog. Not necessarily his type, but he couldn't fault her personality. She liked human interaction. Pats and an ear rub and she curled up beside him. The interesting thing was that Simon seemed willing to share his human. No snarly, pulled-back upper lips or growling from either one of them. There was even an effort on Simon's part to interest Daisy in a game of ball. But dropping the bright red ball in front of her produced panic and a run for the couch.

He wished he had a fenced area large enough for a game—well, at least an introduction to ball tossing and return. But there was no doubt in his mind that without a fenced yard, Miss Daisy would be off like a bullet at the first hint of a squirrel, or a cat…or, God forbid, a real rabbit and she'd be long gone. Up to forty miles per hour and there would be no catching her. He'd work in an extra walk—not as much fun as a sense of freedom, but something.

>>>

She got to meet Stanley. And Elaine was rather taken with him. Peering through the dusk at a shadowy figure outside the storage barn in The Villages hadn't given her a very clear picture of Maggie's love interest. Yet, Stanley was all old world manners—doors opened, bottles of cold water in a cooler for the trip, helping her with her jacket—altogether a sweetheart. A woman's man. Wasn't that the old term? Actually, *womanizer* came to mind remembering the bobbed blonde, elf-finding help-mate in the storage barn.

And it also didn't help that she'd seen the sexting message from Stanley—the picture of a stiffy with a bow on it—wallpaper—background on Maggie's iPhone. Presumably his and presumably Maggie's birthday present. It had caused quite a row with Dan's sister back in Wagon Mound. She referred to her mother as a degenerate if Elaine remembered correctly. But Elaine couldn't suppress a smile—more power to them. If this is what your sixties and seventies could be like, why not? Maybe he made it worthwhile to overlook old girlfriends. Oh, not a good thought—she had to remember she was talking about her future mother-in-law.

But she could imagine Stanley on board a cruise ship. This was a man who could make a tux look good at six one and, maybe, one-eighty. She imagined he probably didn't look too shabby in a pair of swim trunks either. Silvering hair in that way that really dark hair grayed—a cross between a timber wolf in full winter coat and expensive streaking by a top salon. Just enough silver chest hair peeking above the two buttons of the heather blue Henley to quietly say virility. The blue jeans tastefully faded… nothing Ackley or Ames about him much more like New York, New Jersey, or the Old Country—sort of an Italian James Bond. But the mob? Could that be? She didn't want to even speculate.

She offered to drive. The GPS would get them there but they would also be following the carrier—an eighteen-wheeler holding twenty greyhounds recently retired from the track, each in a separate compartment. And they would be picking up twenty greyhounds to bring back for adoption. These would be photographed and introduced to foster homes, then advertised nationally—some with their own websites.

It was a pretty rigorous adoption routine and not inexpensive. Average cost for a "recycled" greyhound ran about two hundred and seventy-five dollars, a home visit to make sure there was a solid, six-foot fence and the means to provide vet care. And an extensive interview to determine level of commitment. Two representatives of the Prison Greyhound organization even traveled with the dogs and interviewed the inmates chosen to receive a dog for training. Very little was left to chance. These dogs were given the best possible opportunity for success—the second time around.

The drive was uneventful. Chatty updates about Dan's sister, Carolyn—her husband, Philip, was getting closer to a run for the governorship of New Mexico—Maggie seemed less than enthusiastic about it. Questions about Elaine's son, Jason, and how he was liking college his freshman year. More interest on Maggie's part about how Elaine had met Dan and had they decided on where they wanted to live. And a wedding…how could she help? Stanley was oddly un-chatty through all the information sharing. Any questions from Elaine garnered only monosyllabic answers. Still the seven hours of drive-time passed quickly.

Pulling in the front gates, minimum security lock-up looked pretty cushy. A four-story sprawling brick building at the entrance, no razor-wire in evidence anywhere. Actually no chain-link or fencing of any kind anywhere—buildings designated as dormitories, another as a kitchen/dining hall combination, immaculate grounds. Was this incarceration? Supposedly, seven hundred and thirty-one inmates were here. Elaine was impressed.

At the gate check-in, they were directed around to the back of what was probably the administration building. Elaine parked the SUV and she, Stanley, and Maggie followed the drivers and two dog-handlers into an office. Not only did they have to sign in, but each dog was weighed, photographed, and its registration number recorded before being handed off to a waiting inmate. Elaine, Maggie, and Stanley each brought a dog from the carrier to the office—back and forth until all twenty had been checked in.

The dogs had been pre-assigned to an inmate and after the hand-off, each inmate waited in line for a brief interview. A manual, a twenty-foot lead, a pinch collar, a sack of dry kibble, and a small box of treats made up a kind of care package. Each dog had arrived with a padded leather collar and appropriate tags showing vaccinations. The collar was mandatory wear when not in training and no dog could ever be off lead. Folded metal wire crates were taken from the carrier and stacked against the office's outside wall. Crates were also mandatory. Dogs were issued blankets if inmates desired them. Most did, Elaine noted.

There was to be a sort of graduation ceremony as yet another set of inmates put already-trained dogs that were to go back with them through their paces—companion dog, service dog, basic obedience, and beginning agility. Elaine was amazed at how well the greyhounds did in each discipline. Only three were

beginning agility training but those dogs were a cut above—
each so attuned to its trainer that Elaine wondered if trying to
place the dog with a new family might cause needless anxiety.
Companion dog training and basic obedience made sense but
it would be difficult to find new homes that would continue
agility training. There was no doubt, however, that the program
was an exemplary one.

There was to be a brief tour of the grounds and lunch before
they loaded the trained greyhounds into the carrier and took off
for home. There was a common area where inmates could introduce themselves and several came forward. In fact, the taciturn
Stanley turned into Mr. Loquacious, shaking hands, laughing
at the jokes of his new companions. The metamorphosis was
pretty impressive. And Maggie looked a little lost hanging onto
Stanley's arm. Elaine started to move in her direction when three
men ushered them forward, presumably to start a tour of the
grounds. Elaine watched them go. One of the men with his arm
around Stanley's shoulders. Chummy. New friends or old? If she
believed Scott Ramsey, these could be former business partners.

Then Elaine noticed a man on the far side of the open area
watching the festivities—his gaze seeming to dwell on Stanley.
Black tee-shirt, black jeans, dark hair combed straight back to
just touch his shoulders. A little squat in stature—more of a "jerk
and press" type than a long-distance runner. Probably Elaine's
age or close. Beside him a cane was propped against the wrought
iron table. As she was about to turn away, Stanley appeared to
acknowledge the man. It was just a glance back over his shoulder,
but the barely perceptible nod he received in return confirmed
a certain knowledge of one another.

Intriguing. But now the man at the table was motioning to
her. Indicating that she should join him. Well, why not?

"Elaine Linden." She held out her hand. "Recent convert to
greyhound rescue."

"Tony." No handshake so she awkwardly let her hand fall
back to her side. He leaned back looking up at her. "It's a good
program. The going will be slow but let me show you around."

"All right." She had to admit this strangely alluring man was more than a little interesting; yet, the name Svengali came to mind. There was something compelling about him—the taunting, smiling eyes that roamed her body—*undressed* her body and appreciatively came back to look her in the eye after lingering on her bust line.

"Nice, very nice." The two-handed gesture seemed aimed directly at her breasts.

It didn't seem to require an answer so she didn't give one but hoped the warmth that was creeping its way up her neck wasn't noticeable. She should just leave—find another guide but by now he'd risen, relying heavily on the cane. And she was a grown woman fully capable of taking care of herself.

"Actually, I'm your best choice for a guide." He took her arm but she pulled away—and felt those brown, almost black eyes studying her.

She found her voice, "And why is that?"

"I can show you the inner workings of this rat's maze."

"Interesting choice of words."

"Do you disagree?"

"I don't know enough to agree or disagree. Have you been here long?"

"Long enough. This way."

The tour was perfunctory. The library a donation by Mrs. and Senator such-in-such, the arboretum a gift of a local doctor and his family, exercise equipment from yet another foundation, electronics including all the latest bells and whistles a loan from a local college and used by their instructors for classes. All in all, the "maze" contained all the comforts. He hadn't made conversation or interacted other than to explain each area and open doors. And she'd stayed out of reach. He didn't try to touch her again, and there were no more comments about her attractiveness, which had seemed limited to above her waist.

"Looks like we're just in time for lunch." They had made a complete circle and ended up more or less back where they started. This time she excused herself and took a chair at Maggie and Stanley's table.

White collar prison. Did it bring back memories? Of course. Her first husband, father of her child, spent seven years in just this sort of facility for flying contraband from Columbia to New Mexico—only to supposedly die in a flash flood the day he got out. What was it about arrogant, the-world-owes-me personalities? She knew she was sitting in the midst of a few hundred. And had just escaped the clutches of a particularly smooth one. One that she noticed others deferred to. Was he some kind of inner prison honcho?

Suddenly she just wanted to go home. Home temporarily being a townhouse in Daytona Beach with a man she dearly loved.

"Are you okay, dear?" Maggie leaned in to whisper.

"Yes. It's just been a long day." Elaine made an effort to finish her avocado stuffed with chicken salad. By the time the flute of chocolate mousse arrived, she'd lost her appetite.

"We'll be going soon. Don't look now but I think you have an admirer over there." Maggie winked. "He's cute."

Elaine didn't need to look. She could feel Tony's eyes on her every move. And it was giving her the creeps. It was a little late now but she should have stayed with a group for the tour.

"I'm going to go back to the car. I'll meet you out front to help load the dogs. I just need some fresh air."

A restroom stop and she walked out into the bright sunny day. A deep breath and she was beginning to feel better. Until she realized that Tony was leaning against her SUV. How could an inmate with a gimpy leg get out here so quickly? She blipped the car open and walked to the driver's side.

"Wait. I want to apologize for bad manners. I've upset you and I didn't mean to."

"No apology needed." She placed her hand on the door handle.

"You're a very beautiful woman. I'm sure you can appreciate that we don't see too many of those."

"Thank you for the compliment."

He stared at her for a few seconds. "Okay. I respect your distance." The gesture was both hands palms outward and Tony stepped away from the car, "Oh, Elaine? Be careful. Don't get mixed up in things you don't understand." He turned back, the smirky, laughing eyes holding her immobile. "Got that, gorgeous? Tony Falco says so—therefore, it's law." A wave of the hand that resembled a blessing, a laugh and a shake of the head. She watched him limp away.

Chapter Nineteen

The newly acquired dogs were watered, fed, exercised, and then crated at the track when they got back to Daytona. The Prison Greyhound people were there to meet them and all went smoothly. Everyone thought the freshly trained dogs were an especially nice group, and there were several new families already waiting to adopt. Happy endings. Elaine liked that. Now for a great ending to her own day. She saw a light on in the living room at the townhouse when she pulled in the drive. Suddenly she realized how much she wanted to see Dan and put the day behind her.

Crackers, cheese, sliced hard salami, and a really good Merlot—could life get much better? He met her at the door glass in hand.

"I take it Mom isn't picking up Miss Daisy tonight?"

"Stanley didn't want to take the time to stop. They have another hour and a half to get home, and he was getting tired. I'm sure she'll run up in the morning." Simon and Daisy were both giving her the once-over—lots of sniffs. Unloading twenty dogs and loading twenty more must mean she smelled interesting.

"So, tell me about dog-delivery. Good day?"

"Mostly." Elaine sank down on the couch. She elaborated on the already-trained dogs—how impressed she was. And then she added briefly and in little detail the guided tours and her bad luck to draw Mr. Mafioso as personal guide.

"Hey, you should be flattered. The man has good taste. You want to nip this little flirtation in the bud? I'll tell him you butter your ciabatta."

Laughing, she smacked him with a throw pillow. "I'll butter *your* ciabatta."

"Promises, promises. Is that what we're calling him now? I know 'walkin' the dog' is a euphemism for—"

"Hush." She took his wineglass, placed it carefully next to hers on the coffee table then leaned in and unzipped his fly. "This is a no talk/no hands zone or I'll have to get the duct tape and cuffs."

"Handcuffs? Wow. I need to send you to prison more often."

⟩⟩⟩

She woke at about three, still wound around Dan on the sofa. She edged to one side, stretched, and felt someone lick her arm. Simon. She gave the big dog a kiss on top of his head. Daisy was watching from a safe distance, not looking very eager to have people slobber on her. Elaine slipped on bra and jeans and let both dogs out into the side yard. It wasn't large but the six-foot white fence made it safe.

"Hey, it's cold. Where'd my blanket go?"

"Your blanket is going up to bed…if anyone wanted to join me, I might not be able to keep my hands to myself."

She let the dogs in but Dan was already upstairs.

⟩⟩⟩

"Is there any way to tell Daisy's age? I don't get the feeling that she's very old." Elaine was pouring their second cup of coffee before clearing the table. Eggs benedict, peach blintzes, juice… they'd stuffed themselves.

"If she came from the track or a kennel that supports the track, she'll be tattooed with not only a registration number, but kennel information. Here, I'll show you." He offered Daisy a piece of English muffin dipped in egg yolk and had the dog's rapt attention. She wasn't going to move just in case there would be more.

"See, here's the National Greyhound Association registration number. And in this ear is the month she was whelped, the year, and this letter indicates she was the fourth puppy in the litter to be tattooed."

Elaine leaned in, "812D. Eighth month, or August of 2012 and D means fourth pup tattooed."

"Got it. 812D. Pretty slick way to individualize each dog." Then Dan looked again at Daisy's ear. "What the hell? I'll be right back." He grabbed his iPad off the dining room table and sat back down. He brought up the initial report on the dogs lost. 812D was at the top of the list.

"I'll be damned. I can't believe this. I knew the number was familiar. What's a good way to hide something? Leave it in plain sight. Now, I don't think that anyone thought one of the lost dogs would end up with my mother, let alone me, but there's more than a little irony in this."

And interesting that a stolen and very expensive dog would be put out for adoption and not be making money racing or used for breeding. Made it seem that the two hundred and fifty thousand was the immediate goal. But for whom? Dixie was the would-be recipient. Was losing the hauler enough for her to want to recoup any way she could? Yet, she was co-owner of the track and the track was big business—a few million, he guessed. Wasn't the insurance money small potatoes? Hauler or no hauler? Or were finances in really bad shape? It would make sense that she wouldn't want the dogs killed or even injured. Still, the insurance money only paid their current worth not projected life earnings. How could she come out ahead? If she wasn't behind the disappearing greyhounds, were they stolen out from under her?

"What are we going to tell Maggie?"

"The truth. I'm going to have to take the proof into custody. You, Miss Daisy, are a very valuable piece of evidence." A pat to the head and the last piece of Canadian bacon.

"Do you want me to tell her?"

"Mom? No, I'll do it." He was dreading it, but sooner was better than later.

Dan picked up his phone and walked out on the porch. He was preparing to leave a message when Maggie answered.

"Sorry to be the bearer of bad news…" Dan went on to explain how Daisy was really a greyhound named ShebaTwo—the stolen property of Dixie Halifax—and one of the dogs he'd been looking for. He needed to take her back to her rightful owner. He paused and braced himself for some sort of outrage, some kind of 'what can we do?' or 'would they let me buy her?' ploy. His mother wouldn't give up something she wanted that easily.

"Well, thanks for letting me know. We're trying to get in a golf game this morning. Talk later."

What was this? She was just dropping the subject? And his mother sounded terrible. Congestion, a lot of snuffling, a cough….

"Mom, are you all right?"

"Allergies. I'm fine. Don't worry."

He was getting the brush-off. Was she covering up? Not wanting to break down on the phone with him? This was the woman who sobbed her way through *Bambi*. Wait. Of course, all the sniffling wasn't due to allergies; she didn't want him to know she was crying.

"Mom, I'm so sorry. I know you really cared for Daisy. She was a great dog but I'm sure there's another dog out there that you'll love just as much. Look, Elaine and I will get you another—a puppy this time if you'd like. What would you say to a baby Simon?"

"Oh no, I mean how sweet of the two of you. But it's quite all right…" the sound of blowing her nose. "Really, I need to go. Stanley is honking the horn." Click.

He walked back inside.

"That was short."

"And strange. I expected a few tears. I wouldn't have predicted necessarily a breakdown but she seemed pretty choked up. I don't think she wanted me to hear how upset she really was. But rushing off to play golf? She doesn't play."

"Maybe it's something she's taken up recently."

"I don't know…maybe…but that was just weird."

"I guess I'd chalk it up to bad timing. She and Stanley could have been having a fight."

"True." Dan made a mental note to try her back later in the day.

> > >

Dan spent a half hour taking pictures—ears, profile, front and rear, head shots—every conceivable angle that would prove who Daisy was—in this case, a very alive Sheba Two.

He didn't call ahead. He expected Dixie to be in her office and wasn't disappointed. She tried to put off meeting with him until after lunch but he just handed the pictures to her receptionist with orders to put them on her desk and mention that they were taken this morning. He didn't have to wait. Her office door flew open and Dixie Halifax strode toward him pictures in hand.

"Where did you get these? Are they truly recent?"

Dan nodded. "We need to talk." He motioned toward her office and then followed her inside. Dixie walked to her desk, turned and leaned back against it, both hands tightly gripping the edge. The desk was conspicuously devoid of doggy urns.

Dan explained the chain of events but was stopped when he mentioned Agnes Halifax as the one who helped Maggie choose a dog.

"My mother? However did she get mixed up in this? She works with a placement group but I have no idea where they get the dogs. There are tracks across the U.S."

"Most of the adoption groups appear to keep excellent records. I'll send copies out of registration numbers on the offhand chance we will uncover another couple dogs whose identification hasn't been altered."

"What happens if we don't find all of the dogs?"

"You will be asked to prove that you have had nothing to do with their disappearance—possibly a polygraph—that's not up to me. If not recovered, Maximillian and Mellow Yellow and the others will be treated as having been stolen. You, of course, will receive the payout for the four. We'll continue to look for those and there will be a reasonable amount of time before the case is closed."

Dixie walked behind her desk and sat down. She looked exhausted, Dan thought. None of this was easy—a fire, two murders, and the suspicious death of a highly visible and important track employee, five dogs that went from life to death to life—and no one arrested as responsible. For any of it. Certainly not the young man the police originally charged. Roger Carter had made a forceful case for Fucher's release after the discovery of Wayne Warren's murder and the possible involvement of three people in Jackson Sanchez's death. There was simply not enough evidence to hold him. Fucher was safely out of the running.

"Who do you think is behind taking the dogs?" Dan wasn't invited but he dragged a chair up to the desk.

A shrug. "I'm baffled. Possibly someone who wanted to ruin my breeding program. Not breeders themselves or they would never have let Sheba go. I know this is going to sound incriminating but there was a time when I would have blamed Jackson Sanchez."

"Why is that?"

"He was highly competitive. About a year ago he had some setbacks—lost two litters to a virus that spread to his racing stock. Three of his best were infected. He wasn't insured."

"Any idea why someone would carve 'thief' on his forehead?"

"I've wondered about that. He owed money...."

"To someone other than Fucher?"

"Yes. Gambling debts."

"But the 'thief' seemed to indicate he'd stolen from someone."

"Sorry. I have no idea."

Did he believe her? Maybe, only maybe. He got the distinct feeling that she thought she'd said too much. Dan got up to leave after promising to bring Sheba to her office later in the day. He felt badly for his mother, but it was the one solid bit of evidence for UL&C. And Dixie was the rightful owner.

Chapter Twenty

The text was brief and had been sent last night.

Last minute decision. Actually a birthday surprise—I have no idea where we're going. Stanley got a wonderful deal on a cruise and we're off. Love to you both. Dan read the message again. His mother's birthday was March 2. Unless he was greatly mistaken this was still October. His mother's furniture had arrived two days ago. What was this about wanting her things around her? Was this why she didn't have a problem with Daisy going back to her real owner? She knew she wasn't in a position to have a dog? His mother could be changeable—sometimes did things more on a whim than solid reasoning, but a cruise? *Another* cruise? Would this be the fifth one in a little over six months?

He dialed her number. And waited. Odd, for some reason it wasn't going to voicemail. Oh well, he'd just answer the text:

Hey, this is a surprise. Let us know when you land somewhere. And have a great time.

Elaine offered to go back to the track with him to deliver Daisy. She, at least, was going to miss the dog. And so would Simon. Dan had never thought of getting a companion dog for the big rottweiler, but Simon had certainly warmed up to Daisy. Once they got a house that could be something to consider. Dan wouldn't feel so guilty having to leave him alone so much. Speaking of which, bringing Daisy and leaving him behind today hadn't set well. He knew he wasn't imagining the howling as they pulled out of the drive.

"Dan, watch out."

The sheriff's cruiser fish-tailed and had two tires in their lane before straightening out and roaring past just as they turned onto the gravel road that led to the casino. No lights and no siren, just in a godawful hurry to get somewhere. And Dan thought he'd recognized Officer Bartlett.

"Oh no, what do you think happened?" The scene in front of them was barely controlled chaos.

Dan pulled the Land Rover to the side of the parking lot. Not that he could go much further due to the police tape and SWAT-mobile and four cruisers sitting in front. "It's something big."

"There's Scott Ramsey. Maybe I can find out something." Elaine stepped out, then turned back, "Should I take Daisy?"

"She'll be all right here. Let's leave her until we know what's going on." Dan lowered all the windows before locking the car and joining Elaine.

Whatever had happened, it seemed to be over. Law enforcement was standing around along with casino workers. Probably a bomb threat, Dan thought. He watched as Elaine waved to a man at the edge of a group of officers who then broke away and walked toward them. Wow. That's all Dan could think of. This was the guy that Elaine was doing surveillance with in a parked car in the dead of night? Tee-shirt hugged ripped abs, jacket barely covered well-developed traps and stretched across bulging deltoids, and his thighs? Well, in all likelihood the jeans weren't spray-painted on and only looked like it. This guy was built and Dan wasn't exactly sure how he felt about all that.

"Dan? Scott Ramsey. Sorry, but I think you've missed all the excitement. Actually, so did the rest of us." He looked back at the casino. "Second time we've had false information."

"Concerning?"

"Money-laundering. We fully expected to storm the place and find around five hundred thousand in cash. Supposedly brought in less than twenty-four hours ago. But if it was here—and we have reason to believe it was—someone tipped off the casino and it's been moved."

"So, there's someone on the inside?"

"Looks that way. We're beginning to get a black eye over it. Too much crying 'wolf' with nothing to prove. Consumer advocates are going to nail us on the cost. Getting all this fire-power out here on the taxpayers' nickel gets damned expensive. Plus, this is the third time in the last year we've just missed a shipment."

"The 'we' means the Bureau?"

"Elaine probably told you I retired a few years back. Actually, I'm enjoying teaching and doing a little PI work. Of course, the powers who be still consider this my territory so I get called upon to lend a hand now and then."

"Money laundering sort of screams 'Mafia.'"

"Yeah. Great place for it. Out-of-the-way casino, a small operation not on Indian land but with enough traffic to move things in and out. In reasonable amounts. They're not trying to move a few million—conservatively a few hundred thousand. Perfect setup in a lot of ways."

"What do you think happens to the money if it isn't laundered here?"

"It finds its way out of the country. Foreign businesses. An international electronics firm was a repository until recently."

"Seems like a pretty sophisticated operation."

"Sophisticated enough to keep us guessing and a couple of steps behind."

"No ideas on a kingpin? It would seem like there needs to be some sort of central control or directives given by one person?" Elaine voiced what Dan was thinking.

"I agree. Apparently, they change up their method of delivery. Our informant never has advance knowledge of a shipment. Nothing more than a few hours. And it would appear that one person is in charge of orchestrating that."

Was Scott dodging sharing information? Seemed that way, Dan thought.

Then a deep breath, and "I probably should say that we're looking at 'retired' Mafia. Those either relocated to the area or in prison in the state. Your mother's boyfriend is new on the scene and other than being a bit of a lothario, he seems to be minding his own business."

"What about Tony Falco?" Elaine was remembering the posturing and proclamation of telling her what to do—not just suggesting.

"Interesting. He's top of our list. How do you know Tony?"

Elaine explained how she'd volunteered with the Prison Greyhound group and met him on a visit to Pensacola.

"The prison—if you can even call it that—is so open. It would seem that you'd know immediately if there were messages going in and out."

"Not really. All mail is opened, private phones are not allowed, and public phones are monitored. There's no easy way for anyone inside to communicate with someone on the outside."

"So just who is this Tony Falco?" Dan was wondering if he should have paid more attention to Elaine's comments about the guy.

"Second-string Mafia. Took the fall for someone above him on a drug trafficking charge. Pulled seven years at a minimum-security lockup. He'll be taken care of. Probably worth seven in exchange for how his family's being treated while he's on the inside. And in prison he's become this big frog in a little puddle— we suspected him of being the mastermind behind an offshore gambling operation earlier this year but couldn't prove it."

"But you think he's behind money moving through here?"

"He's probably our best guess. We just don't know how he's pulling the strings. We've set up people on the inside to buddy-up but Tony isn't sharing. We'll keep at it. You guys here for the races? Don't think they're going to start up again much before three."

"Just here to drop off a dog." Dan briefly explained the circumstances. "Any chance we could get in to see Dixie Halifax?"

"Things are probably a little crazy inside. The kennel's up and running, leave the dog there. I'll make sure Ms. Halifax knows where to find her."

>>>

The mournful whining was almost too much to take. Daisy reluctantly went into a crate then turned and sat down by the door. And cried. Elaine was beside herself. "We can't just leave her. She thinks she's being abandoned."

"Not sure I know what we can do. Wait. Let me see if Mel is here." If she was working, Dan knew she'd make time for the dog. He called the reception area and had Mel paged. She called back right away. Not a problem, she'd be over after she finished lunch. She'd give Daisy a good long walk and make sure Dixie knew where to pick her up. And she couldn't congratulate Dan enough on finding Daisy, aka ShebaTwo. This was just the best news and made her believe that he'd find the others. Dan could only hope so. He still had Fucher working on recorded races but there hadn't been any new sightings.

"I still hate to leave her." Elaine made the mistake of looking back when she reached the door. Daisy was quiet but looked dejected, head hanging, ears drooping.

"We don't have much of a choice." Dan wished there could have been a different ending to the adoption, but he didn't look back.

>>>

There were still people milling around the parking lot when they reached the SUV. Fewer agents and cops but Scott Ramsey was there and gave them a wave.

"Did your mother ever text back?" Elaine voiced what he was thinking—why hadn't she gotten back?

"Nope. Not a word. Of course, if they've just boarded they may not have access to Wi-Fi."

"Dan, I don't want to be an alarmist but is there any way we could make certain she's on a cruise?"

"I'm thinking the same thing. I don't have a good feeling about this." He reached in the glove compartment for his iPad. "We could start with travel agencies."

Chapter Twenty-one

After a salad at Frappes in Ormond they divided up the eight travel agencies that specialized in cruises listed in the local online yellow pages, sat in the parking lot, and called every one. Nothing. No Margaret Mahoney and Stanley Evers traveling from Florida to anywhere. Next Elaine went online with her iPhone and Dan with his iPad and they did the same with direct booking cruise lines. Bingo. Mr. and Mrs. Evers—Dan tried not to cringe—left Fort Lauderdale at seven yesterday morning on a one-hundred-and-eleven-day world cruise. He thanked the booking agent and hung up.

Something was very, very wrong. For starters—one hundred eleven days. Wasn't that over three months? What was his mother thinking? In fact, it didn't sound like her at all. She simply wouldn't take off for that length of time—not without saying something and making plans first. You didn't go on that kind of trip with forty-eight hours' notice. At least not his mother. She could reason and plan things to death. There was nothing spur-of-the-moment about Maggie Mahoney.

So how could he find out for certain that Mr. and Mrs. Evers were truly where they were supposed to be? He could pretend there was a family emergency and have the company contact them. He called the agency back. Yes, of course, they could help him. They were so sorry that there was an emergency and hoped it was not life-threatening. If he could hold, the company would contact the ship's captain and set up a time for Mrs. Evers to call the states—ship to shore.

The agent sounded young but competent, "Would six Eastern Standard Time be convenient for your mother to call you back? They're at sea now but are scheduled to dock around four."

"That would be fine," Dan checked his watch. Just after noon, six hours to wait but he was toying with the idea of going to The Villages. Maybe she'd talked to a neighbor, left a list for someone taking care of her house…He had no idea what he would find but he suddenly felt the need to keep busy.

"I'm sorry about this extra work," he told the agent. "My mother's spur-of-the-moment trip unfortunately came at a bad time."

"Did you say spur-of-the-moment? Oh no, Mr. Evers booked this cruise over two months ago."

Dan was stunned, "Are you certain?"

"Oh, absolutely. He was on our hold list for over six months waiting on a cancellation. This is a very popular cruise. Your mother and her husband were very fortunate to get a spot."

Dan felt sick but left his number and Elaine's before hanging up.

"Why didn't she say anything? And then to adopt a dog…"

Dan nodded and knew he'd have a difficult time waiting until six that evening.

"Didn't she say it was a surprise? A birthday surprise?"

"Yeah, I'd forgotten. But three months early? With a truck-load of household goods to put away…I can't imagine he'd just assume she'd go." Dan thought for a minute. "Do you have plans for the afternoon?"

"No. What are you thinking of?"

"A trip to The Villages."

〉〉〉

He didn't like the place any better the second time. And he had no idea what he expected to find. But then he realized he didn't even have his mother's address. Phone listings revealed only a handful of realtors within the community, and he found the one who had worked with his mother on the third try. Then a tiny fib—his mother had left on a cruise and he needed to pick up her car. Not a problem. If he could run by the office, she'd have a duplicate key ready.

The townhouse was perfect—perfect in size at around eighteen hundred square feet with a small fenced backyard, on a corner so neighbors were only on one side and in back. The generous side yard along the street sported mature trees—a couple of palms and an oak laden with Spanish moss. Clematis on trellises, petunias in beds and in hanging pots gave the place that *Better Homes and Garden* look. He idly wondered if she had a neighbor watering plants while she was gone. Had she contacted anyone to keep an eye on the place?

He unlocked the front door. The house was hot, stuffy, and the smell of rotting garbage was overwhelming. Boxes were stacked three and four deep and furniture haphazardly piled together in the living room and dining room. The bed frame in the master bedroom was leaning against the wall with the mattress and box springs balanced against it. Elaine quickly checked the guest room and found the same arrangement—non-functional beds, furniture just pushed through the door. An Armoire kitty-corner to the bed but well away from the wall, pushed through the doorway and then abandoned.

"I don't think anyone's been here for days." Elaine covered her mouth and nose against the ripe garbage.

"I'll take care of the smell." Dan walked toward the kitchen—easy to find in the open, circular floor plan—and located the offending plastic bag next to the sink. He tied the bag shut, removed it from the plastic container and left the cabinet door open to air out. A quick search of the garage found the city-issued rollaway receptacle with a tight-fitting lid. He had no idea what day was earmarked for pickup in this area but maybe he could find a neighbor to ask.

"Monday. And they come early…sometimes seven. If the lid fits tightly, you could put it out the night before. But the city is very wary of attracting birds. One time I had four turkey vultures going through a weekend's barbeque throwaways. It was awful. Took me the entire morning to pick up after them."

Dan had knocked on the door of the house to the north and hadn't been disappointed. The woman who introduced herself as "Claire" seemed willing to chat.

"I didn't know your mother, of course. She seemed very nice—always waved when she saw me, but we never talked."

"Do you know if she might have talked with someone else in the neighborhood?"

"Well, perhaps Tom Fitch. He lives in back." Claire stepped out of the doorway and pointed to the house behind his mother's. "He's such a busybody. You know the type—everybody's business is his business. I saw him over next door when your mother's furniture came."

Dan thanked Claire, excused himself and walked through his mother's backyard to the lot and house behind. Interesting, but Tom Fitch must have seen him coming because he suddenly popped out the back door and rushed up, hand extended.

"You just have to be Dan." A singularly vigorous pumping of Dan's hand and then the smallish man stepped back. "Your mother's not home, you know."

"Yes, she said she was leaving on a cruise. Did she mention anything to you? Like who might be looking after the house."

"Your father asked me to do that. Just the small stuff—collect the paper and the mail."

Dan felt himself visibly wince but didn't try to correct the "father" misconception. Too complicated. "Did he say when they'd be back?"

"Oh my, the cruise is a long one. I think it must have been a total surprise to your mother—a bribe, so to speak. You know, offered out of guilt."

"Why do you say that?"

"Well, I don't want you to get the idea that I listen in on my neighbors…"

"But you heard something?" Geez this man could be irritating.

"Two, three nights ago? They had a fight. A doozy of one."

"Could you hear what about?"

"Mostly your mother wanting her own place. The reason she moved in here. Apparently she rented the house without your father knowing it. Had plans of forcing a separation. She said she just didn't want to live with him anymore. There was, um, a rather loud discussion of supposed indiscretions—his dallying with someone—you know, behind her back. He denied it, but personally I didn't feel he was very convincing—I have to say I took her side. It also seemed like she'd ticked him off by snooping through his things—don't know what exactly she was looking for—probably trying to get the goods on the lady he was seeing. Of course, your dad was steamed—likes his privacy—but who doesn't? Honestly? I think he had a point. Key to a lasting marriage? Have a few secrets. Doesn't hurt to keep a little mystery in place. Maybe if she hadn't found out about the other woman, they might still be living together."

Dan didn't care about his opinion, "How were things left?"

"They both stormed off in her car."

"And this was two nights ago?"

Tom nodded, "Maybe, three. Yeah, more like three."

"And you haven't seen them since?"

"Nope. Not around here. I take it they've already left on the cruise—isn't that what you said? Believe me, it was the least your father could do after all that fighting. But I'm not sure—"

"Are you saying that you don't think they've gone? According to the travel agency they boarded the cruise in Fort Lauderdale two days ago."

"Well, it just seems odd to me that there wasn't any luggage. I never saw either one of them come back to the house. Not that night, not the next morning, or the next. And a three-month plus trip requires stuff—lots of it. It would have taken my poor dead wife a year to plan and six months to pack." A laugh, then, "I don't want to sound an alarm or anything. But, you know, just saying."

Too late, an alarm had been sounded—at least one was going off in his head. Big-time. A fight and no luggage? Three days ago? His mother could never have prepared for that kind of trip without substantial notice—surprise makeup gesture or not. He asked Tom to set the garbage out and bring the container in—Dan would leave the garage open. Then, he gave Tom his card and a hundred dollars to water plants and keep the lawn mowed. He wasn't sure what arrangements his "father" had made, but a little payment in advance never hurt.

Elaine met him at the kitchen door. "Her car's gone and there's a complete set of luggage empty and sitting in the guest bedroom. Dan, I really don't like this."

Dan nodded, "Guy in back says they had a fight. Overheard Stanley go ballistic about Mom snooping through his things. And I guess Mom wasn't too happy about Stanley seeing someone else. Apparently they left in her car."

"When was this?"

"Three days ago."

"Do you think they ended up at Stanley's?"

"I have no idea but we need to find out."

Another quick call to the realtor—Mom was supposed to have left her car at the townhouse but apparently forgot and took it to Stanley's—and they had the address, combination to the gate and a key to the front door in no time—thank God, Stanley and his mother had worked with a realtor.

>>>

Mom's Lexus SUV was in the drive. Dan pulled in alongside. Maybe, just maybe, she hadn't gone on the cruise—no, the booking was for two. And there had been the text. Dan simply couldn't get his hopes up and he knew he was just trying to shut down the panic. The feeling in his gut that was beginning to mimic the flu.

"Maybe—" Elaine began.

"Don't even say it." He took her hand. "Whatever we're facing, I'm glad that you're here." He drew her to him and just held her. Dread was making him put off even getting out of the car, let alone going into the house.

"Get the fuck out of this car." Two large fists slammed against the passenger-side window. Elaine shrieked and Dan was out of the car, gun drawn. If retrieving a firearm from the glove box and exiting a car in record time was an Olympic event, he'd just gotten all tens.

"Step away from the car."

"Not until you tell me who you are." The man's face was flushed bright red—anger? Booze? He guessed a little of both. The guy was big, probably had twenty pounds and fifteen years on Dan.

"I'm looking for my mother. This is her car." Dan pointed to the Lexus.

"Well, you won't find her here. That son of a bitch ran off with my wife. Just took off. Made her cut her hair and dye it red. Looked like a cheap whore." Then instead of just stepping away from the car, he crumpled to the ground sobbing. "I don't know what to do. I gave her a good life. Thirty-six years. Do you believe that? A lifetime and she runs off with some gigolo." Elaine was out of the car and helping the man up. "I knew things weren't right but don't two people work things out? Give it a try anyway. She told me she wasn't seeing this guy anymore. I thought it was over. Last year I caught 'em up in Palm Coast. His wife had just died, for God's sake. I laid the law down then and things died down. Next thing I know he's moved down here. I knew it'd started up again. I paid to have her followed but she said she was only helping him move in. That I wasted my money and it served me right for not trusting her—then she takes off." Dan heard Elaine making soothing sounds and watched as she helped him cross the driveway and go back into his house.

Dan turned away. Red hair? Stanley made the man's wife look like his mother. And a haircut? She was about the same height—five-foot five, according to Elaine's report. It would be total camouflage. Anyone seeing them at a distance would easily mistake her for Maggie. Was the woman traveling with Maggie's passport? In all likelihood. Had Stanley always planned on taking the world cruise with the neighbor's wife? And that's why it had been planned six months ago? And he only picked up Dan's mother when he thought the affair was over? Was that why he'd moved to The Villages? Hoping the affair could be rekindled? But keeping his mother in tow just in case it couldn't?

One way or another at this point it was fairly obvious that his mother was expendable. Stanley had killed her because he caught her snooping and needed her out of the way. But he also needed to cover up the deed—throw Dan off the trail by making him think his mother was alive and well. What better way to do that than leaving town with a Maggie-lookalike? One who would occasionally text and send pictures of the cruise and continue the ruse. Until they were safely in some foreign country that didn't have an extradition treaty. Far-fetched? No, not at all.

Now the gnawing in the pit of his stomach felt more like an open wound. He took the front steps of Stanley's house in twos, and by the time he was turning the key in the lock, Elaine was right behind him.

"This could be bad." He turned to look at her. Elaine didn't say anything, just squeezed his arm and stepped inside the house with him.

What a mess. They stopped just inside the door simply because any forward movement was thwarted by piles of clothing, toiletries, overturned end tables, ottoman, and a china cabinet that had crashed down against a sofa. Someone had fought for his or her life.

Elaine picked her way to the kitchen. This room was more in order. Someone had made coffee in what looked to be a new appliance and a quick check of the fridge revealed half and half, salad makings, cheese, butter, eggs—all apparently fresh. But three months of lock-up and this would be ruined. So why the fresh groceries? To keep Maggie from guessing he had an ulterior motive?

"I'll check the bedrooms." Dan headed down a short hall leading to the stairs.

Elaine stuck her head in the utility room—new washer, new dryer, cabinets empty. She moved down the hall opening doors.

These closets were also empty, hangers on the floor like clothes had been hurriedly pulled from them. She guessed the last door on her right was the guest bathroom.

A turn of the knob and a gasp. "Dan." She hadn't meant to yell but he came running.

"Oh, my God." They both stared. The smear of red that started at the corner of the vanity mirror continued across the pedestal sink and puddled on the floor. A bloody hand had pulled a bath towel off the rack and left a trail of fingerprints that slid down the wall. The glass shower door was open and streaked in long red smears that were both horizontal and vertical like someone had been pushed up against it and held even though they tried hard to get away.

"Do you think she's…" She had meant to say 'here' but the thought that she could be dead pushed that word aside. Dead. She could be dead. "Oh, Dan, I'm so afraid."

"Let me finish checking upstairs," was all he said and left her standing in the hall.

Elaine braced herself for a yell to come up. She heard doors opening and shutting, and finally Dan came back down and just shook his head. "Nothing. Wait, the garage. I'll look." Again, he returned shaking his head. "She's not here. The Chrysler's gone. Maybe they took her to dump somewhere along the way."

"Please, don't talk like she's dead."

"It's a reality and things don't look good."

"You know, there's one other place to check."

Dan looked up expectantly. "The storage barn—remember I told you about it. Supposedly Stanley was keeping some garden things there along with the elf and his bass boat. I saw a ring of keys on a peg in the utility room; I'll bet one of them opens the padlock."

"Can you find the place again?" Elaine nodded. "Then, let's go."

>>>

It looked different in daylight. More like an oversized Quonset hut than a storage barn. Ballet flats made the going a little rough but Elaine's sheer will to get there as quickly as she could helped her keep up. Dan was half running up the slight incline to the front door. Both of them were a little out of breath but it didn't take long to match the "master" key to the "master" padlock.

Dan threw open the door. There was enough light coming in from openings near the top of the roof's overhang to see fairly clearly. The place was packed. And with big things. Portable basketball stands, party tents, a golf ball picker cart, kayaks, fishing gear leaning against the wall…Stanley couldn't be the only renter.

"Mom?" Dan yelled, and started down the center aisle at a jog stopping every few feet to yell again. "Nothing." His voice seemed to bounce off of the high ceiling. "If she's here, she can't answer us. We're going to have to turn this place upside down."

"Where do we start?" Elaine sounded defeated.

"Let's start at the side walls and work to the center. I'll take the left."

Elaine moved what she could, looked behind, under, in, and over everything else. She found a stepstool and dragged it along for things over six feet and worked her way to a covered boat in the back corner. A canvas tarp was stretched tightly in place and snapped down around the edges. An outboard motor was leaning against the open-bed towing platform underneath.

Elaine set up the stepstool and climbed up. The snaps were rusty in places and resistant to being undone but she was persistent until she could gather a handful of canvas and just pull the covering back a couple feet. And she wasn't sure what she was looking at. A pile of rags? Bedding? She reached down and grabbed a corner of fabric and lifted.

"Oh no, oh no…" She squeezed down into the boat and reached for her phone. Nine-one-one. Directions to the barn—a brief description of the injuries as they appeared to an untrained eye. Then Dan was beside her lifting his mother out from under the boat's plank seating. Her breathing was barely discernible but there—a slow in and out that hardly ruffled her tee-shirt. But breath—life-sustaining breath, no less. The side of her head bloodied, hair badly matted and stuck to her forehead, an arm that dangled at a precarious angle, a cut lip, black eye... Elaine wanted to burst into tears. She couldn't bear to think what would have happened if they hadn't come when they did. Maggie Mahoney had been left to die. What kind of monster could do this? But then, she knew, didn't she?

The rest of the afternoon was a blur. An ambulance to The Villages Regional Medical Center, Police reports, then a run back to Stanley's to open the house to members of the crime lab. A couple hours of swabbing and photographing evidence, another trip back to the hospital waiting until Mom was out of surgery—not out of danger but the doctor was hopeful. They'd know more in the morning. All this and far too many cups of black coffee to even count before Dan and Elaine could just sit and take a deep breath.

And then Dan's cell rang.

Chapter Twenty-two

"Mr. Mahoney, Kristen here with Dream Vacations, I don't know how to tell you this—I mean we're still investigating the matter but your father and mother seem to have left the ship. Well, what I mean to say is that they did not rejoin the ship after an afternoon in port. I want to assure you that we have every bit of security personnel addressing the problem."

"What do you mean *left* the ship? You mean you can't find them?"

"Well, yes. Oh my, nothing sinister has happened—they didn't fall overboard." A chuckle that was supposed to denote humor but fell flat. "I think they just missed the shore curfew and we've been instructed to sail without them. Schedules, you know. We can't hold up a few hundred people for two. Once they're found they will rejoin us at the next port. There are nineteen resorts on the islands. Countless restaurants and bars. A seven-mile stretch of absolutely pristine sand. It wouldn't be the first time that a couple has wandered away, fallen asleep on the beach—"

"And where would this be?"

"Our first stop, the Grand Cayman."

Bingo. Dan knew Stanley Evers, or whoever he was, and Miss Look-Like-His-Mother might not be rejoining the ship. They probably weren't even in the Cayman Islands as they spoke. No, a large amount of cash had probably accompanied them on the cruise and was either deposited on the island or was still with them. He'd give Scott Ramsey a call because he'd bet there had been a charter—boat or plane—with two passengers aboard leaving the islands for parts unknown earlier in the day. Or maybe they *would be* rejoining the cruise ship after securing the money in an account. One or the other. He just had no idea which.

And if someone would check dates, he'd also bet that the rumored delivery of large amounts of cash to the casino would coincide with Stanley's wanderlust and cruise fetish over the last six or so months. Stanley was a money-mover. Large sums would find their way offshore, thanks to a little help. And Dan knew who had provided that help. He just wished his mother had never met him.

He thanked Kristen and hung up. The thought that his mother had been left for dead was too upsetting to dwell on. They had found her. She would be all right. That's what he had to keep telling himself.

He quickly filled Elaine in. Mr. and Mrs. Evers seemed to be missing. No surprise. He'd let Scott Ramsey know and trust that the right people would get the information.

"Let's sleep at Mom's tonight. I'll call Joan, tell her what's happened, and ask her to walk Simon and then feed him. I want to be here just in case and sit with Mom in the morning. I think she's out of the woods but I don't want to take a chance."

Elaine nodded. She looked as tired as he felt.

〉〉〉

Elaine helped him put the bed frame together in the master bedroom, flopped the box springs onto the frame, then lifted the mattress into place, and rummaged through boxes until she found a set of queen-sized sheets. Pillows were another story and remained an enigma. Maybe they could use folded up towels—those she'd found. Under any other circumstances it would be fun to sort of be roughing it. Light candles, order in pizza....

She gave Dan Scott's number, started a pot of coffee and collapsed on the couch.

"I bet you get an 'A' if I give you all the credit." A sort of lopsided grin but the first relaxed, attempt to be funny all day.

She grinned back. "Interesting business you're in. I'll be glad when it doesn't hit so close to home."

The call was short. She could only imagine Scott's reaction. This would be a big breakthrough for the FBI. She poured two mugs of coffee with extra half and half and returned to the sofa, handing a mug to Dan.

"Your instructor was one happy man. I think ol' Stanley will be a little surprised that he's about to be caught. Shouldn't take them too long to pick up the trail—especially when Stanley's not looking over his shoulder. Of course, we screwed up his grand plan. I hate to think that his plan might have worked—kept us from guessing the truth."

"It's just so ruthless, cruel—no, even those words don't touch leaving someone to die."

"It's difficult for me to get my mind around. Scott said he'd let us know when he had him. But I'm not too sure I ever want to see Stanley again."

Elaine scooted the coffee table closer to the couch and opened her laptop. "I think some kind of mindless bit of frivolity is in order. Anything you'd like to stream?"

Dan was saved from having to figure out if that was an opportunity to name a chick-flick and get some points or a chance to name the most recent sci-fi thriller and snag something he'd really like to watch. His phone rang.

"Marie Hunt here and, yes, I know it's after-hours. I just haven't had the chance until now to follow up on something that's been bothering me. Do you have a minute to talk?"

"Yes, this is a good time." Dan shrugged his shoulders and mouthed "lab."

"When you brought that latex glove in, I tested it for blood—what was obvious—and then put it aside. There was a large amount of talcum in the glove, and I didn't bother to look for prints. And, well, long story short, I should have." The sound of her clearing her throat, "I was able to lift a pretty good index fingerprint. But the interesting thing is when I ran it through the print bank looking for a match, there was one, but the guy's been dead for eighteen years. A Franco Marconi. Former Mafia. I checked the FBI files and according to them he lost his life in a shoot-out. I'll turn the info over in the morning but I thought you might like to know there's another suspect out there—if you can find him. This one tied directly to the death of the casino owner or maybe that kennel owner, too. But it's definitely good news for that young man you mentioned. I think the motives just moved beyond a little name-calling."

Marconi, Marconi…yes, of course, now Dan remembered. He reached for his iPad and brought up the Wikipedia entry on Dixie Halifax. Bingo. The merry widow might not be so merry. Was the husband F. Marconi really Franco Marconi? Still very much alive?

"Would you happen to have any pictures of this Marconi?"

"A couple from the eighties or nineties, probably. Nothing recent. Obviously, no reason to update records on the dead."

"Email them to me if it wouldn't be too much of a problem." After profuse thank you's, Dan hung up.

"What was that all about?"

He quickly told Elaine what Dr. Hunt had found and passed her his iPad. "It'd be interesting if we knew this Marconi."

"Wow. Dead Mafioso still alive, witness protection program makeovers, dead dogs that still race—I guess I was hoping we'd found out Stanley's real name. Do you think we know this Marconi?"

"We'll see soon enough—looks like I just got the pictures." Dan opened his email and enlarged the first picture. A young man in a baseball cap—a Yankees cap. Thick, long dark stringy hair just touched his shoulders. A tight-fitting tee-shirt strained against muscled arms and ripped torso. The man was short, maybe no more than five eight or nine. This was not Stanley Evers. The next photo was a headshot, same cap, face in the shadows but his hair was pulled behind his left ear and something in his ear caught the light. Dan enlarged the photo. The man was wearing a sizeable diamond stud. Dan sat back. What do you know? He was pretty familiar with a guy who wore a diamond in his ear.

Add twenty-five years and some short, curly, white hair...was Fred Manson really Franco Marconi? The husband, supposedly deceased, of Dixie Halifax? Dan reached for his cell and left a message for Scott Ramsey. Talk about making a guy's day.

〉〉〉

Dan slept fitfully. Visions of calzones, diamond studs, and pistol-whippings danced in and out of his semi-consciousness. A vivid picture of his mother lying in the bottom of Stanley's stored boat brought him bolt upright—shaking and sweating.

"Are you okay?" Elaine turned on a bedside lamp.

"Tough to shut down my mind. Too many what-ifs."

"Will Dr. Hunt turn over the glove evidence to Scott or local police?"

"Probably to Scott. The perps are more in their ballpark. I just wish I'd taken a firm stand with Mom—I feel guilty not trying to dissuade her from snooping around to get information on Stanley. I'd like her to stay with us for a few days when she gets out—or for however long it takes her to heal and feel comfortable being alone."

"Of course." Elaine took his hand. "Simon will be absolutely spoiled having someone here all day. It's five-ten, do you want to try for another hour or so of sleep or should I go make coffee?"

"I wouldn't mind getting to the hospital by six. Guess it's coffee." He glanced over at Elaine prepared to apologize but she was already out of bed pulling on a tee-shirt.

"See you in the kitchen."

〉〉〉

A bright blue cast and sling offered the only color, aside from tufts of flaming red hair pushing out from underneath the wide strip of gauze across her forehead. Otherwise, Maggie Mahoney could have blended in with the white sheets. But she was awake. Dan tried to hide his concern but knew he'd failed.

"Oh, for God's sake, get rid of the long face. I'm not dying. Unless utter stupidity can be fatal. Actually, it almost was, wasn't it?" The attempt to laugh brought a groan and a left hand pressed to her forehead. "Of course, he broke my right arm. The son of a bitch. But I put myself in a compromising position. I absolutely have no one to blame."

"Mom, don't beat yourself up."

"I never saw the anger, the viciousness before…before this." A feeble wave of her left hand to include her right arm and head. "But I uncovered who he is. Stanley Evers from Ackley, Iowa, my ass. Try a Mafia has-been who ratted on a mob leader and got federal protection. Yes, do you believe it? I was swept off my feet by Joey D'Angelo. The Feds told me he was in the program, but I'm not sure I really believed it. They thought he'd gone back into the mob—was doing odd jobs for an organized crime group here in Florida—but couldn't prove it. That's where I came in. Do you know why he tried to kill me? I found a briefcase crammed with receipts—including deposit information. Huge sums of money being taken out of the United States and put into foreign bank accounts."

"I can't believe I let you put your life in danger."

"Darling, there was no way to stop me. It never occurred to me that I might be in danger."

"Getting the goods on criminals is a tough business. Frankly, I'm surprised the Feds set you up."

"Oh, I had my suspicions—nothing as sinister as a Mafia connection—but I insisted on helping. Just never thought the payoff would be this." Maggie pointed to her right arm.

"Hey, I think we match." Dan pulled his sleeve back to reveal the wrist brace—also in bright blue and the last physical reminder of the rollover accident in Wagon Mound.

"Sorry, matching my son with broken bones is nothing I've ever aspired to." His mother might be banged up but it hadn't softened her withering look. The one that used to freeze him in place as a child and meant his mother was entering the no-nonsense zone of parenting.

"On top of everything else, I'm sure losing Daisy was a shock." Elaine had pulled a chair up to the bed. "I'm so sorry you won't have her to go home to."

"Daisy? Oh my God, what happened? What do you mean I've lost her?" Maggie tried to sit up but fell back breathing quickly and biting her lip. "Oh, I get so dizzy."

"You remember, Mom, Daisy turned out to be one of Dixie Halifax's lost dogs—one of the insured ones. I called you when I found out."

"We didn't talk. I'd remember that."

Had his mother suffered a concussion? Worse? Maybe impaired brain functioning? Or, his mother had been out of the picture longer than they thought—how long had she been incapacitated lying in the bottom of the bass boat? Had he really talked with the mom impersonator? Something was telling him he had.

"Were you getting ready to leave on a cruise?" Dan might as well figure out a timeframe for all the duplicity.

"A cruise? I'm not even moved in yet. My furniture was only delivered three days ago. He was thoroughly pissed that I was renting the townhouse and wasn't moving in with him. I could call him a control freak but the term doesn't do him justice. He simply cannot stand to be crossed, refused anything. We had a knock-down, drag-out over it—guess that term is applicable—I can't believe he thought I'd even consider living with him after the garden elf incident. Separate houses made sense and then we could work together on common interests—like the greyhound placement program."

Dan and Elaine exchanged a look. How much should they tell her?

"I saw that, you two. Don't keep secrets. Now's not the time."

Dan quickly brought his mother up-to-date: world cruise for one hundred and eleven days, had reservations for six months before sailing and, oh yes, they were for two. Mr. and Mrs. Evers sailed three days ago.

"*Mrs. Evers*? The tart who helped with the elf?" This directed to Elaine.

"Yes. There's reason to believe that she dyed her hair and had it cut to match yours. I think the plan was to impersonate you, giving them ample time to get away before you were found. We assume she's traveling on your passport."

"I'll be damned." Then a short laugh, "If she is pretending to be me it must gall her to be somewhat older." A look of smugness and Maggie settled back against the stack of pillows. "I would like to see their faces when they realize I'm alive."

Dan purposefully bypassed any discussion of money laundering and suspicions that all Stanley's cruises were booked around deliveries of large sums of the stuff. He'd save that for another time, but she'd probably guessed that much anyway. She was alive; she needed to work on getting well—that was enough—at least for now.

Chapter Twenty-three

He left the hospital feeling a whole lot better. They were keeping Mom for two more days, and then he and Elaine would pick her up and bring her home—to their house. It remained to be seen if she'd even want to go back to the townhouse in The Villages. But her furniture was there and Stanley wouldn't be so he didn't rule out Maggie giving it a go. In the meantime he still needed to prove conclusively that the insured, Dixie Halifax, was not involved in the disappearance of five greyhounds—three of which proved to be alive. It was like one part of the puzzle was only partially completed and there was a jumble of other pieces sitting on the side. Pieces that seemed to resist fitting in anywhere.

So far, the facts were slim. Thanks to Stanley or Joey, there was Mafia involvement in moving money through the casino and getting it out of the country. And Stanley, thanks to Dan's mother being alive to testify, would be put away for attempted murder. Dan would bet on there being no chance of parole. But that left two completed murders with murderers still at large. Had Jackson Sanchez helped himself—got caught with his hand in the till? Found out that there were large sums of money lying around just waiting to help him pay off gambling debts? Not too difficult to believe he could have dipped into funds and earned a painful death and the epitaph "thief." But Wayne Warren. What was his crime? Discovering how his casino was being used? He could have simply been in the wrong place at the wrong time. And it might be tough to prove otherwise.

By now the fingerprint of Franco Marconi would be FBI fodder. Old dead Mafioso come to life. Or should he say old dead husbands come to life? Where did that tidbit of info fit in? Too coincidental that Franco was working "for" his wife. Dan smelled conspiracy. The two of them scheming together. He still thought of the maintenance barn as a house of horrors. Would the Feds check? He made a mental note to chat with Scott and share his suspicions about how Jackson Sanchez got smashed toes. He certainly hoped a fingerprint inside a bloody glove would get someone's attention. But that still left the greyhounds and his particular part of the puzzle. Who had them now? Only one was accounted for—in the flesh.

"I've put off viewing the recordings for the perimeter cameras from the night of the fire." Dan was doing a quick inventory of things left to do and running the list past Elaine. "I assumed they would have been monitored and checked as part of the investigation by Police Chief Cox's men. But maybe what would be a red flag to me wouldn't raise a question for someone else. I have no idea what I expect to find but it's one more rock to turn over."

"Let me come with you. I'd like to pick up Simon and give him an outing. And I want to make sure that Daisy's been taken to Dixie's farm."

"You know, it might make sense to see if Fucher can come, too. He'd be able to explain anything about the track's routine that I didn't understand. Anything that might be different— outside the norm that night."

⟩⟩⟩

They presented quite the entourage pulling into the casino parking lot and walking toward the reception area—a very beautiful woman playing a make-believe game of hopscotch with a young man who quickly bested her by hopping the furthest distance on one foot. Dan brought up the rear, pulled forward by a very large dog straining on his leash and obviously reacting to an olfactory overload of dog smells. Even a sharply ordered "heel" was ignored.

"I'm going to take Simon around back." Elaine took the leash, and after a quick kiss, walked toward the side of the building.

Simon was beside himself but, Dan noticed, remembered how to "heel." Damn. His own dog. How did she do that? Did animals really have opposite-sex preferences when it came to humans? He guessed it could be true. Or maybe he should remember to put the food down more often.

"We need to see Ms. Taichert." He turned to Fucher who was continuing a one-footed approach to the front door. "Then I'm going to need you to help me." Dan needed to put a "work-face" on this outing and curb just a little of Fucher's enthusiasm. But he could sympathize; Fucher had been more or less on house arrest for awhile. And not working or being able to care for the dogs must be frustrating. Let alone watching the track recordings of races—now that was tedious.

"I like Carol. She's nice. She has candy."

Dan wasn't sure about the candy part but it was obvious that Fucher had friends at the track. It took them twice as long to get to Wayne Warren's office because of the people coming up to wish Fucher well. Lots of inquires about his coming back to work.

"I don't know, can I?" Fucher turned to Dan.

"Not up to me. If it were, I'd have you back here tomorrow. We could talk with Ms. Halifax later, if you want."

"Yeah, I'd like that." Fucher was beaming and Dan realized it might have been best if he'd felt out Dixie first. What would happen if she refused? Fucher had been exonerated. Bail returned—and put in the bank, Dan noted to himself. No need to broadcast that bit of news. But where did Dixie stand? He really had no idea. She had certainly talked like she thought he was guilty. He hoped he hadn't put his foot in his mouth.

Carol Taichert looked worn out. Sallow skin, gray circles beneath her eyes, the woman probably had slept badly since learning about her boss. But she had candy. Fucher retired to the leather sofa against the opposite wall with a large Snickers bar.

"I know this is probably not a good time, but I mentioned a few days ago that I'd like to view the footage captured by the surveillance cameras on the day of the fire."

"That won't be a problem.

"I'm assuming the cameras are manned at night?"

"Oh yes, security is in charge of that. We have three full-time guards."

"Do you have the name of the guard on camera duty the night of the fire?"

"Oh, that was so unfortunate. That person was already standing in for a guard who had called in sick. Then the stand-in was also taken ill and couldn't complete the shift. I don't think he called a replacement because he didn't leave until three, and the first shift comes on at five-thirty. On any other night backup wouldn't have been needed. It was the wrong call but who could have known what was going to take place?"

Uh oh, something's a little fishy. Dan made a note of talking with the guard and his replacement. Did someone pay him to leave his post? "I'd like to talk with the man who covered for the ill guard. Do you have a name?"

"Well, yes, you see this was a bit out of the ordinary. We had a young man on the custodial team who often helped out at night in the camera room. Only in emergencies, I might add. Roddy Stack. An unfortunate young man who we've all tried to help. He's no longer with us, and I have no idea how to reach him."

"I see." In fact, Dan did see. Roddy. No wonder he disappeared. Roddy probably had had a pretty lucrative month between ducking camera duty and collecting ashes from certain urns. He could only hope the money hadn't gone up his nose or in his veins.

"Are you familiar with the technology or should I find a security officer to walk you through it?"

"I'm familiar with most systems. I'll need passwords but that should be all."

"Well, just in case, here's a cheat-sheet. The system is brand new. Even saves to the Cloud." A little shrug indicated that that bit of technology might be beyond her. "Spare cameras, dedicated PCs, and other recording equipment are kept in the office/mechanical room in the maintenance barn. It's security's thing. Maintenance was the only place big enough for all the equipment. We have eleven outside cameras—four are infrared for night-viewing and nine interior cameras for the casino. The system is really state-of-the-art. Of course, the four cameras from the kennel area were burned to a crisp. Not one escaped unscathed. Give me just a minute, I'll get you a key to Mr. Manson's office."

Damn. No record of inside the kennel but did he really expect there to be? Well, to tell the truth, he'd hoped one or two of the cameras might have been out of range of the fire. He'd like to see them anyway but that was probably impossible. Carol came back into the room and handed him a ring with two keys.

"First key is to Fred's office. This key is to the mechanical room. Do you know where the office is?"

"Yes, I recently had a latte there."

A roll of the eyes. "Can you imagine? Lattes? He treats that place like his own. You probably noticed the cot? I think…" she lowered her voice, "that he, uh, *entertains* there." A knowing nod and pursed lips. "I've discussed it with him. How he's breaking rules—how it looks to the other workers. And he just says he's boss. His word is law."

"Molly." Fucher offered, pushing a large piece of candy to one side of his mouth and yelling from across the room.

"Who's Molly?" This from Carol.

"The one who visits. Fred likes to entertain her a lot."

"Visits? What do you mean by 'entertain'?" Carol asked as both she and Dan turned to look at Fucher. Dan noticed a red flush creep up Carol's neck. Sort of a spinster's reaction to hanky-panky. Must lead a sheltered life.

"You know, coffee and stuff. She's always hanging around. She came to my house day before yesterday. She brought me a present. Fred likes her a lot."

"I don't doubt it." Carol's hands were clenched and the pursed lips were now a tight line. "He knows better. Boss or no boss, he knows better. Mr. Warren read him the riot-act—he simply cannot use the facilities for personal…pleasure. This could mean trouble. Trouble with our license."

"Yeah, Fred says girls are a lot of trouble. He says that I should stick with dogs and leave girls alone. Dogs are your best friends."

Some wisdom in that, Dan thought. He really wanted to change the subject but thought he'd ask, "Is Fred off today?" Dan had been wondering why he was going to need a key. He didn't relish meeting the man who in all likelihood had been detained and questioned about a bloody surgical glove and why, just possibly, he was living under an assumed name and closely connected to a track owner. He was counting on Scott having acted on his phone message, but he hadn't heard back. He'd feel a lot more comfortable if he knew he wasn't going to run into Franco Marconi.

"Just taking a sick day." Hmmm. That could mean the Feds had made a move. He should have called Scott earlier and double-checked that someone had received Dr. Hunt's submission of information. Or maybe she had sent her results to the local police chief.

"Can I have another?" Fucher had walked to her desk and was eyeing a bowl of miniature candy bars. "I could take a little one."

"Just one. We'll have some trick-or-treaters here tomorrow night. I have to have candy for them."

Good God, Halloween. Dan had totally forgotten it was this week. It wasn't like all the papier maché and plastic yard ornaments shouldn't have given him a clue. Joan had put out a five-foot-high black spider at the entrance to the complex right in front of a three-foot-tall fake tombstone. He still wasn't sure how those two images fit together. But he guessed each was suitably scary. He'd remind Elaine that they would have to pick up candy on the way home.

>>>

If Dan could say one thing for Fred, aka Franco, his office/apartment was neat and clean. He hadn't noticed before but there was a door off the kitchenette—a ten-by-ten-foot room of walk-in closet size with one wall a solid bank of electronics—monitors, computers, and fans all humming and whirring and blinking as the screens changed. Dan counted eleven screens: four for the front of the casino, three along each side, two at either end of the kennel, and two keeping tabs on the maintenance building. Another nine screens showed the lobby and front door, the restaurant, each of three gaming rooms, the hallway leading to the corporate offices, including Dixie Halifax's office, the kitchen, and two on the betting windows—one in front, one behind. Those monitors were on the opposite wall.

Dan sat down at the central computer with its oversized monitor sitting on the desk and the tower on the floor underneath. The machine was in sleep mode but sprang to life when he entered the passcode. Files were numbered as to week and day of the week and kept in a separate folder for each month. It was Fucher who pointed out that there were fifty-two weeks in a year and seven days in a week and three hundred and sixty-five days in a year…unless this was a leap year and then he'd have to look it up.

If Dan's calculations were correct, he needed to be looking at weeks forty-two, forty-three, and forty-four. The fire occurred on a Tuesday, but did security start the numbering on a Sunday or a Monday?…Looks like Monday is the first day—if he could trust the circled days in red on a paper calendar hanging above his head. Dan idly wondered if the software lacked a calendar. Tech savvy but someone still used red pen on paper. Interesting. Dan popped a flash drive in a USB port, opened the file marked Oct42 and clicked on 42-2-6A(1-4).

All the days seemed divided into A and P segments—of course, a.m. and p.m.—he should have known. The "6" must mean six in the morning and the tapes were simply numbered one through eleven or if grouped together must mean they overlapped a particular area. Dan looked at the cheat-sheet from Carol Taichert. He was right; cameras one through four were mounted on poles at the four corners of the parking lot according to the attached diagram. These cameras seemed to have a sweep mechanism. Whatever restrictions as to border one camera might have, another seemed to cover that ground for it. And all four were infrared, night-sensitive.

"Pull up a chair." Fucher was hovering and Dan needed him to give his attention to the screen. "I want you to tell me what's happening as I play the video. For example, give me approximate time of day, whether you're on the grounds or haven't come to work yet, and pinpoint the exact location of what you see on the screen. I want to know if that's normal activity for the time and place." Dan could only hope Fucher had gotten all that. Oh well, no time like now to find out. Dan pressed "enter."

He'd start with the parking lot, get a feel for the equipment and then check out possibly more meaningful areas. Camera One had recorded the right side of the parking lot in front of the casino. Camera Two from the left side alternated with Camera One capturing the front door. Inside, looking out was recorded on an interior camera; Camera Seven, he thought. Time for that later and probably only if he wanted to check something.

A lot of people came to work at six a.m. Dan watched as twenty or so workers swiped their cards and entered the casino with another ten close behind. The parking lot was filling up. A forty-something-foot tour bus pulled up to the entrance and thirty-five Q-tips exited and lined up in front, their white hair under the floodlights standing out in sharp contrast to the muted pre-dawn gray shadows that crisscrossed the driveway. There was lots of excitement—selfies and pictures of each other before falling into a single file formation to enter the casino.

"That's me. There. See?" Sure enough, a fairly grain-free image emerged of Fucher getting off of his bicycle, securing it to a bike rack, opening up the compartment on wheels he pulled behind and letting Sadie literally uncoil from the cramped "wagon" and step onto the asphalt. "She likes to ride in the cart." Dan wasn't so sure about that but he'd take Fucher's word for it. She certainly didn't seem to be afraid of riding behind a bicycle.

He watched as Fucher and Sadie disappeared around the corner of the casino. Dan would bet a camera that recorded the road that ran in front of the kennel would be picking them up about now. Enough of this. He needed to spend his time looking at footage of the back of the kennel; he could always come back to the parking lot recordings if he thought they might be of help.

He was just about ready to close out this file when an eighteen-wheeler came into view. It was obviously a dog carrier—doors to the outside each with slots for air, all stainless steel.

"Fucher, did you get a load of dogs that morning?"

"Nope."

"Look here—at this truck. Isn't that a dog carrier?"

"Yeah. It picked up dogs."

"How many?"

"Um…maybe fifty."

Dan quickly opened the file from the camera that would be recording the back of the kennel directly. "There doesn't seem to be any activity around the truck. When did they load the dogs?"

"After the races…the dogs eat first and exercise. They like to drive at night."

That made sense. It would be cooler; the dogs would be tired and would settle down quicker after being fed. He did a fast-forward to six p.m., still no activity around the hauler. Seven p.m. and someone who could have been the driver walked around the transport checking tires then opened the back double doors and pulled down a loading ramp. Two workers pushed a large flat utility cart up to the back of the truck. Four crated greyhounds were lifted off the cart and carried into the transport.

"What's that hanging on the cages? Every cage has one."

"That's their collars."

"Why are they taken off?"

"Safety. Collars get caught in the wire."

Dan hadn't thought of that. It made sense. "So each dog has his or her own collar? And they stay with the dog?"

"Yeah. They write their names on them."

Dan watched as more crates of greyhounds were brought to the truck. It was slow going. There was paperwork with each dog and it took time to situate each crate on board. One man walked among the crates with a clipboard seemingly matching paperwork to an envelope of papers with each dog. Crates of dogs were now lined up along the drive waiting to be loaded. It was quarter to eight.

"Do you remember where you were at this time?"

"With Fred. We ate supper."

"What time was that?"

"Late. Maybe, eight o'clock. Maybe later. We got burgers and played foosball. When I stay the night, I get to take a break. Sometimes I go home."

"What time did you get back to the track?"

"Ten, I think."

"What did you do then?"

"It was real quiet. I went to bed."

"Did you check on the dogs first?"

"No, they'd only bark and want treats." Fucher turned back to the screen. "Stop. Stop. Look there. Mr. Mahoney, it's them—that's Maximillian, Sheba, Sandy's Dandy, Roger Dodger and Mellow Yellow." Fucher excitedly pointed to each dog and touched them on the screen as he named them. Each waited in a wire crate to be loaded. Dan zoomed in on each crate. He recognized ShebaTwo or Daisy with the white chest and blaze and knew he could trust Fucher to know the others.

Paydirt. Finally. In almost two weeks this was the first solid lead and proof that the dogs were nowhere near the fire when it broke out. Of course, their crates were empty—Fucher hadn't made that up. Fucher and Dan watched as each crate was carried into the hauler. Then they waited and watched until the ramp was removed and both doors were closed. The truck was on the road by five minutes after eleven, according to the time-stamp. Dan made a note of the license plate and slipped the flash drive in his pocket. It had been a stroke of genius to bring Fucher to view the tapes. Not too many people would have recognized the five "dead" dogs.

Chapter Twenty-four

The next morning was a busy one. He had the name of the hauler, the license plate number, the bill of lading from Carol Taichert and basically all he had to do was sit and wait. He'd put in the calls to trace the load—he needed to know signatures of authorization, and drop-off destinations for starters. These could be revealing. Carol was following up and would have paperwork faxed to her office. Dan needed to prove the whereabouts of the original five dogs and he was close. Daisy, aka Sheba Two, was the only one safely back with her owner. Someone at the track had initiated that shipping. The owner? A handler? Dixie Halifax needed to answer a few more questions.

〉〉〉

Dixie met him at the door to her office—all solicitous and ingratiating as she clasped his one hand in her two. A little squeeze before she dropped them and ushered him inside. It was killing him not to be able to ask if Fred Manson was Franco Marconi, but he knew better—however the Feds wanted to handle it, it was their territory.

"First of all let me say how relieved I am that your mother is going to be all right. Mom has had nothing but good things to say about Ms. Mahoney—I think they quickly developed a very strong friendship. Do you know if she plans on returning to The Villages? I know mother would be thrilled."

"As of now, that's her plan."

"I've spoken with Scott Ramsey and Chief Cox. I just cannot believe that the casino was being used for money laundering and that your mother's friend was involved. Such ugly business. But I think all this will give us a fresh start. You know, a time to reflect and then start over and be better."

"It does offer that opportunity."

"Oh, and one other thing. I'd like your mother to have Sheba-Two. There comes a time when a dog's happiness should be foremost in any consideration of its future." Dixie stood beaming. And Dan could only think, "bribe." Was he being callous? Could this be a sincere, altruistic offering? Or was he being asked to look the other way about something? Could he have been in this business so long that he was becoming jaded? Suspected a dark motive to everything? Yeah, maybe. He needed to be more nonjudgmental.

"That's very generous. I know Mom will be pleased." But why was she giving away a fifty-thousand-dollar dog—the cornerstone of her breeding program?

"And now what can I do for you?" The half smile, smug even, as Dixie leaned forward elbows on the desk, hands clasped, steepling fingers indicating authority.

Dan shared the camera findings—proof that all five dogs left the kennel some six to eight hours before the fire. He needed to know who authorized the shipping, purpose, and destinations.

"This is fantastic news. Oh, I just knew this would have a happy ending."

"I'm not sure Jackson Sanchez or Wayne Warren would agree with you. And I suppose I should throw Kevin Elliott's name in there, too."

"Oh, of course not. I didn't mean to put the lives of my dogs before the lives of three dear human beings. God rest their souls." Did Dixie just cross herself? Dan had looked up from his iPad in time to see some kind of hand flurry in front of her chest. "Let me pull up a copy of the shipping papers." Dixie busied herself at the computer. "Here it is. October 21, a Tuesday…I signed the order. That's not unusual. That sort of thing falls to me when Wayne is gone. Let's see. Looks like there are three separate destinations. Forty-five were delivered to the track outside Jacksonville, three dogs were dropped off at the white-collar prison in Pensacola—we work with the Prison Greyhounds Program—another two, the last two, were apparently also picked up in Pensacola. I don't have a name, per se, just Radcliffe Kennels."

"Any reason listed for Radcliffe Kennels to have had two dogs shipped to them?"

"None. Just a minute, let me check something. Here's a bill of sale for the two. Two neutered males, three years of age... Apparently from the Jackson Sanchez kennel. It appears he sold them for seventy-five thousand." Dixie sat back. "These had to be racing prospects. Between the two of us? I don't think Jackson had any top prospects left—he'd sold off so many."

"My guess is that Maximillian and Mellow Yellow were the two sold. I bet there are papers somewhere with altered registration numbers. I think your other three dogs ended up in the Prison Greyhounds Program and, for whatever reason, at least one that we know of was adopted out. I'll alert the program to check registration and kennel identification. I suspect we'll find the last of your five dogs."

"That would be terrific. But Jackson...I'm just in shock. It's just so hard to believe. I considered him a friend. But to alter ear tattoos and sell my own dogs...steal my dogs?" She seemed at a loss for words.

"You had no idea that these dogs, your dogs, were being transported that evening?"

"None. I initialed the paperwork—I'll admit that I don't read these carefully. I was expecting a shipment going out and kennel personnel takes care of the details. Transports are paid for by kennel owners. I never expected my own dogs to be involved."

"The pressure of owing money makes people do things out of character. Perhaps his life was threatened—"

"Yes, I'm afraid Jackson's reasons are transparent. But it's Kevin Elliott that simply baffles me. I still find it difficult to believe that he would cremate a human being, maybe even kill a human being, lie about my dogs, cause so much suffering… then be murdered himself."

"Elliott was a threat. He knew too much. But any idea as to why Wayne Warren might have been killed?"

"Oh," Dixie replied. "I'm sure it's because he uncovered the money-laundering scheme. Probably threatened those involved with exposure. I don't think the Mafia takes kindly to ultimatums. It was just a stupid thing to do—it could have been handled so differently." A grim smile.

Interesting. She seemed to have an answer for everything—just like she'd rehearsed it. What wasn't she telling him? Damn. If Fred or Franco was her husband how much of what had happened had been planned together?

>>>

Elaine was picking up candy for trick-or-treaters and food for a cook-out. Fucher was coming over for burgers around six along with Joan and Roger. Dan would have time to run up to Scott's office before going home in addition to stopping in to see his mother. She had been moved to the hospital at Ormond Beach. More observation, nothing serious. She'd developed an infection in the arm that was broken, which led to an elevated temperature and the precautionary measure of detaining her. Not a popular decision, but the hospital at Ormond had all the latest test equipment. The doctors were being thorough and he applauded that. His mother was in her seventies and what could have been four days drugged and bound and bleeding in a storage barn had to have taken a toll. But Maggie had begged him to intervene and "spring" her. It took a lot of cajoling and the promise of a visit later in the afternoon to keep her there. He knew she'd be thrilled to learn that Daisy was going to be hers.

The only other thing on his afternoon agenda aside from visiting his mother was the carving of two big pumpkins, but there would be time for that. He called ahead, assured Scott that he just wanted to touch base—compare notes, catch him up on finding the dogs. Scott had an hour—more than enough time.

>>>

Scott took a sip of what must have been fairly cold coffee and offered Dan some. He must have been ready to leave for the day. Dan noticed the coffeemaker was already turned off and opted for a bottle of water instead.

"I've been put on retainer by the state's racing commission. Florida doesn't take kindly to money laundering or anymore black eyes for their racing program. Believe me, the last five years have taken a toll. It would be nice to put this whole thing to bed. I think you're closer than I am. The dogs have been proved to be alive. That alters any payout that your company needs to make. Mission accomplished, so to speak."

"Not if they've been stolen. UL&C is still on the hook. Only one is back with its rightful owner so far. But I'm close to getting the other four returned. Wayne Warren's administrative assistant is doing the follow-up."

"I know your mother almost paid the ultimate price, so she might be happy to know we picked up Joey D'Angelo this morning, aka Stanley Evers. Mr. and Mrs. Evers had made it as far as Venice. We believe his traveling companion was an accomplice—helped Mr. Evers hide your injured mother, then knowingly represented herself as Margaret Mahoney and used a passport under that name. She'll get prison time for her part in aiding and abetting a would-be murderer."

"Joey D'Angelo, Franco Marconi—"

"By the way, thanks for the tip on that Fred Manson, or Franco Marconi. Dr. Hunt sent everything over. The connection with Ms. Halifax was an eye-opener. However, we're not having any luck finding him. Any reason he would have thought we were on to him?"

"Possibly. Maybe my asking questions put some pressure on. But what about Warren's murderer? Or Kevin Elliott's?"

Scott looked up and paused, a slight lean forward, "Where did you hear that Kevin Elliott was murdered?"

"Officer Bartlett…let's see, I think he said that his bike's tires' walls had been shaved, set up to collapse at speed. He was still trying to pin something on Fucher, the young handler at the track—had a handful of Snickers' wrappers to try and prove involvement."

Scott sat back. "Interesting. The fact that Elliott was murdered is information that law enforcement knows but the general public doesn't. It was kept out of the papers on purpose. Only the murderer would know there was a killer involved."

"Unless Officer Bartlett shot off his mouth to Dixie Halifax. She just referred to Elliott's death as a murder."

"I'd like to know her source." Scott rummaged through some papers on the desk. "By the way, ever hear of an A.J. Bowman?"

"No, doesn't ring a bell."

"That's the name on the account in the Caymans. Our boy, Joey, deposited an even million but it was withdrawn by this Bowman five hours later."

"Joey…" it was difficult not to say, Stanley, "has been questioned?"

"He's not going to give up any of the players. And I'm not sure he knows. He was a transport, a mule, who probably pocketed a little with every deal—not sure he was taken into anyone's confidence. The less the grunt labor knows about what's going on at the top, the better. Joey already ratted on one biggie in his lifetime. I don't think he's going to do that twice. And he's out of bargaining chips. Beating up your mother and leaving her for dead will guarantee a lifetime behind bars. If this A.J. Bowman isn't just a pseudonym, we'll find him soon enough."

"It would seem that there's a mastermind out there—got to be someone pulling the strings."

"Yeah. I'd put money on Tony Falco. We just don't know how he sends and receives messages."

〉〉〉

Dan pulled into the hospital parking lot at a little past four. He was doing great on time and wouldn't have to rush a visit with his mother. Her room was on the fifth floor of the building that resembled a spaceship on I-95. But the place was new and sparkly clean and inviting—for a hospital.

He hadn't expected his mother to have company, but when he opened the door Dixie Halifax's mother and father were there.

"Move it A.J., let the man have your chair."

"A.J.?" Dan wasn't sure who Dixie's father was referring to.

"Oh, I've been called A.J. all my life—Agnes Jane. I must say that I prefer a nickname." Dixie's mother crinkled her nose.

A.J. Why did that sound familiar? Then he had it. "Is your maiden name Bowman?"

"Why, yes it is. How did you know that?"

"Something that Dixie said, I think. But I like A.J., too."

It was tough to contain his excitement but he shared the good news about Daisy, promised to visit the next day, waited until dinner was served at five, then made his escape. He called Scott from the parking lot, missed him but left a voicemail. Something told him A.J. Bowman didn't have an account in the Cayman Islands but he'd bet the farm that her daughter did.

> > >

He barely got the pumpkins carved before the first trick-or-treaters showed up. All the really little guys who were held or pushed in strollers came while it was still light. An assortment of bees, tigers, sharks, princesses, and pirates came up and down the front steps. Fucher was beside himself putting candy in an array of pillow cases, plastic pumpkin buckets, and just plain sacks. In between interruptions everyone helped themselves to burgers and dogs and all the trimmings—including Simon and Sadie. It was fun, sort of a family gathering, and everyone shared Fucher's excitement.

The call from Carol Taichert came as a surprise. Was he coming to the casino party that night? To tell the truth he'd forgotten about it. Well, she had the information on the hauler and the missing dogs. It would be on her desk—an envelope with his name on it. If they missed each other later, help himself. She was pleased to say she had information on all four dogs still unaccounted for. Oh yes, speaking of the five dogs, Ms. Halifax had left ShebaTwo in the kennel—could he pick her up? Something about her being adopted by his mother?

Dan decided he could run by the casino and get back to help with the bulk of handing out candy. He'd waited too long to learn the whereabouts of the dogs and curiosity was, in fact, killing him. Fucher wanted to go with him but had to run home for his "costume." The percale sheet with large holes cut for eyes would have been a great costume had the sheet not been part of a pink and green flowered set. Took the edge off of the ghost being very scary.

When they got to the track, Fucher wanted to get ShebaTwo and bring her back to the car. Dan thought that would save time and watched him go—flowery sheet flowing behind him as he headed for the kennel.

He checked in with Carol who was arranging trays of cookies and bottled drinks just inside the front doors. Her long flowing black dress just lacked a tall pointed hat to make her costume complete.

"I'm so excited. The man outside St. Augustine who bought the two race dogs from Jackson had no idea they were stolen. Giving the ear numbers to various tracks paid off. He's bringing them here tomorrow. But everything's in the envelope—including transcripts from phone calls. I left my office open."

"Great. Thanks for your help."

"It was the least I could do…under the circumstances. Mr. Warren put his life into this casino and track. Oh dear, literally, I guess." Her eyes welled up and she immediately turned back to the table.

Dan thanked her again for her help. She had certainly been loyal to her boss. He skirted the restaurant full of costumed workers—including several greyhounds in various costumes. He wondered how the jaunty black beret stayed on the head of one dog whose black cape and white scarf made him some kind of artist. Did dogs really enjoy all these trappings? Actually, the greyhounds seemed to be okay with it. If more people knew how great these dogs were, adoptions wouldn't be a problem. He was really pleased that Daisy/Sheba would have a good home.

As Carol promised, her office door was open. Dan flipped on the lights and picked up the thick manila envelope. And couldn't resist a peek inside. As Carol said Maximillian and Mellow Yellow would be returned to the track tomorrow. Sandy's Dandy and Roger Dodger were still at the Pensacola prison. Those two would be entrusted to a warden and brought by car. Relief. A huge sense of relief. He'd email UL&C later.

Now to find Fucher. Dan headed back through the main entry, grabbed a frosted pumpkin-shaped cookie from the table, looked for Carol but didn't see her, and continued out the front doors into the parking lot. It had filled up in the last half hour and he was jostled by skeletons, a couple Obamas in rubber masks, and to top it off a woman with her arms and legs sticking out of a large rounded, padded egg and carrying a live chicken. He wondered if there was going to be a costume contest—he'd put that one up for honorable mention at the very least.

He continued to the car but didn't see Fucher and Daisy. He didn't remember saying to meet him back at the car so maybe Fucher was still at the kennel. Dan put the envelope on the front seat and locked the car again. He jogged toward the side of the building. Two of the lights were out at the edge of the parking lot, which made the south side of the casino pitch black. He made a note to mention it to security. Interesting, but the "sweep" cameras on this side were stationary. Were they inoperable? That made him vaguely uneasy. Lights off, cameras not working…he turned back and made another trip to the SUV. Just a precautionary trip. His .38 was always in the glove box when he wasn't carrying. He tucked the gun in his belt and checked the flashlight in a side pocket. A bright, strong beam illuminated the car's interior. Great. Batteries working.

This time he could see clearly. He tried the back door to the kennel office. It was locked tight but the next door down that opened next to the vet's office and lab was open.

"Fucher?" No Fucher answered his shout, but about twenty dogs set up a chorus of barking.

"You lookin' for that Crumm guy?"

Dan could thank the Lord for strong sphincters, the skeleton-clad worker with a rubber "howling" mask who stepped out of the shadows gave them a test. Now if he could just get his heart to stop racing. "Yeah, know where I can find him?"

"Don't know for sure. He took off with Fred, but I know he's coming back to pick up Sheba."

Fred. Wow. He hadn't expected to hear that. Dan thanked him and tried not to let himself overreact to knowing Fucher was with Fred, alias Franco. If Fred knew the Feds were looking for him...he'd bet he wasn't in the casino at the party. Dan walked back outside and stared hard at the maintenance barn. The lights weren't on but he'd swear he'd seen a flicker. Just an instant of illumination like someone had switched a flashlight on and then off.

He quickly ducked back under the overhanging eaves, put his back to the siding-covered exterior wall and stayed in the deep shadows of the kennel as he moved forward. He slowed his pace. No noise, no light, no advanced warning if he could help it. There was approximately fifty feet of exposed ground between the gate at the end of the exercise area and the maintenance barn's double doors. The barn's outside spots were also off along the south and west sides of the building and above the entrance. Still, he was definitely an exposed target. Someone had the advantage of cover and maybe night-vision goggles. And he felt someone watching—waiting for him to make a run toward the barn. But who? And why? What was supposed to happen tonight that required darkness?

At the muffled burst of gunfire coming from the casino, he jumped forward and eased through the gate of the exercise area. What the hell was going on? His .38 was in his hand but by the sound of the ammo being sprayed about inside the casino he was probably outmanned and underpowered. He hesitated—gunfire was being returned. Whatever was going down it wasn't all by the bad guys. Suddenly five figures—a cowboy, a surgeon, a cop, an astronaut, and a priest slammed through the back doors of the restaurant, ran to a parked car next to the kennel, and took off.

"I'm going to need the keys to your car. And I'll take the .38"
Dan felt the muzzle of the Glock before he heard the words.
How could he have been so stupid? He'd taken his eyes off of
the maintenance barn and was about to pay for it.

"Where's Fucher?"

"Where he won't cause trouble."

Dan didn't need to see under the mask to know the replica
of Popeye who just pocketed his .38 was Franco Marconi. And
the arms weren't pumped-up, fat-suit fakes. The guy worked out.

"Now, turn around and walk away from the building. Nice
and easy. Yeah, that does it."

Suddenly his peripheral vision caught movement. Dan saw the
witch step out of the shadows. Crooked hat, black flowing dress...a
perfect costume right down to the wart on her rubber nose.

"Put the gun down, Fred." The voice was cold, calculating,
very familiar and the .45 loomed like a cannon held steady in
two hands. "I found Wayne's letter—what to do in case he didn't
return. The day before we're going to have a service because you
fucking took that away from me, too. Ashes. Not even a body. I
know everything—the money, how he found out, how he begged
you to just leave. But you couldn't do that. Not some old Mafioso
has-been. Wayne knew you tortured and killed Jackson Sanchez.
Why? Because he stole something you thought was yours—he
was needy and flat broke. Then you threatened Wayne with his
life if he reported what he'd seen. But you couldn't leave it alone.
What did he do to you? How could you butcher that dear soul?
The love of my life. I never wanted anything else. Just Wayne
Warren."

"Hey, Carol, com'on sweetie, we can talk."

Popeye should be wetting himself about now. Not a good
situation. Dan eased his head a slow half-turn to the left trying
to keep an eye on the Glock now pointed at his back.

"You've run out of talking time. Put the gun down. NOW.
I will not let you kill again."

Dan watched Fred lay the weapon on the ground in front of
him and then was slow standing back up. Hesitation, a slight

almost imperceptible move forward, knees remaining bent. Oh shit, he was going to launch himself at Carol and knock her gun away. The decision to intervene was taken out of Dan's hands when the .45 thundered and Fred fell backwards—the second and third shots probably weren't needed. Fred or Franco was very dead and a sobbing witch had dropped her gun, ripped her mask off, and buried her face in her hands. Just to make certain, Dan knelt and checked Fred for a pulse. All three bullets had hit the chest in a tight circle. Ms. Taichert was one hell of a marksman.

"This doesn't bring Wayne back but it makes me feel good." Carol turned a tear-stained face toward him. "I found Wayne's letter this afternoon. He wrote everything down. Everything. And it wasn't just the money laundering, Wayne found out how the group got messages back and forth from their leader."

"Who was in charge?"

"Tony Falco. He directed everything—when the money was delivered, picked up, the accounts…and it was all in the collars of the dogs."

"I'm not following you."

"Dates, amounts, destinations all were in code and written inside the collars of the greyhounds transported from this track to the prison. They left here with individual collars and returned with collars. In the meantime, a little information had changed hands."

"Pretty slick."

"Only Wayne figured out what was going on. Oh, Mr. Mahoney, he gave his life to try and save this track."

Dan found a tissue in his jacket pocket. There was a time when he wouldn't have had one. Domesticity. Could he admit to that?

"Glad to see you two are among the living. Franco Marconi?" Scott Ramsey pointed to the body on the ground and waited for Dan to give the affirmative nod before slipping on latex gloves. He then picked up the .45, next the Glock and bagged each separately. "Am I going to find another firearm out here?"

Dan pointed to his .38 sticking out from the edge of the body. Scott carefully pulled it out and slipped it into a clear plastic bag.

"I know you know the drill. Gotta keep this for awhile. Want to tell me what happened out here?"

"Ms. Taichert saved my life." Dan proceeded to reiterate how he happened to be in a compromised position and let himself be ambushed. "I was on my way to find Fucher. My guess is he's in the barn."

Scott motioned for two officers to join them. "Check the barn area. Be careful. Take someone with you. We're not sure everyone's accounted for." The two men took off at a jog.

"Ms. Taichert, I presume?"

"Yes, formerly Mr. Warren's personal assistant. I think you may be interested in this." Carol pulled an envelope from a skirt pocket. "He left a detailed account of what he'd discovered going on here at the casino including first-hand knowledge of Jackson Sanchez's death and a warning that his own death might be next."

Any comment by Scott was interrupted by Fucher running toward them with Daisy bounding along at his side. He stopped when he saw the body, then sank to the ground beside it. No one said anything. Dan kicked himself for not doing something, preparing Fucher for seeing his friend dead, trying to explain that sometimes we find out people we trust can do bad things. He watched helplessly as Fucher fumbled for Fred's hand and then held it. No one moved but Dan would bet everyone was feeling just a little of Fucher's pain.

"Fred was my friend. But he did bad things."

"I know, Fucher, but I believe he liked you very much."

"Maybe." He stood up. "He locked me in the bathroom. With Daisy." Fucher waved a hand toward the barn. "He said I had to be quiet. Then I heard lots of guns. I was scared. But I had to be brave for Daisy. I held her tight. She was shaking."

Dan stepped forward and put an arm around him. "Let's go back up to the casino. I bet I could find you a cup of hot chocolate."

"And candy?"

"I saved two Snickers bars just for you. Those Halloweeners didn't get everything. I'll make sure you get them before you go home." Carol added.

"You can go inside in a few minutes. The forensics team will be here soon and a couple ambulances are on the way." Scott turned to Dan, "The boys were able to stop the guys with the money but not until after a shoot-out."

"Money? I thought that had left the casino earlier in the week—with Stanley and mom's look-alike."

"That was a decoy. We were getting close so only a part of the loot was handed off. The majority was here…pretty much right under our noses but we'd missed it. Had a tip as to where to look. There was a false bottom to Kevin Elliott's freezer in his lab. We'll debrief inside—make certain we're all on the same page."

Scott stayed behind and waited for the forensics team who took swabs of Dan's and Carol's hands before they were allowed to leave the scene. Who had fired their weapons wouldn't rely on testimony but rather evidence or residue. Finally, the three of them were allowed to walk back to the main building with Agent Ramsey. Officer Bartlett met them at the casino's back door and directed them toward the restaurant where several tables had been pushed together. "The chief wants you over there." The man didn't look happy but, then, he never did, Dan thought. Funny, but he wouldn't have put money on Officer Bartlett being one of the "good" guys. Perhaps he was wrong.

"We'll do a little debriefing in here." The chief motioned for them to take a seat. Carol, Fucher, and Dan found places at a round table in the corner. Scott was detained at the door but soon joined them. The wail of ambulance sirens could be heard in the distance and the casino itself had been cleared of party-goers. It was a relief to not see witches and skeletons and Popeye…

"Oh, thank God, you're all right." Dan barely had time to stand up before Elaine was in his arms. "I saw what was happening on the news. Three people were killed. But, of course, they couldn't give names." She had thrown her arms around his neck and was holding him so tightly, he was afraid to swallow. But, hey, who was complaining. He was lucky in more ways than one. After a deep breath, she let go and stood back, "I was so afraid."

Dan put his arm around her and pulled her back close. "It's over now. We're all safe. Carol, Fucher, Mom, you, and me." He turned and smiled at the group. "And five greyhounds."

"I have a couple questions then you can all go home." Chief Cox indicated the chairs across from him.

"First, I have something I want Fucher to do." Dan leaned over and whispered, "Go to the kennel and bring back a half dozen collars—ones the dogs wear when they are transported. Remember? We talked about them."

Fucher nodded, pushed back from the table and headed for the side door. Dan restrained Daisy who tried to follow. Fucher had a great way with dogs, maybe someday he'd apply some of his magic to Simon.

"I want him to know he's making a contribution—maybe take his mind off of what happened earlier. And Carol shared some information with me that will make a difference to the case. If we can find the evidence," he nodded at Carol, "we'll be able to see a pretty sophisticated information exchange system. Proof that this was a fairly well thought-out scheme overall."

It didn't take long for Fucher to come back through the doors with a handful of collars. "These are old."

"All the better, I think." Dan reached into the pile on the table and handed a couple to Carol. Then he turned one inside out and looked at the series of numbers, letters, and dashes penned onto the leather collar's underside.

"These are not simple registration numbers." Carol read off a series from one of her collars that was mostly letters. "I don't know the code but this shorthand let Mr. Falco call the shots—lock up or not."

Chief Cox took a collar from Dan, turned it over and studied the inscription, "Not bad. A pretty good system."

"Yeah, the trucks delivered and picked up dogs every month or two and Falco could stay on top of operations long-distance." Actually, Dan was impressed.

He didn't have a timeframe but it had obviously been working for awhile.

"As a precaution, we had Tony Falco transported to Jacksonville earlier today. He wasn't too thrilled to go from minimum security to maximum. But he filled in a lot of blanks for us—all in the name of blaming Franco Marconi. I imagine Tony's testimony is going to become a lot more explicit and incriminating now that Franco is dead."

"In retrospect, Franco *could* be held accountable for a lot. And there's Dixie's tie-in to all this. Do you think you'll be able to separate fact from fiction when it comes to who instigated what?"

"Probably not, but we'll have enough to take away Tony's minimum lock-up privileges and give him a real long vacation at the government's expense. Probably no way to pin a murder on him but Tony simply outranked Franco—he would have stayed in charge—ordered things done. The dog collars prove he had a finger on the pulse. However, it's a toss-up as to who hired whom. Tony says Dixie brought in Franco and Franco brought in Joey D'Angelo. That part's true but we believe that Franco was already working for Tony. The casino was a nifty little setup for a modest money-laundering operation. Must have been a feather in Tony's cap to run a few hundred thousand through the casino and race track every other month or so. And they didn't overdo it—no amounts that would have called attention to the casino. Excess funds needing laundering were kept nearby and funneled into foreign banks via Joey D'Angelo."

"But didn't you say that there was a mole? Someone on the inside giving you guys information as to shipments?"

"Kevin Elliott. We'd been working with Kevin for a few months. He'd come to us after sharing his suspicions with Wayne Warren—alerted him to the fact that his casino was being used illegally. Seems the excess money had been hidden in his lab. He found it and saw who was putting it in and who was taking it out. We don't know what happened next, but somehow Kevin was able to figure out that Franco was behind the scheme. We think Kevin's punishment for talking to Wayne was having to cut up his friend's body and dispose of it. At least that's Tony's story. Played right into Dixie's wanting to get rid of five greyhounds.

The crematory served two purposes. I think if there hadn't been a murder, the dogs would have just been 'stolen.' Looks like she thought death certificates would hasten the payoff. A break for you that Sanchez decided to double-cross her and sell a couple for racers."

"And then Sanchez got caught stealing from the mob?"

"Yeah. And he couldn't be trusted—too much booze—the old loose lips sinking ships sort of thing."

Dan hadn't heard that one in awhile. "What brought you here tonight?"

"We checked into A. J. Bowman and came out to arrest Dixie Halifax. Using her mother's name on the offshore account maybe wasn't the brightest thing to do. But we were here for an arrest, not a robbery. It was a fluke that the robbery had been set up for this evening. Of course, with a cover like Halloween, the costumes helped the men blend into the crowd. Again, some good planning. Two of Tony's men were killed tonight but we're hoping the third will share what he knows."

"Do we know who killed Jackson?" Dan was curious.

"Franco. You were right about maintenance being a torture chamber. We think we found where Jackson was tortured and killed—at least there's some rubber tubing that will probably test positive for alcohol and Jackson's DNA. Looks like they needed to find out just how much he knew and who he'd told."

"I can believe the etching of 'thief' on his forehead, but the stabbing? That doesn't make sense."

"Not unless you look at the interior surveillance footage from the kennel."

"Wasn't all that lost in the fire?"

"The new system makes use of the Cloud for storage of data. We have a very clear picture of Dixie Halifax bending over the body in the hallway, stabbing an already dead man, and then wiping the knife handle off."

"Do we know why?"

"Dixie wanted the two hundred and fifty thousand insurance payout and she didn't take kindly to Sanchez potentially ruining her plan to claim it—and stand to profit from selling two of her dogs to boot. She didn't want to kill her dogs and she didn't want them found. They were supposed to have been placed in homes—never raced. Jackson helped her with the plan but then got the bright idea to sell the two best racers. He changed their tats after they were loaded that night, forged their registrations, and had sold them without her knowing about it. The hauler probably left a copy of the shipping papers in her office and took off. Either someone told her what was going on or she simply found the bills of sale for the two dogs and went to confront Jackson about pocketing an extra seventy-five thousand. I'm certain she was more than mad enough to kill him. Imagine how convenient to find him supposedly passed out in the hallway."

"The money would have come in handy—might have helped get her hauler back."

"Wasn't sure you knew about that. The track was struggling. The perfect setup for the mob boys to move in. Who could refuse?"

"The insurance money still seems small potatoes compared to the rest."

"It was money totally separate from the mob. Dixie wasn't above getting every penny she could. Her dealings with United Life and Casualty were never meant to interfere with the money laundering—two separate entities. Actually I'm surprised that Franco didn't nix the deal. I can't think that he'd want anything to call attention to the track. But Dixie went ahead. There didn't seem to be any reason that money laundering and missing dogs would overlap—but that's when you showed up. And thanks to your mother there was a lot of overlap."

"Who started the fire?"

"We're guessing Dixie. She needed to cover-up the murder she thought she'd committed and have a vehicle for the greyhounds to supposedly die. We're not sure when Franco decided to get Kevin to cremate human remains and claim the dogs' deaths. Somewhere along the line, Franco also moved the body around to implicate Fucher. He may have known Dixie did the stabbing and was protecting her. Or maybe he just needed a fall-guy. Knew if he provided a 'murderer,' it would keep the cops busy. He may have seen Fucher remove the knife and knew Fucher's fingerprints would be on the knife handle—he just had to make sure the body wasn't burned. Nice way to set up his pal. And everyone knew Sanchez owed Fucher money. That would explain the "thief" carving—which is something Franco probably did to further implicate Fucher."

"And Wayne and Kevin Elliott?"

"Both deaths also the work of Franco. Thanks to your investigation, Kevin Elliott became a liability. Or maybe Franco found out he was working with the Feds. Someone thought threatening him wasn't enough; he couldn't be trusted—not after having to cut up his friend. Smart move to check the ashes in the urns. Franco had a nice little network of people working for him in the neighborhood. It wouldn't have been a problem to have someone alter the tires."

"I guess it's my turn to offer an apology." Officer Bartlett stood up. "We arrested Mr. Crumm to keep up appearances. We knew someone had gone to extremes to implicate him, and we didn't want to give the real killer a chance to run for cover. We especially needed you…," a nod toward Dan, "to believe we had our man."

"I understand. Let me say how sorry I am about Kevin. I know you were good friends."

"I knew he was a mole. He thought it was his civic duty. I tried to get him to talk about what was going on, but he refused. It was something we argued about all the time. He thought he was safe—thought he was needed too much around here to be expendable. And I know him—doing what they made him do to Mr. Warren scared him to death. He had a former wife and two teenage kids; he was convinced that they'd be harmed."

Elaine and Dan sat holding hands. There was finally a sense of closure.

"What's going to happen to Dixie?" Elaine asked.

"Attempted murder, defrauding the government, and United Life and Casualty—we don't know the extent of her involvement in the other deaths, but based on what we do know, I doubt Ms. Halifax will be out of prison any time soon. Franco seemed to be Tony Falco's puppet—his eyes and ears on the outside. Maybe, so was Dixie. Tony didn't have much choice but he seemed to trust the two of them with his money scheme."

"What will happen to the track?" And Fucher and Mel's jobs, Dan thought.

"I think the State Gaming Commission will get involved. I doubt they will even close it—unless they take some downtime to give it a face-lift—I think they'll bring in new personnel and keep it open to the public. It's been a viable part of this community for a long time."

"Ms. Taichert, I know it's getting late but I need you to come down to my office for a statement. Shouldn't take long." Chief Cox stood. "Mr. Mahoney, I'd like you to stop by in the morning."

"Can I have some candy now?" A sleepy looking Fucher interrupted.

"I think I can handle that." Officer Bartlett turned to Fucher. "I was pretty hard on you, pal. Even after we knew you hadn't killed Jackson Sanchez. But it gave us the extra time to build a case against the bad guys. Do you understand?"

"That's okay. Can I come back to work now?"

"I imagine you can." Officer Bartlett looked at his boss and got a nod from Chief Cox. "How about I give you a ride home in a cruiser? You could help me with the lights and siren maybe."

"Yeah. I'd like that. But I have to take Daisy home."

"We'll do that. You need to get some rest for work tomorrow." Dan watched as Officer Bartlett pulled a Snickers bar from his jacket pocket and handed it off as the two headed toward the exit. Fucher's happiness was complete.

Every retired racing greyhound wants

A TICKET HOME

But each ticket costs $75. The cost of a long distance haul from racetrack to waiting adoption groups in nonracing states has risen to $2,400. A full "haul" ships 32 dogs, or $75 per greyhound.

Here is how your tax deductible donation would work:

A TICKET HOME: $75 donation guarantees one ticket home for a greyhound

SEND A LITTER: $375 donation sends home five greyhounds

FILL THE WHOLE TRAILER: $2,400 donation sends a trailer of 32 greyhounds home!

There IS a home out there for every retired racer ... if someone can finance their ticket home. Every $75 sends another former racing greyhound home, somewhere, to the home he truly deserves.

Make checks payable to: Greyhound Pets Daytona Beach
960 S. Williamson Blvd
Daytona Beach, FL 32114

Let them know it is **A TICKET HOME**. Or donate online at www.greyhoundpetsdaytona.org, and designate **A TICKET HOME**. *The ticket's destination will be at the sole discretion of GPA Daytona, according to the need. They decide, not the donor.*

Why GPA Daytona?
By long standing tradition, GPA Daytona pays 100% of the cost. As a greyhound adoption group, they own the equipment, pay fuel charges, upkeep and maintenance, registration, insurance, hire drivers, etc. This is on top of their regular expenses like dog food, vet bills, etc. to house the dogs until they each get their ticket home. The racetrack generously provides GPA Daytona a kennel to house 110 dogs waiting for adoption. (There is always a waiting list of 150 more retired greyhounds wanting into this adoption kennel.) The Daytona racetrack is also setting an industry standard by paying for the majority of the broken legs, and pays the kennel staff that work in the adoption kennel. So, it is a good working relationship. GPA Daytona pays the total cost of each greyhound's ticket home. Adoption groups that receive the dogs are only charged basic pre-adoption vetting, never transportation for the dogs. The full Ticket Home has always been paid by GPA Daytona. This financial burden now puts the long distance hauls at risk. Yet if the dogs can be shipped to states that do not have race tracks, there are many potential adopters waiting for a new greyhound.

To receive a free catalog of Poisoned Pen Press titles, please provide
your name and address through one of the following ways:

Phone: 1-800-421-3976
Facsimile: 1-480-949-1707
Email: info@poisonedpenpress.com
Website: www.poisonedpenpress.com

Poisoned Pen Press
6962 E. First Ave. Ste 103
Scottsdale, AZ 85251